CONSUMED BY DECEPTION
RINA KENT

*To the little girl in me who found heroes boring
and fell head over heels with villains.*

AUTHOR NOTE

Hello reader friend,

If you haven't read my books before, you might not know this,
but I write darker stories that can be upsetting and disturbing.
My books and main characters aren't for the faint of heart.

Consumed by Deception is the second book of a trilogy and is
not standalone.

Deception Trilogy:
#0 Dark Deception (Free Prequel)
#1 Vow of Deception
#2 Tempted by Deception
#3 Consumed by Deception

Sign up to Rina Kent's Newsletter for news about future
releases and an exclusive gift.

My husband. My monster.

The truth isn't always what it seems.

Lia doesn't realize that, but she will. Soon.

I chose this life. This road. This twisted arrangement.

For her, I made a deal with the devil.

For her, I toyed with fate and death.

There's no going back.

I stole her and like any thief, I won't return her.

Lia is my addiction. My obsession. My love.

Mine.

PLAYLIST

True Love—Coldplay
Let it Go—James Bay
Infinity—Jaymes Young
Flying High Falling Low—Walking on Cars
Breath—Breaking Benjamin
Lost it All—Black Veil Brides
Fallen Angel—Three Days Grace
Everyone Changes—Kodaline & Gabrielle Aplin
Learning to Breathe—Switchfoot
Remedy—Thirty Seconds to Mars
Closer to the Edge—Thirty Seconds to Mars
Make Believe—The Faim
My Heart Needs to Breathe—The Faim
Never Know—Bad Omens
Second Chances—Imagine Dragons

You can find the complete playlist on Spotify.

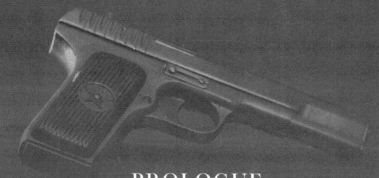

PROLOGUE

Adrian

Age ten

I'M THRUST INTO THE COLD, DARK NIGHT.

At first, I can't keep up with my dazed head as I blink the sleep out of my eyes.

I take a moment to focus on my surroundings and make sure I'm not daydreaming about the last book I read.

Books have been my only escape since Aunt Annika left. She died all alone in a brutal car crash and my father wasn't there for her. Instead, he was with us. My parents had taken me to the hospital to put a cast on my arm that Mom broke.

I didn't cry. The pain in my arm didn't hurt as much as the constant, unending ache in my chest, and the fact that Aunt Annika wouldn't be there to hug me, that she couldn't take the pain away anymore is what put a halt to my crying.

Dad was proud of how strong I was and that his son didn't shed any tears. I thought about telling him everything, but before he came to take me to the hospital, Mom said she'd get rid of me as she got rid of Aunt Annika if I mentioned anything to Dad.

I wanted to hit him and Mom. I wanted to throw them both from the car because back then, I thought I'd have Aunt Annika again if they disappeared.

But she was already gone and merely has a tombstone now. One that no one visits anymore.

All the warmth and joy she brought to the house has vanished ever since Mom took her place.

Dad married my mom, even though his friends from the Bratva don't like her.

She's too smart for her own good. I heard one of them say.

I guess it's because she insists on knowing everything and gets involved in as much as possible.

She fights with Dad a lot because he doesn't want her to be 'part of the business.' Once, Mom said that if he would listen to her, he could be the *Pakhan* and he hit her across the face.

I don't like it when Dad hits Mom. Because she hits back and then they're both screaming, breaking things, and bleeding.

If I get in their way, Mom shoves me against the nearest wall and Dad hits her harder.

But I guess it's better if they're fighting, because when they're not, Mom slaps me for the slightest mistake and Dad makes me memorize books and meet his friends from the brotherhood.

Judging by the pain in my arm, it's Mom who's dragging me. She's the violent one, at least at home. Dad gets violent with her but never with me. He loses his temper whenever she hurts me, and that's why she only does it behind his back.

I blink as I'm hauled to my feet, unsure why she's yanked me out of bed and barely given me time to put on my shoes before she's leading me outside.

She doesn't usually bother me after I'm asleep.

"Hurry up, Adrian!" Mom shoves me forward, her red nails digging into my wrist and her expression pale under the soft light coming from the street.

"Mom…? Where are we going?"

"Now, hush!" Her gaze darts sideways, then she dashes to her Jeep and pushes me into the passenger seat. "Fasten your seatbelt."

Before I can ask again, she hurries to the driver's side and gets in. The tires screech and the car races in the direction of the exit.

My hands are unsteady when I loop the seatbelt around me. Mom doesn't bother with hers as she drives down the empty street at a speed that physically draws me back and steals my breath.

I hold onto the seat with both hands while I study my surroundings. It's dark but for a streetlight every so often. No other people or vehicles are in sight. I crane my head and see '2:25 a.m.' in neon red on the dash in front of Mom, who keeps hitting the gas harder with each passing second.

She's never been a careful driver. If anything, she's the type who honks and shouts at people and calls them names. However, this is the first time I've seen her knuckles white and trembling on the steering wheel.

"Mom? Where are we going?"

Her head tilts in my direction and she's wearing a weird expression, as if she's just realized I'm here. Then she focuses back on the road. "Away from your fucking father."

I know they've been fighting lately and that Dad's guards have been whispering about her, but I thought they would reconcile, as usual. They have phases where they're tolerant of each other's presence, but it barely lasts before they start hitting and calling one another names.

She takes a turn while speeding and I hit the door, bruising my side. My hold tightens on the seatbelt. "Why?"

"Because he's an idiot," she snarls. "He could be so much more, but he's letting his fear overrule him. If he's taking away my ambition, I'm taking away his precious heir."

"Does that mean we'll live together, just you and I?"

"That's the plan. Until Georgy stops being a fucking fool."

I don't want to live alone with Mom. At least she doesn't hit me in Dad's presence. If he's not there, nothing will prevent it.

At the same time, I don't like the fighting, so maybe if they're not together, it'll be better.

"The asshole doesn't even know how far he could go or where I can get him. That jerk, Nikolai, doesn't deserve to be the leader."

"But he's the *Pakhan*," I say softly.

"That doesn't make his reign absolute. Remember, Adrian, power is seized, not given. If there's a chance to win, don't ask questions or hesitate. Take it."

"Even if it hurts others?"

"Even if it hurts others. They're the ones who allowed themselves to be hurt, so you needn't worry about such idiots…" she trails off as she stares at the rear-view mirror and then smacks the steering wheel, cursing in Russian.

I look behind me and find several cars on our tail.

"Motherfucker!" Mom hits the breaks hard when a car cuts in front of us horizontally and stops.

I tumble forward, only the seatbelt holding me in place. Three men rush out of the car, and before I realize what's going on, both of our doors are jerked open. Mom is yanked from her seat by two of them while Pavel, Dad's senior guard, undoes my seatbelt and leads me out, much more gently than the way the other guards handled Mom.

Pavel makes me stop in front of him, his hands on my shoulders as we stand between Mom's car and the one that blocked us.

She's fighting against the guards who are detaining her, cursing in a mixture of Russian and English. She tries kicking them with the pointy heel of her shoe, but they mobilize her.

I'm a few feet away, completely still in Pavel's hold. Not that I would leave or even have an idea of where to go.

Dad strolls in from the side. Although Mom is a tall woman, he's taller and more buff, and he has a scowly face that never changes. I can count the number of times in my life that I've seen him smile on one hand, and that only happens when he's with his Bratva friends.

As soon as he approaches my struggling mom, she spits in his face.

He raises his hand and slaps her on the cheek so hard, her head reels back and blood explodes from her bottom lip. It trails down the fair skin of her chin and to her graceful, long neck.

I wince, still not liking that he hits her. He never did it to Aunt Annika, at least not when I was around. But he always becomes violent with Mom.

"Stupid bitch." Dad wipes his face with a napkin. "I knew you'd be more trouble than you're worth."

"Fuck you, Georgy!" she snarls, trying to kick him, but it ends mid-air because the guards are holding her hostage.

"Fuck me? *Me?* Fuck *you*, Dominika, and all the trouble you've put me through since I married you. I told you not to get involved in Bratva business. I told you to keep your conniving mind to yourself. But what did you do? You met Italian capos and their wives behind my and Nikolai's backs. Did you think we would never fucking find out?"

"I did that to get you the power, you fucking asshole! Nikolai is old-fashioned and you could be stronger than him, *better* than him."

"He's my *Pakhan*! One does not plot a coup behind their Vor's back. That's not how it fucking works, as I've told you a million damn times. Any act of betrayal is punishable by death."

"No one will punish you if you're the damn leader!"

"But I'm not." He releases a long breath. "You betrayed me and the brotherhood, Dominika."

"No." She squirms and fights, kicking and screaming.

I hate this sight of Mom. I've always known her to be larger than life, stronger too. Sometimes, downright hateful. I've never forgiven her for taking Aunt Annika away, but I also don't like seeing her this helpless and with no way out.

"You can't do this to me! I'm the mother of your son!"

"Doesn't make you exempt from punishment." Dad retrieves his gun and motions with it at his guards. "Put her on her knees."

The men push her down until her knees hit the ground, her shoes making a haunting sound on the concrete as she thrashes. "No! Don't! Are you picking Nikolai over me?"

"I'm picking the brotherhood over you. If you're not punished properly, Nikolai will never forgive what he thinks is *my* betrayal." He pauses, looking at me for the first time tonight. "Come here, Adrian."

Pavel gives me a slight push, then releases me but follows close behind. My legs feel as heavy as bricks as I drag them to where Dad is standing.

"You're old enough now, so listen carefully, my boy." Dad jams the gun against Mom's forehead and she stares up at him with her usual haughty defiance, not even a single tear escaping her lids. "This is how you punish traitors, no matter how close they are to you."

He pulls the trigger.

A loud bang echoes through our surroundings as hot liquid splashes onto my face.

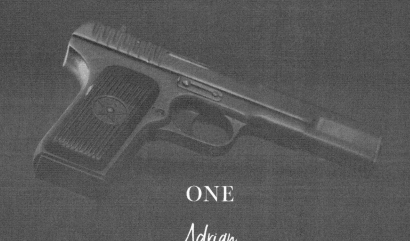

ONE

Adrian

Age thirty-six

I'VE WITNESSED LIFE ENDING RIGHT IN FRONT OF MY eyes.

Not once.

Not twice.

But countless times.

After I saw the life leave my mom's body when I was ten years old, I had an epiphany.

Ah. Death is that easy.

Death is a pull of a trigger, a splatter of blood, and empty eyes.

If Mom, the fearless Dominika who was stronger than life itself, was killed that easily, then the act couldn't be that hard.

That's why I've never feared death. Never looked the other way from it. Never hesitated in front of it.

In fact, I barged straight into it. I conquered it and shoved it to its knees in front of me, like Dad did to Mom, then shot it in the face.

I've eluded the merciless clutches of death so often that I thought myself immune to it.

That in a way, death doesn't imply to me.

Doesn't touch me.

Wouldn't touch me.

That was my mistake. The error in my system.

Even though I've never feared the end—or anything, actually—since Mom's execution, there's something I've feared losing.

Or someone.

The world goes in slow motion, but it's still too fast and impossible to stop.

When I followed Lia here after she sent a doppelgänger home and attempted to escape, this isn't what I thought would happen.

Lia tumbles down the cliff like a leaf. Light, tiny, and so fucking fragile.

I reach out a hand, but all I grab is air.

Panic like I've never felt in my life snaps my shoulder blades together and freezes me in place.

Fuck no.

This isn't how it's going to end.

I skid down the side of the cliff, sliding over the dirt until I nearly hit the water. My bicep wound screams in pain and my tendons ripple with every movement.

Pulling out my phone, I hit the flashlight icon until a beam of light spills in front of me, illuminating the violent waves hitting the rocks.

The thought of Lia being stuck out there, ripped apart by the angry water, tightens my body and assaults my nerves.

I make out a small figure clinging to a rock while it floats in the water, but it doesn't drift away.

My men's voices grow near, and Kolya's large build is the first to appear as he makes his way down the side of the cliff.

"Get ropes!" I bark, then place my phone on a small rock, directing the flashlight forward before I dive straight into the freezing water.

Shock ripples through my body and my wound, the wound she caused in her attempt to escape me, but I ignore all the discomfort as I swim against the harsh current.

The crashing waves are stubbornly trying to whisk Lia away, to slam her delicate body against the merciless rocks and suck out her life essence.

When I reach her, I find out why the water hasn't succeeded in taking her. I thought she was looped around one rock, but it turns out, she's stuck between two. One of them isn't visible but is imprisoning her lower half.

I grab her cold, wet wrist and stop breathing while I wait for her pulse.

One fraction of a second passes.

Two…

Three…

A tiny beat thumps beneath my frozen finger and I finally inhale in a large breath of air.

I use one rock as an anchor as I pull Lia from between the other two. The moment she's loose, I loop an arm around her waist and hold her freezing body close to mine.

Dark strands of her hair cover her face and I push them back. Even under the faint glow of the flashlight, I can see that she's pale and her lips are blue, darkening a shade with every second.

She needs medical help and she needs it now.

"Boss!" Kolya calls from the shore.

I stare up to find him, Yan, Boris, and a few of my men standing at the edge of the cliff. My senior guard throws the rope, but it's whipped away by the water.

He does it again, and I grasp it at the last second and loop it around Lia's middle. I pause when my fingers meet the torn material of her dress, then I carefully feel around.

My hand slows when I find a gash at her lower abdomen. A deep as fuck gash that swallows my finger.

I quickly remove my hand while keeping her immobile. This is a lot more fucking serious than I thought if she's also injured. This complication could be fatal in her freezing state.

"Pull us out!" I shout over the current.

Kolya and Yan yank the rope while the other men stand as a second line of enforcement.

I place Lia in front of me to keep from touching her wound, one of my arms wrapped around her chest and the other holding onto the rope.

The water carries our weight as my guards drag us to the shore. Kolya hands the rope to the others while he and Yan hurry toward me.

I let Kolya take Lia's body only so I can come out of the water. My muscles ache from exertion and my bicep wound pulses with red-hot pain. However, as soon as I'm on solid ground, I yank the rope from around Lia and pull her fragile body to me. She's still freezing as fuck and her lips are blue and...wrong.

"One of you give me a jacket," I order in Russian.

Yan removes his and throws it over Lia's body, not bothering to hide his malicious stare directed at me.

"The hospital, now!" I start climbing up the side of the cliff, keeping her as steady as possible.

Life is slowly leaving Lia, and soon, it'll be all gone.

Everything about her will be only a part of my memories.

Not if I have a say in it.

She might have jumped from a cliff to escape me, but that won't be happening in this life.

She's my wife.

My son's mother.

Fucking *mine*.

And I'll go through hell itself if it means keeping her there.

TWO

Adrian

LIA'S CONDITION IS CRITICAL.

I haven't been able to get over that piece of information ever since Dr. Putin said it. He's on our payroll, but since I was the one who brought him to the Bratva, he knows when he should keep secrets for me.

He won't tell a soul about Lia's injury. Not even the *Pakhan* himself. That is, if he wants to protect his family from my wrath.

Lia's abdomen wound was indeed deep and she needed stitches for it, and fortunately, no internal organs were harmed. Her freezing temperature has returned to normal, thanks to how quickly we got her here.

But the fact remains, she's still not opening her eyes.

Dr. Putin said there's no brain swelling, but she must've hit the water hard enough to cause a blackout.

That was yesterday.

It's been a whole day since she threw herself off the cliff.

A whole day since she last opened her eyes.

A whole day of me pacing the length of her hospital room or holding her delicate hand in mine.

After I changed into dry clothes, I never left her side. Dr. Putin had to stitch my bicep wound while I was in her room.

I thumb the soft flesh of her wrist, gliding my finger over the visible blue veins. "What have you done, Lenochka? Why?"

If she hears me, she doesn't show a sign of it. The question is useless, anyway, since I already know the answer. I know why she thought about giving up.

To leave me.

I was suffocating her, she said.

I was *torturing* her.

Those words dug a deep black hole into my soul, perhaps even worse than when she confirmed that she was cheating on me.

I've become insufferable in the past months. Every time I looked at her, I recalled that she let another man touch her, that she was protecting him from me, and my anger grew worse with each passing day.

It mounted and heightened and I took it out on her cunt, ass, and flesh. I marked her and hurt her to chase away the red mist.

But that wasn't enough.

Whenever I finished, the mist returned with a vengeance, and all I could see was her opening her legs for another man. Her moaning and whimpering and crying in front of someone that's not me.

My anger turned into rage and I had to take a step—or a few—back so I wouldn't hurt her to the point of no return.

I hated what she had done.

I hated *her* sometimes.

And because of that, I apparently tortured her, smothered her, and drove her to the edge of a cliff where death was better than being with me.

"Fuck," I curse under my breath, running a hand through my hair.

How will I be able to take a step in a different direction now? Because I have to or I will lose her for good.

The door slides open, then closed. I don't lift my head as heavy footsteps echo on the floor.

Both Kolya and Yan stand in my peripheral vision, hands crossed in front of them. My two guards have been with me since I was young because my father groomed them to keep an eye on me. Kolya is my age while Yan is a few years younger than Lia. They're both orphans and originate from the slums of Russia, which made them the perfect target for Dad's schemes.

What he didn't count on was that I would form a connection with them and that their loyalty would be absolute to me. Not him. Not the brotherhood. Me. Or at least Kolya's is. Yan has been switching sides between my wife and me ever since she came into the picture.

The fact remains, I trust my men. Not only did we go through my father's tyranny together, but also our military training. A bond formed between us after we saw each other at our worst, and that can't be bought with material things.

"Who was it?" I ask with apathetic calm. "Who helped her?"

"We traced the signal to the *Pakhan*'s house before she headed to the forest," Kolya says. "So she could've met anyone there."

I tap my forefinger against my thigh. "Not Sergei since he dislikes her. If Vladimir was there, he wouldn't have cared enough about her. That only leaves Rai."

"What are you going to do about it?" Kolya asks. "If you attack her openly, everyone else might know about Mrs. Volkov's accident."

"I'll find a way."

"That's not what's important right now," Yan snaps. "Lia almost died."

My head tilts to the side to meet his harsh glare. "Watch

your fucking tone if you don't want your tongue cut out, and she's Mrs. Volkov to you."

"I don't care if you cut my tongue or my limbs, but someone obviously needs to tell you this, Boss."

"Yan," Kolya warns.

"Shut the fuck up, Kolya. You should've told him this a long time ago, but you chose not to and blindly took his side." Yan breathes harshly through his nostrils, his anger still directed at me. "She was suffering and you knew it, but you chose to believe she cheated on you and let her bear your ruthless wrath. When the fuck could she even cheat on you when we shadowed her every step? She lost her previous life and was adapting to yours. She never tried to escape after that one time, because deep down, she wanted to be with you and Jeremy, but you had to suffocate her."

I release a long breath, choosing to ignore Yan's insolence for now. "Are you done?"

"No." He swallows, his voice losing some of the anger. "I don't know why the fuck she said she cheated on you, but I'm guessing it was because she figured out you were using her for being Lazlo's illegitimate daughter."

I narrow my eyes. "She said that?"

"She didn't have to. I could feel it."

"So now you share a telepathic connection with her?"

"No…?" he asks, unsure. It's the right choice of words. If he had said he did have that connection, I would've killed him.

I already hate that she shares an easy friendship with Yan. That she smiles at him more than she does at me lately. And while I've wanted to snuff it out since the beginning, even I realize how much she's needed a friend. Kolya also said that it would be smarter to let her be friends with her guard rather than seeing him as a threat.

"Just talk to her without being closed off." Yan sighs. "Then you can kill me."

"I also don't see why she shouldn't know her place in the great scheme of things," Kolya says.

"What?" I ask.

"She's been your wife for six years and if she learns about everything, it will prepare her in case something happens."

Yan holds him by the shoulder. "Fucking finally! That's what I've been saying all along."

I stare back at Lia. They think I'm doing this to keep her in the dark, when everything I've done was to protect her.

Her childhood wasn't the best and I know how she feels about my world, so I've been trying my fucking hardest to keep her as far away from it as I can.

That, and I didn't want her to meet my mother's fate if her true identity is discovered.

I halt tapping my finger. "How about the other one?"

"The other one?" Yan frowns.

"The fake Lia." I give him a glare. But on the bright side, even he couldn't tell her apart from my Lenochka.

"Her name is Winter Cavanaugh, twenty-seven, American," Kolya starts. "She's been homeless for a few months after having a stillborn. The child's father is unknown. She has an alcohol addiction and she comes from a lower-class background."

"Is there more information about her parents?"

"Not really, but I'll look further into it."

"How about her medical condition?"

"She's in a coma."

"Keep her in the guest house until I figure out what to do with her. I don't want Lia's lookalike roaming the streets."

"Yes, Boss."

Lia's fingers twitch in my hand and her eyes move beneath her lids before she slowly opens them.

"Call Dr. Putin," I order, then lean forward as Kolya gets out of the room.

My wife blinks a few times, and as I witness life slowly

creeping back into her, I make a vow to get her back, to make things right.

Somehow.

"Hey." I stroke her chin and cheek. "How are you feeling, Lenochka?"

She stares at the ceiling, blinking slowly, but shows no signs of hearing me.

"Lia. I know you're mad at me, but look at me."

She doesn't.

Instead, she's limp, her numb expression making her blue eyes muted, almost like a haze has covered them.

"Lia," I call again.

No sound or movement.

"There's something wrong with her, Boss." Yan is on the other side, watching the rapid rise of her heartbeat on the machine, which beeps at an alarming rate as she remains still, staring at nothing.

Her lips twitch and she releases a sound. I lean over to be able to hear her words. They're low, haunted, and stab me straight in the fucking chest.

"Winter... My name is Winter..."

Then her eyes roll to the back of her head and she loses consciousness.

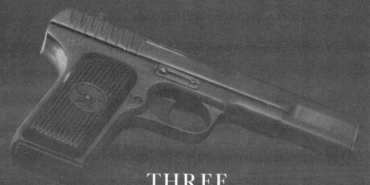

THREE

Adrian

WINTER.

Lia said her name is Winter.

Not only that, but she also didn't say anything beyond those five measly words. She's been going in and out of consciousness for the past three days.

And when she comes to, she stares at nothing, not even acknowledging my—or anyone else's—presence.

Dr. Putin said it's purely mental at this point and that her bodily reaction is related to that.

I called in her shrink, or more accurately, I threatened her so she'd come to check on Lia. Dr. Taylor is a small brown woman with short black hair and an upright posture, who insisted on talking to my wife alone.

But that doesn't stop me from watching through the glass window. Surprisingly, Lia is talking to the therapist, and she doesn't seem to be repeating the fact that she's Winter over and over again.

Kolya remains silent by my side after I send a grumbling Yan back home to look after Jeremy. I've had to go back for short intervals during the past few days to keep him company before putting him to sleep. He cried the first time I told him his mother had gone on a trip and would return for him soon. Then he refused to sleep anywhere but on my lap and in my company.

Jeremy has always been used to having his mother around, and I have no fucking clue how to ease him into the change of circumstances. For now, he needs to believe that she's away and will come back.

Because she *will* come back.

Even if I have to threaten and coerce all the doctors and psychotherapists.

Dr. Taylor smiles at Lia, then walks to the window and pulls the shutters to block my view of them.

I'm about to barge inside, but I'm halted when the therapist steps out and closes the door behind her.

"Why did you do that?" I ask in a calm that's laced with deep-seated anger.

The fact that Lia doesn't talk to me, let alone recognize me, has been like being pricked by tiny needles. The sting isn't sharp, but it's constant and without reprieve.

Dr. Taylor slides her gold-rimmed glasses over her nose. Her hand is shaking and I can tell she's intimidated by me, but she meets my gaze head-on. "Because you're scaring her."

"She recognized me?" I ask slowly, hopefully, and even Kolya's body leans forward in anticipation of the answer.

"No, she doesn't, but she recognizes you as a danger."

I pretend those words don't cut through me like a blunt fucking knife. "She said that?"

"Yes."

"What else did she say?"

"That there are scary men outside her room and that she didn't do anything wrong. She also seems to believe she's Winter Cavanaugh and even relayed her life events. From what you told me, she already met Winter and talked to her, so the fact that she knows all the details isn't a surprise."

"What's wrong with her?"

"She's dissociating, Mr. Volkov."

"Dissociating?"

"It happened due to the traumatic event she experienced, and other factors from her childhood, combined with adulthood traumas, are most likely what led her to this state. I believe her case to be a form of dissociative fugue. She doesn't realize that she's experiencing a memory loss and has invented a new identity to fill the gaps."

"And how do I stop her from dissociating?"

"You can't. She currently believes herself to be Winter and if you tell her otherwise or force it on her, she might get worse and develop other critical types of dissociations."

"Are you telling me to sit by and do nothing?"

"Something like that. She needs to find her old self on her own. Her neurosis is quite strong right now. In other words, her mind is very fragile and she's the only one who can build it back up. Any form of duress will have the exact opposite effect. In fact, victims of dissociation escape into their minds as a response to trauma or *abuse*." She stresses the last word even as she tries to avoid my gaze.

It takes everything in me not to snap her neck and show her what true abuse is like. Instead, I hold onto my cool so I can get the answers out of her. "What does she need now?"

"A change from her usual habitat would be great. She also needs a supportive entourage and no judgmental dialogue. In order to open her mind again, Lia has to feel safe."

"And you don't think that will happen if she's in my company."

"I didn't say that."

"You were thinking it."

"Well, yes, Mr. Volkov. I told you, she considers you a

threat, and since she doesn't really remember you, being in your presence will make her case worse."

"How about our son? He's five years old."

"I'm afraid that in her current state, he'll do more harm than good. She thinks herself to be Winter and that she lost a child. If she sees another child this soon, it might backfire and lead to further complications. Her psychosis is quite volatile and unpredictable right now and it's better not to put pressure on her mental state. Give her time and try to fill the gap for him as much as possible."

"What if I talk to her?"

"You talking to her is the reason she's been having those panic attacks. She believes herself to be Winter and you keep calling her Lia." She pauses. "It'd be better to put some distance between the two of you for now."

I want to tell her that won't be happening.

That there's no way I'm leaving Lia alone.

Fuck psychotherapy and all its nonsense. Lia and I will write our own story, and for that to happen, she needs to stay by my side.

However, I've seen my wife's panic attacks. I've witnessed the numbness in her eyes, and before that, I experienced her complete surrender when she jumped off that cliff.

Deep down, I know I need to let her go.

Even if only temporarily.

Even if it means shredding a fucking piece of my chest.

Dr. Taylor says something about recommending a fellow psychotherapist so that I'll leave her alone, but I shoo her away with two fingers. She hurries down the hall, her heels clicking along as she keeps staring back at me and Kolya.

I face the window with drawn shutters and although I can't see Lia inside, I can feel her.

She's become a part of me.

At the beginning, I only got close to her because of who

she is and the role she plays in my system. However, she slowly but surely has become an integral part of my life.

She made me lose control more than once when I thought myself incapable of such blasphemy.

Lia didn't just challenge me, she also seeped under my skin and clashed into my bones.

Now, I have to let her go for her own good.

Because even though I need her in my life and crave the softness she brings to my ragged edges, I have apparently cut her too deep that I didn't only reach the flesh, but I also severed tendons and veins.

I told her I would be there for her until her scars healed, but I ended up adding a few of my own.

"Hey, Kolya." My voice is lethargic, low.

"Yes, Boss."

"Do you also believe I suffocated Lia?"

My second-in-command hesitates before touching the short blond hairs at his nape. "Honestly? I believe you suffocated each other."

I face him. "How so?"

"You didn't give her many choices and she retaliated by being cold and putting distance between you two. She did that to protect herself, I believe, but you're not a patient person, so the situation kept mounting until we reached this phase."

"You've had those beliefs all along?"

"Yes."

"Then why haven't you voiced them?"

"You didn't ask for my opinion, so I didn't see the need to give it."

"I thought you'd be in Yan's camp."

"I am, partially. However, Yan can be reckless. Due to his friendship with Mrs. Volkov, he sometimes forgets about your character, Boss."

"It'll get him killed one day."

"He just cares about her."

"And you think I don't?"

"Of course not. You just…show it differently." Kolya pauses. "What do you plan to do about this situation?"

A long sigh leaves me as I study the pattern of the closed shutters through the glass. When the therapist said that Lia needs a change of habitat, an idea has been building in my head.

I hate it, but it may well be the only solution possible right now.

"I will let her be Winter."

Kolya watches me intently as if I've grown a second head. "You…will?"

"It's either that or I'll lose her."

"And how do you intend to go about that?"

"Do you still keep in touch with your colleague from the Spetsnaz who was excellent at disguise makeup?"

"Yes. What do you need him for?"

"Yan."

"Yan?"

"Your colleague will disguise Yan so he can keep an eye on Lia."

"He can't keep an eye on her as he is?"

"No. She knows his face. It might remind her of me and complicate her state. He needs to look different and have another background."

"What do you want him to be?"

"A homeless person. Put Lia in the shelter that's under our protection and make sure to tell Richard that she's to be treated with care, but hide her identity from him. He's never met her before, so it shouldn't be hard."

"Boss, are you sure about this?"

"Yes, Kolya. I'll let her believe the lie. If she wants to be Winter, so be it."

Because sooner or later, her path will be a one-way road to me.

FOUR

Adrian

A month later

IT NEVER GETS ANY EASIER.

Not the part about watching from afar.

Or the part about going to an empty home without her.

Or the part where Jeremy asks me when his mother is coming back.

I tell myself it's for her sake, for her mental health, and to kill whatever reason she had for jumping off the cliff.

I tell myself that she'll remember me, that she'll one day recognize Yan, then tell him to take her home.

Hasn't happened so far.

If anything, she seems to be more invested in her fake life as Winter.

I hate that fucking name and the woman behind it who's still comatose in my guest house. If Lia hadn't met her, she wouldn't have jumped off that cliff and we wouldn't be here.

Though, it was probably only a matter of time before Lia

attempted her escape. Meeting Winter was the last straw that broke the camel's back, not the first.

What I hate the most about this situation are the conditions she's living in. My Lenochka isn't supposed to sleep in shelters or on the streets. She shouldn't be wearing charity clothes and torn gloves.

She shouldn't be homeless.

Her home is with me and Jeremy.

Every day, I battle the urge to whisk her up and take her with me, to drive her to our house where she was always meant to be.

Something stops me, though.

The change in her.

Unlike before, Lia's often smiling now and even laughing with Yan—or Larry, as she knows him. Watching her interactions with him give me different urges, like strangling the life out of him.

I don't like that she laughs with him yet doesn't even remember me. I hate that she bonded with him in no time but had only panic attacks when I was by her side at the hospital.

But at the same time, I like that she's more carefree, that her demons aren't getting the better of her.

Yan also mentioned that she hasn't had a single nightmare since the day she became homeless.

A few weeks ago, I had Emily, one of our department store managers, give Lia a makeover while she was on sleeping pills. The store manager changed my wife to look like the pictures of Winter we found on surveillance cameras. When she woke up in the hospital, I had a different doctor than Putin discharge her in case she remembered any details from the past and recalled his face.

Lia didn't have any trouble believing she was Winter or adapting to her life, as if it had always been her own. It could be because she was used to being around the homeless due to the amount of volunteering she took part in.

She did mention once that they were free.

I never forgot her expression from back then, the sadness in it, and how much her eyes shone with a secret yearning for that freedom.

That night, I made up an excuse to spank her, to punish her forever thinking about leaving me. Then I fucked her like a madman as if intending to purge that idea out of her head.

But deep down, I recognized that she believed in it. In fact, she probably buried it in her subconscious until this moment.

Being homeless is akin to freedom to her.

Kolya stops the car at the back of the shelter she stays in and we wait. My second-in-command retrieves his phone, probably to check on the hackers' emails. Boris opens and closes his cigarette pack but doesn't light one.

I sit in the back seat, my whole attention zeroed in on the door of the shelter. Every time someone exits and it's not her, my stomach falls with a pungent type of disappointment.

When she comes out, I feel her before seeing her. It's a strange connection that I didn't realize I had with her until the day she fell from that cliff.

I shake that gruesome image out of my head as I focus on her. She's gotten thinner, but her features are still the same—soft, delicate, and so beautiful.

She's still the fragile rose I want to shield from the world, lure her into mine, and swallow her in my darkness.

Lia shoves her hands in her coat and hurries down the street, probably to get a beer and get drunk.

I motion at Boris. "Follow her."

"Yes, Boss." He opens the passenger door and steps out, keeping his distance as he trails her from afar.

My attention remains on her until she rounds the corner with Boris on her tail.

I'll probably join him after I talk to Yan. To say I've been neglecting my work these past couple of weeks would be an understatement.

I can't focus on anything when Lia is fucking gone. In the past, I was used to watching her in the garden or knowing she was somewhere at home, safe and sound. Now that she's not there, my mind feels scattered and I can't get anything done.

Though I have to. In order to keep protecting her and Jeremy, I need to be on top of things and not let anything slip past me.

The back seat opens and Yan slides to my side, smelling of trash. He rubs his nose with his dirty gloves and retrieves a cigarette.

He looks like shit.

But he doesn't seem to mind as long as he gets to protect Lia.

Kolya's ex-colleague did wonders on Yan's features. Not only did he make him look a few decades older, but he also changed his face map in a way that gives him a completely different appearance.

Yan is currently Larry, an ex-veteran who has high cheek-bones and graying hair.

He's always by Lia's side unless he needs to touch up on his disguise, and that's when either Boris, Kolya, or I keep an eye on her from afar.

Sometimes I watch even when Yan is with her. Partly to see her smile and partly to give my fucker guard strikes in case he touches her.

"Did she mention anything?" I ask the same question I do every day.

He shakes his head once, blowing a cloud of smoke. "The usual. She really does believe herself to be Winter."

I tap my finger against my thigh to keep from punching something. I should be used to it by now, but I never am.

Every day, I hope that she'll remember me. That she'll come back.

Dr. Taylor mentioned that the fugue state could last from days to months, and that Lia would eventually remember who she actually is.

It's been a month already and yet, my wife seems more interested in being a different person altogether.

Yan drags a deep inhale of his smoke, then releases it. "There's something you need to know, Boss."

"Talk."

"That motherfucker Richard put his hands on her."

My body goes rigid. "*What?*"

"He harassed her and she kicked him in the balls—among other things—before she left."

Two emotions rush through me simultaneously. The first is rage. A dark foreboding grips me by the gut at the thought of Richard or any other bastard touching my Lia. I'll rip every last one of them limb from limb and bathe in their blood so they learn to never fuck with what's mine.

The second is pride in my Lenochka. She fought because that's what she is deep down.

A fighter.

The first emotion is stronger and more potent, compelling me to shred Richard's heart out of his chest and tear him fucking apart.

I tighten my hand into a fist. "Where is Richard?"

"In his office." Yan taps his cigarette. "Why are you asking?"

"Why do you think?"

"He's the Bratva's mayoral candidate, Boss," Kolya interrupts from the driver's seat. "Not only would Sergei not like it, but he would also consider it a betrayal."

"What Sergei doesn't know won't hurt him."

I step out of the car and stalk to the back entrance of the shelter. Since I've been here countless times either to talk business with Richard or to keep an eye on Lia, I know my way around.

The director of the shelter isn't aware of who my wife is and he would never suspect that she's under his roof. When I first had Kolya talk to him about it, he thought she was a prostitute I intended to fuck.

That was his mistake.

At first, I let him believe that because I couldn't care less what he thought.

But who the fuck is he to believe he could touch her?

That he could put his filthy hands on her?

I twist the doorknob of his office, opening the door and slipping inside. The place is shabby with a faux leather sofa and a desk made of cheap wood.

Richard stands by his chair, dabbing a piece of cotton against his cheek that has fingernail scratches.

My lips twitch as that feeling of pride hits me again.

That's my Lenochka.

The shelter's director is a middle-aged man with a flat nose and bushy brows. He dresses in cheap suits that make him look like a wannabe clown.

Upon noticing me, he straightens, ugly greed shining in his bland, mud-colored eyes.

"Oh," he stumbles over his words. "A-Adrian. I didn't know we had a meeting today."

"We didn't."

He throws away the blood-soaked cotton and retrieves another one from the top of the desk. "Hold on, let me take care of this. A stupid bitch clawed me and kicked me in the balls…" he trails off when I pull out my gun and the silencer, then take my time attaching it.

Sweat breaks across Richard's forehead as he watches the weapon with widened eyes. "W-what is that for?"

"Continue." I stalk toward him. "You were at the part where the *stupid bitch* clawed you and kicked your minuscule balls."

He lifts both hands in the air. "H-hey…we can talk about this, yeah? I'm an asset to you."

"Not when you touch my fucking wife." I place the muzzle to his forehead, then think better of it and grab my knife.

I'm going to make this fucking personal and stab him until all his blood pours out.

No one touches Lia and lives.

No fucking one.

꙰

After I'm done with Richard, I don't rejoin Kolya and, instead, choose to walk on foot.

To watch Lia.

She's marching in front of me, oblivious to her surroundings and me. She keeps sipping from a drink that she shoplifted when Yan wasn't around. Lia was never an alcoholic and she's not one now either. She just believes she's Winter—and because Winter was an alcoholic, Lia thinks she is as well.

I make sure Yan dilutes her beer when she's not looking. I won't allow her to develop an addiction that she'll regret.

My wife is wearing a coat and shoes that are a few sizes too big. Yan mentioned that she always complains about the cold and the winter weather. I wish I could take her home, wash her, and tuck her in a warm bed.

After what happened with the shelter's fucking director, I'm paranoid that the incident will repeat. That she's no longer safe, even if my guards and I are almost always watching her.

What if I lose track of her and can't get to her in time?

She stops in front of a New York City Ballet poster, her brow furrowing as she studies it. My feet come to a halt a small distance away, but as usual, she doesn't notice me.

Will she ever?

Lia remains there for several long seconds, her body

slightly trembling before she crunches her can and throws it in the trash.

Well. That's interesting.

At least she remembers her connection to ballet.

Winter was never a ballerina. However, Lia somehow has it in her mind that she was and even told Yan that she was pushed out by an evil prima ballerina who asked her to seduce her husband.

Per my knowledge, Winter was never married, nor has she had a long-term relationship.

Dr. Taylor mentioned that Lia invented her version of Winter and she could have used references from her own life to fill in the gaps.

I wonder if Lia asked Winter to seduce me. After all, she did want a stranger to take her place in my life.

As if that would ever be fucking possible.

After throwing away the can, Lia starts to cross the street without lifting her head. A van speeds down the street and she's completely oblivious to it.

I don't think as I grab her by the elbow and pull her back. For a second, I bask in the feel of touching her, even though layers of clothing are separating us.

Even though she doesn't smell of roses right now.

I haven't gotten this close since the hospital. And she didn't even remember me at the time. She had memory lapses later and didn't recall the first encounters with me. Dr. Taylor, who visited again, said it was normal for someone in Lia's state to erase everything from their previous lives. Apparently, only her new identity matters and my attempts to talk to her only caused her to escape deeper in her mind.

To a place where I couldn't reach.

Lia startles but then flips off the driver when he calls her names. I make sure to memorize his license plate so I can cut out his tongue later.

"Are you all right?" I ask.

I probably shouldn't be talking to her, in case she has a panic attack like in the hospital, but I couldn't resist.

I miss her.

I miss my Lia, and the fact that she doesn't remember me has been eating at my soul like the crashing waves that swallowed her that night.

Lia finally looks at me and she pauses, her aqua eyes widening and her breath audibly hitching.

She observes me intently as if she knows me. Maybe not on the surface, but deep in her heart.

Hope blossoms in my chest because I know, I just know that I can have my wife back.

FIVE

Lia

Four weeks later

I THINK I'M CRAZY.

Either that or everything I just learned is true and I've lost nearly two months of my life.

Two months of believing I was Winter.

Two months of escaping my true identity.

Two months of…lies.

Flashback upon flashback slice through my battered head with the wrecking force of a thunderstorm.

My life plays in front of me like a distorted movie, one where the audience doesn't know the ending until it strikes them in the face.

My name is Lia Volkov.

It's not Winter. I'm not homeless.

I have a husband, and Jeremy is indeed my son.

Winter has always been a figment of my imagination. No, not my imagination. She's a real person whose identity I used so I could escape my own.

Why…? Just why…would I do that?

I sag against the wall in the dim, narrow alleyway and stare up at Luca through my blurry vision. When I planned to escape with Jeremy and texted my childhood friend for help, I didn't think he'd plot an entire masquerade. I never would've anticipated it was he who sent the circus clown to where I was waiting in the park in order to distract the guards and Jeremy so that he could pull me into this alley.

This is the same Luca who wanted me to not only spy on Adrian, but to also kill him—because I killed the mercenary he hired for the job.

Bile rises to my throat and I slap a hand on my mouth as the realization coils inside me, twisting and tugging on my heartstrings.

I *killed* someone.

To protect Adrian, I didn't think twice about ending a person's life. That's why I went mad. That's why somewhere in my mind, being Winter made more sense for my sanity.

She might have been homeless, but she was free and definitely not a murderer.

Luca snaps two fingers in front of my face, his impatience etched in his hard features. The leather jacket, black baseball cap, and mask give him the anonymity he religiously tries to achieve. I don't remember him ever showing up in public with his face entirely visible. The stench of bleach coming from him fills my nostrils. He always has that distinctive smell, because he's obsessed with cleaning. Before, I thought he had an OCD, but maybe it's more to do with cleaning bodies and killing.

Somewhere in the gloomy corners of my mind, I recognized the smell when I was Winter. I was close to identifying him but couldn't.

"I don't have all day, Duchess."

Hot red emotions bubble in my veins as I let my hand fall limp at my side. "What have you done to me?"

He lifts a shoulder. "I opened your eyes to the truth. I told you that Adrian has been using you all along because you're Lazlo Luciano's daughter."

I jam a stiff finger in his chest. "The only one who's been using me all this time is *you*, Luca. I considered you a friend, but you've been manipulating me all along. You've endangered my, my son's, and my husband's lives just because it serves your agenda."

"My agenda? What the fuck, Duchess? Have you forgotten why Adrian is keeping you by his side?"

"That's for me and him to sort out. You have no damn business to get between us."

Luca's eyes flash with unmasked rage and he grabs my arm, his gloved fingers digging into my coat. "You're choosing him over me?"

"I'm choosing *me* over you, Luca. I don't want anything to do with you anymore. Leave me and my life in peace and go away. If you ever hurt Yan or anyone else I care about again, I won't hesitate to shoot you like I shot your man."

It might make me crazy once and for all. I might lose my identity and become someone entirely different, but if it's to protect my family, I'd do it again in a heartbeat.

My family.

My heart squeezes at that thought. Adrian and Jeremy are my family.

Believing that I had no relation to them for two months was the cruelest thing I could have gone through. I thought I was an imposter, that I was taking another woman's husband and son when I had Adrian and Jeremy all along. Well, at least Jeremy.

Adrian is…another story.

The last time I saw him as Lia, I jumped off the cliff. My demons got the better of me and I didn't think about Jeremy. I didn't think about my life and the people I was leaving behind.

That's what happens when your mind becomes your worst enemy. When its sole purpose is to destroy you from the inside out. It's impossible to think past the demons' whispers and the need to end it all. Past the thought that by ending it, I could make everything fine.

I was wrong, of course. So utterly wrong. And I would've made a huge mistake had it not been for Adrian.

He brought me back.

That thought causes my heart to thump wildly in my chest, slamming against my ribcage. Even when I chose to be Winter, my husband got me back and treated me as Lia.

He also refused to call me Winter, even when I begged him to. Even when I threw tantrums and demanded it.

Even when he could've easily made me into Winter.

And that touches a deep, dark corner of my soul. One that had no light, no hope, and no way out.

One that considered the cliff my last resort.

"You think you can go against me, Lia?" Luca steps closer until his chest nearly flattens against mine. His grip on my arm is unyielding, as if he plans to twist and break it.

"I don't want to, but I will if I have to."

"I thought we were friends."

"I thought so, too, but I'm not friends with people who use me."

"What about Adrian?"

My chest squeezes at the mention of his name. I think it's impossible for me to be unaffected whenever it comes to my husband. "What about him?"

"I'll tell him everything you did over the years."

"I'll talk to him. He'll understand."

"Adrian?" he scoffs. "You're so delusional, Duchess. He's the type who executes people if they have the mere thought of crossing him. Now, if he learns his wife has been spying on him, how do you think he'll react?"

The thought of being the target of Adrian's wrath makes me flat out shake. He's really terrifying when angry and not only because he hurts me, but also because of his silent treatment. I'd rather he fuck me and punish me until I can't move instead of giving me the cold shoulder.

As if I'm meaningless.

"He'll forgive me if I explain," I lie to Luca.

"Will he forgive this, though?"

Before I can make sense of his words, he smashes his lips to mine with a blinding force that leaves me momentarily stunned.

His lips, harsh and unpleasant, provoke a deep sense of disgust. All I can think about is Adrian's kisses, the passion behind them and how they're able to lift me yet mess me up.

I slam a hand on Luca's chest and attempt to push him away, but he grabs it and continues kissing me. Even when I tighten my lips.

"So this is why you wanted to get out?"

My body goes still at that voice.

The same voice that exists in both my dreams and my nightmares. The deep voice with a slightly husky tenor that saves me from my mind most of the time.

Only, that doesn't seem to be the case now. Judging from the frightening calm beneath his tone, he's here to unleash his wrath.

The wrath that makes me tremble all over.

Luca pushes off me, forcing my hand to release him, and then he's sprinting in the opposite direction.

Adrian quickens his pace after him, not sparing me a glance. He's holding a gun, and although his grip seems effortless, his body is so rigid, he appears on the verge of breaking all hell loose.

If he goes after Luca in his state, I have no doubt that my ex-childhood friend will kill him. He won't hesitate to put a bullet in him and finish his life. He's been planning my husband's assassination all this time, after all.

I grab Adrian's hand, the one with the gun, but he pushes me back without looking at me. I don't let him go, though, my nails digging into the sleeve of his jacket.

For the first time since he caught Luca kissing me, Adrian's eyes meet mine.

I wish they hadn't. They're sharp, hard, and resemble the merciless sky overhead. When he speaks, the tenor of his voice is calm but harsh. "Let. Go."

I shake my head frantically.

"Protect him all you like, Lia, but I'll fucking murder him. Today or tomorrow or a decade from now. It will happen."

"I'm not protecting him…" I choke on my tears. "I'm protecting *you*."

My husband faces me and slams his free fist into the wall over my head, the hideous sound echoing in the small alleyway. His body magnifies, almost like it's doubling in size, while his features sharpen. Being in Adrian's company has always been an experience, but actually being the subject of his anger is no different than slamming into a volcano at the point of eruption. He might not burn me, but the threat is there, waiting, biding its time to swallow me whole.

"So now you're protecting me? What's next? Are you going to say you're fucking him for *my* sake?"

I release a shaky breath, my hold tightening on his jacket sleeve. "I never have, Adrian. I lied."

"He just had his tongue down your fucking throat. Which part of that is lying?"

"He didn't have his tongue inside. If you weren't so blinded by your anger, you would've seen that and the fact that he forced that kiss on me."

"So now it's *my* fault?"

"No…" I wrap both of my hands around his wrist, staring up at him, waiting, imploring the Adrian I think I've lost.

Turns out I haven't.

Even as Winter, he came back to me. He treated me like I mattered.

He kissed me.

He sat down and smiled at me.

I want that Adrian, not the closed off monster he becomes when he's enraged. Or worse, when he thinks I've cheated on him. He saw Luca kissing me, so my case isn't looking so good, but I want to fight.

For him.

For us.

For the relationship we've never properly had.

"I remember… I know I'm not Winter and that I'm Lia. I know you must've kept an eye on me the entire time I thought I was homeless and that you eventually brought me home."

Adrian studies me intently, his inquisitive gaze piercing through me, tearing me apart to reach the very marrow of my bones.

If I expected any joy or relief, I get nothing. A muscle works in his jaw and he pulls his fist back so that he can slam it against the wall again. I flinch, but it's more out of worry at the thought of him hurting his knuckles.

"Apparently, the first thing you did upon remembering was to meet your lover."

"No, no…" I hold onto his hand, needing the closeness. "I know how it looked from your perspective, but that wasn't the case."

"You obviously planned to meet him, Lia."

"It's because I saw Winter in the guest house and thought I had no place in your life. That's why I wanted to leave."

I realize how wrong my words are the moment they're out.

"You wanted to leave," Adrian repeats slowly, menacingly.

"I don't want to anymore. I swear."

He lets his hand fall from the wall just so he can grab me by the chin using two fingers. They're rough, meant to punish and hurt, but the only thing I'm focused on is the blood marring his busted knuckles.

Before I can reach for them or try to soothe them, Adrian tilts my head back with a tight grip. "You might have forgotten a few things, so let me remind you, Lia. You are my wife. Fucking *mine*. That means you don't protect another man in my damn presence. No matter how much you try to shield him, I'll find the bastard and kill him. Then, I'll keep my promise and fuck you in his blood."

I see it then. The closing off. The simmering anger that will eventually cool into indifference.

That's what happened before. He was so angry that he refused to touch me for fear he'd hurt me and then he drew away.

I was stupid enough to let it happen in the past. And by doing that, I ultimately hurt myself. I gave up all control to my demons and let them dictate my fate and my life.

That won't be the case anymore.

Even if my insides are shriveling at the thought of being rejected, even if my mind is still swimming with a million gloomy scenarios, I know one thing for certain.

I need to keep Adrian.

I have to stop him from closing himself off to me.

And the only way to do that is to use the methods he did when he wanted me with him.

Before my nerves get the better of me, I lower myself on my knees.

This time, I'll be the one who gives.

SIX

Lia

FOR THE FIRST TIME SINCE I'VE KNOWN ADRIAN, I GET on my knees.

Not so he can punish or fuck me from behind, but for *him*.

Because I want to give *him* something.

Usually, he's the one who initiates sexual activities and I'm there for the ride. I love his rough handling and unapologetic sexual drive. I love that he never seems to get enough of me.

And now, I want to use that so he doesn't retreat back to his highly built walls.

Due to his indifference, I went crazy the first time. I went so crazy that I thought it was a good idea to send a strange lookalike to him, and then I jumped off a cliff.

I don't think I can do that anymore. I can't handle that side of him.

So I choose to do something I never have.

Adrian stares down at me with drawn brows and eyes so gray, they blacken in the darkness. I don't even care that we're in a semi-public place and that anyone can walk by and see me on my knees in front of him. I feel that if I don't do this now, I'll lose him. Maybe not right away, but it'll happen in the long run like before.

I reach for his belt and unbuckle it, my thighs clenching at the reminder of the amount of both pleasure and pain this belt has brought me over the years.

He lets me free his cock, and I have to use both hands to clutch him. They tremble slightly around his length as it hardens in an instant at my touch.

"What are you doing, Lia?"

Staring up at him, I offer him what we both want. "Fuck my mouth, Adrian."

"You actually think I want to after what I just witnessed?"

I glide my hand from the root up and then down, adding pressure until I'm jacking him off, mimicking the same level of violence that he usually uses on himself before he comes all over my breasts, ass, or pussy. "You do. You love punishing me."

My pace picks up, relying on pure instinct as I lean over and lick the precum from the tip and suck him into my mouth.

A deep groan spills from his lips and I use it as an incentive to quicken what I'm doing. A weird sense of empowerment mixed with arousal hits me. My thighs clench and my heart thunders so loud, it nearly bursts my chest open.

I'm the one who's giving him pleasure now, the reason he's releasing the appreciative noises and thickening in my mouth. Right in this moment, I'm the only one who can grant him release.

Adrian sinks his strong, lean fingers into my hair, then tugs me back by it. I don't release the tip of his cock or loosen my hands as I stare up at him.

His height is blocking the dim light coming through the entrance of the alleyway and he looks like a general, a warrior.

Or maybe he's just still the devil.

Because despite the lust shining in his ash eyes, his features are as hard as granite, glinting with the promise of pain.

"Remove your hands, Lia."

I drop them to my lap, eager to let him take control. I might love having these reactions from him, but I think my real pleasure has always been when Adrian owns me wholly.

Body.

Heart.

And soul.

"I know you've been texting him," he says with a feigned calm that chills me to the bones. "Did you think I wouldn't know just because you deleted the texts?"

I shake my head and start to inch away so I can speak, so I can explain, but Adrian thrusts his cock to the back of my throat. My gag reflex kicks in and I slap both palms on his thighs.

My nails dig into his pants, but that doesn't deter him as he pulls back the slightest bit before slamming back inside and holding it there. He chokes me, confiscating my air and leaving me hanging by a thread.

"I only let it slide to see how far you'd go, Lia. How fucking much you'd betray me."

I want to deny it, to tell him that I thought I was an imposter, that I was jealous of my own self because I didn't have him. Because I believed he loved another woman and not me.

However, Adrian doesn't allow me any room to breathe, let alone talk.

My lungs burn from the lack of oxygen and tears cling to my lids at the way he keeps holding his dick at the back of my throat.

"Did you let him fuck your mouth, too? *My* mouth?"

I attempt to shake my head, but I'm too dizzy and without air.

I think I'll faint.

That I will blackout from being choked by his cock.

However, he finally pulls his length out, and I sputter for air, coughing, my lungs aching from exertion.

"A-Adrian, I—" Before I can take a full gulp of air, he's pounding in again with a merciless rotation of his hips, pushing all the way in.

Even with him fucking my throat, he's still not completely inside my mouth. He's too big for that and his cock is too thick.

His other hand grips my jaw with two fingers and tilts my chin up. "Did you look up at him with these fucking tears in your eyes?"

I shake my head, but the gesture is barely-there as Adrian powers in and out of my mouth with a mad rhythm that's out of control. I'm lightheaded, unable to breathe, and my hold on his thigh is more for balance than anything else now. I feel like if I let him go, I'll fall.

Or maybe worse.

My husband uses my mouth like it's his own vessel of punishment. He drives in, keeping his cock at the base of my throat, then pulls out, allowing me a sliver of air before he rams back inside.

I don't attempt to stop him as he uses me, punishes me, and takes out his anger on me.

If anything, my thighs tighten every time he confiscates my air. Every time he thrusts in with unapologetic force, manhandling me, taking what he wants from me.

Drool drips down my chin and tears streak my cheeks, but I still keep my mouth open whenever he pulls out. I still want him inside, even if my jaw aches.

However, punishing me doesn't seem to take the edge away from his savage features. Instead, it seems to deepen, heighten, *sharpen* them.

"I spend two months, two fucking *months*, entertaining your belief that you're Winter, and just when I think I have you back, just when I start to believe you'll be different, you fuck up everything."

A sob tears from my throat, but it's lost in the sound of him fucking my mouth—or more accurately, my throat.

"This mouth is mine, Lia. Only mine."

I nod frantically, even though he didn't ask a question.

Adrian's grip tightens on my hair and his body goes rigid. I think he'll come, but that doesn't seem to be the case.

He keeps going on and on, his hips thrusting with a ruthlessness that steals my thoughts and my breath.

"Open your mouth wide," he finally grunts.

I do, sticking my tongue out the slightest bit.

Adrian releases my jaw and tugs my head back using my hair. "Fucking mine."

And with that, he comes all over my lips, tongue, and throat. I swallow as much as possible, but some of his cum rolls down my chin, mixing with the saliva and tears.

I'm panting and aching between my legs, but I ignore all that and focus on Adrian.

He's still gripping me by the hair, and even though he just came, his cock is already semi-hard as if ready for more.

I don't stop staring at him. In part because of how utterly beautiful he is, but also because I've always loved witnessing the moment of ecstasy on his face right after an orgasm.

But the most important part is because I need to know he still wants me. That what happened just now wasn't only him punishing me or the mere fusing of our bodies, but something more.

Adrian tucks himself in with one hand and does his zipper, not bothering with the belt. His hold is still harsh and unforgiving on my hair as he pulls me up by it.

I stumble to my feet, gripping his bicep for balance. We're standing toe-to-toe, one ragged pulse against the other, and my heart flips in my chest at being this close to him.

It's never felt ordinary over the years. Adrian will always have a part of me in the palm of his hand.

He'll always make me stop and stare.

He grips my chin again. This time, his fingers trace over my lips that are still coated with his cum. "Whose mouth is this?"

I don't even think as I whisper, "Yours."

"Whose tears are these?"

"Yours..." He leans over and licks them off my cheek, then bites down slightly.

I shudder, my whole body drowning in a shockwave of emotions as he nibbles his way to my ear and murmurs in hot, dark words, "You'd best remember that, Lenochka."

SEVEN

Lia

"**M**OMMY!"

I open my arms and crouch as Jeremy runs at full speed toward me. Tears are shining in his huge eyes when he slams into my embrace.

As I hug him to my chest and smell his marshmallow and apple scent, I feel like everything will be okay. As long as I have my baby boy, I'll be fine.

"I thought you went away, Mommy." He sniffles against me. "I was playing with the clowns, but then Boris stopped them and you were gone."

"It's okay, my little angel. I'm right here and would never leave."

I mean it this time, because there's no way in hell I'm abandoning Jeremy again. He's suffered enough for his young age. I don't care what happens to me as long as he's safe.

Even if it means facing his father's wrath.

When Adrian and I emerged from the alleyway after he fucked my mouth, turning me on without having to touch me, Kolya, Boris, and a few other guards were waiting for us near a small parking area with Jeremy.

Adrian ushers us into the back seat of the car without saying a word. God, I hate his silent treatment. It gets on my last nerve and it also hurts because I know he uses it as a method to pull away from me.

He hasn't always been talkative, but he's at least used his voice—aside from ordering me to do sexual things.

Soon after, we're leaving in the car, with Kolya and Boris in the front and the three of us in the back. Jeremy is sitting between us, apparently unaware of the tension brewing in the air while he excitedly tells me about the clowns and how they were so funny.

I answer him when he asks questions, but my attention is divided as I keep stealing glances at Adrian. He's focused on his phone, seeming to cut us both out, although he does talk to Jeremy when he asks him something.

So it's only me.

If it were still old times, I would've focused on Jer and given Adrian the figurative middle finger. But that lack of communication is what ruined us in the first place.

Handing Jeremy a bottle of juice that I had in my bag for our picnic, I pretend to be preoccupied with fixing his scarf as I ask Adrian, "Did you follow us?"

He doesn't spare me a glance, but he doesn't ignore me and nods.

It was a redundant question anyway, considering he appeared not long after Luca took me. He must've suspected me since I asked him if I could go out with Jeremy last night.

And here I thought I was being smart.

I should've known from everything that's happened in the past that Adrian is always one step ahead. However, I couldn't really recall those years when I was being Winter.

Though a part of me felt a certain familiarity that I did my best to ignore.

My instant connection with Adrian makes sense, too. The fear, the lust, and the affection all came from deep within me.

"Why did you follow us, Papa?" Jeremy asks and it takes everything in me not to kiss his adorable cheeks.

"Because I wanted to see you, Malysh." Adrian ruffles his hair before going back to his phone.

Jer takes a slurp of his juice, then frowns. "How about Mommy? You didn't want to see Mommy?"

"Of course I did," he says with no emotion.

"Maybe you can come with us next time, Papa."

"Maybe."

"Your papa has work to do, Jer." I stroke his hair away from his face, adopting my softest tone. "He doesn't have time for us."

Adrian glares at me beneath his lashes, but I hold onto my defensive line through Jeremy. I hate using him, but he's always been the only solid thread keeping us together. And if that's the best way to get to my husband, so be it.

"Maybe he doesn't want to be with us," I continue, stroking Jeremy's hair.

I wouldn't have dared to say such words a few months ago. I always kept my words to myself, was mad on the inside but refused to let it show on the outside.

However, something's changed ever since I mistook myself for being Winter. I freed myself in ways I never thought possible, and it's only because of that freedom that I'm able to embrace my true self.

I'm able to talk aloud about what I want.

As much as I hated those couple of months and the loneliness I felt, I don't hate my newfound freedom.

Or my voice.

Jeremy grips the bottle of juice as he stares up at his father. "Is that true, Papa?"

"Not at all, Malysh. I love spending time with you."

"And Mommy?" Jer, bless his little heart, is the first member of my fan club.

"And your mother."

He's insincere, judging by his apathetic tone, and that's why I need to strike the iron while it's hot.

"Then go on a vacation with us," I say nonchalantly.

A muscle tics in his jaw, but he quickly masks it. "We'll talk about it later."

"Or we can talk about it now, isn't that right, Jer?"

"Right! Go on vacation with us, Papa."

Adrian stares at me and I stare back. When I was Winter, his eyes started making me uncomfortable at some point, because I didn't recognize that I knew them, intimately so, and he can get scary whenever he directs his impenetrable intense gaze at me. However, I refuse to cower.

I meet him stare for stare, tipping my chin up for good measure.

Jer clutches his sleeve, gazing up at him with those huge eyes that neither of us can resist. "Papa, *please*."

Adrian releases a sigh. "Fine."

"Yay, Papa!"

"Next week? The one after?" I push.

"We will see."

"In two weeks, then. Hear that, Jer? The three of us will go on a trip."

My son's eyes widen as he looks between us. "What type of trip?"

"We'll let your father surprise us."

"Yay!" Jeremy kisses me and then his father.

Adrian tightens his hold on the phone and I can tell he doesn't like the fact that I indirectly forced him, but I need more time with him outside his work and the house. I need to rebuild our relationship before it's too late.

That is, if there's anything left to build.

The thought sends a shiver through me and cripples me to my bones.

As soon as we reach the house, Adrian gets out first, followed by Boris.

Kolya lingers a bit behind for the first time ever, not eager to be on his boss's heels.

"What?" I ask when he keeps staring.

"You...shouldn't have done that."

"Done what?"

"Used Jeremy to force his hand. That's what his mother did. She used Boss so his father would do things her way. Needless to say, he hates it."

Shit.

Just when I think I'm making things better, they end up being way worse.

EIGHT

Lia

ADRIAN SPENDS THE REST OF THE DAY COOPED UP IN his office with Kolya.

No surprise there.

Unlike before, however, I don't sit around and wait. I don't have a pity party for myself, bottling up the pain of being neglected or moping around because he doesn't come for me.

That Lia was killed at the bottom of that cliff.

I might not have come out normal after the fall, but now I'm well aware of who I am.

Something changed in me after that night and I'll embrace that change. It might not be the best, but it's better than how I was before.

I wait until it's Jeremy's bedtime, then read him a story that makes him giggle. He hugs my waist, fighting the sleep from his metallic eyes as they droop. "Don't leave me, Mommy."

"Never, my angel." I kiss the top of his head.

Soon after, he loses the battle to sleep. I gently pry his fingers from around me and tuck him under the blanket before

I stand up. For a moment, I remain there, watching him and noticing how much he's grown up.

It feels like yesterday that he was born and we had to flee for our lives. My baby boy has been resilient since the very beginning.

Abandoning him with a strange woman, even at the promise of reuniting with him, worsened my state of mind. I recognize that now. That's why I used the information I learned from Winter about losing her own child and mixed it up with the emptiness I had for not having Jeremy with me. Then I came up with a completely different identity.

I need to pay Dr. Taylor a visit because I have to prevent that from happening again. Feeling like another person, a *stranger*, in the company of my son and husband was the worst experience I've ever had to endure.

Worse than being trapped in the black box as a child.

Worse than the ending of my career.

At that moment, I saw myself as an imposter who was stealing another woman's family, and God help me, I wanted to steal it.

I wanted this life. I wanted Jeremy and Adrian to be all mine.

It's ironic, considering I spent a great deal of effort trying to escape from being me. I never knew how much I was attached to my life until I nearly lost it.

Until Jeremy and Adrian were no longer my family.

Turns out, they always were. Or at least, Jeremy is. I need to do something about Adrian so that he doesn't treat me like a stranger.

And the best way to do that is to learn some information before facing him.

Thankfully, I know the right person for that.

After kissing Jeremy's forehead one last time, I step out of his room and go downstairs. I throw on a coat and slip out of the main house.

The freezing air chills my bones and I tighten the coat around me as I cross the distance to the guest house.

Boris and another guard stand out front, smoking and talking in Russian. Upon seeing me, they toss their cigarettes and Boris hurries to block my entrance.

He's about the same build as Kolya, but has mean features with thin lips and a pointy nose.

"Evening, Boris," I say in my most welcoming tone.

"Mrs. Volkov," he greets back in his gruff Russian accent.

A sudden frisson goes through me at that name. When I thought I was Winter, I hated it because I was jealous of her—me. But when I was Lia, I refused to admit how much I loved having that last name attached to mine.

"I need to see Yan, Boris."

He clears his throat. "That won't be possible. Boss's orders."

"Are you going to use force to stop me?"

His and the other guard's eyes widen at the suggestion. "Of course not. Boss would slaughter us if we touched you."

"In that case, let me in."

"I'll have to report it to him."

"Do it then. Tell him to come and stop me himself." And with that, I brush past Boris, slightly scared, slightly excited about the fact that Adrian might come to fetch me.

But before that, I have to get the information I need.

The room in which Yan is resting is on the ground floor, but I stare at the stairs. Winter is up there and probably has been for the past two months. She's another mystery I need to solve.

If Adrian knew from the get-go that she wasn't me, why did he hurt her? My chest squeezes at the thought that I put her in danger.

At the same time, I swear I saw her staring down at us when Adrian and I were playing with Jeremy in the garden at that time. Was that also a figment of my imagination?

Shaking my head, I go to Yan's room and softly knock on the door.

"Come in," he says in a weary voice.

I push the door open, then go inside and settle on the chair beside his bed. The one Kolya would be occupying if he were here. For a stoic dude, Kolya cares about Yan and shows it through action, though he'd probably never admit it in words.

Yan is sitting in bed, wearing a blue hoodie. His long hair is loose, falling to his neck and giving his face a softer edge. His skin's color has returned to normal and the ghost of death has slowly retreated from his features.

He's browsing through the TV channels without focusing on one in particular. Upon seeing me, he switches the TV off and leans back against the numerous pillows surrounding him.

"Are you okay?"

He lifts a shoulder and winces. "If bored out of my mind means I'm okay, then sure, I guess I am."

A small smile paints my lips. His attitude is something else, I swear.

"How did you get here, anyway? I thought Boris was standing like a hell guard at the entrance of my prison."

"I have my ways."

"Your ways? You're going to get us in trouble again, aren't you?"

"Wouldn't it be worth it?"

"Fuck, no. I still need my neck, thank you very much."

I laugh softly, then pause as it dies away. "Hey, Yan."

"Yes?"

"I remember."

"You…do?"

"Yes. I stopped thinking I'm someone else or whatever."

His lips part before he releases a long breath. "Fucking finally. I thought I'd have to start forcing info down your throat."

"Why didn't you?"

"Did you forget the part where I still need my neck? Boss is already on a mission to cut me into pieces and exhibit them in the entrance hall. I don't need to give him more incentive. Besides, the head shrink said you were dissociating, and forcing information on you would have the exact opposite effect and could worsen your state."

I inch closer. "Is that why Adrian let me live as Winter?"

"Exactly."

"I assume he watched me from afar?"

"We all did. You have no idea how grumpy he was during that period—more than usual, I mean. Yours truly had to take his wrath. He beat everyone up during our daily workouts."

"I'm sorry."

"Don't apologize for a situation you had no control over. Mental illness isn't something to be sorry about."

Tears surge to my eyes and I widen them to stop them from spilling. "Thanks."

"We ride together and die together, woman."

"Oh my God, Yan!" I shriek from excitement, a wide grin stretching my lips. "You're Larry?!"

He winks. "The one and only."

"I can't believe it. You look nothing alike, except for the nose deformation. You even spoke in a different accent."

"A disguise took care of the looks. As for the accent…" He clears his throat and switches to an American one. "I lived here most my life, woman. I can speak like an American. I just choose not to because a Russian accent makes me sound scary and badass."

"You little bastard." I'm still laughing, overjoyed at the fact that Larry and Yan are the same person. They were the only people I could consider a friend, whether as Lia or Winter.

"Who are you calling little? I'm twenty-five, thank you very much."

"You're still younger than me. Deal with it."

"Whatever." He rolls his eyes. "Does Boss know you remember?"

My humor vanishes as I recall what happened today. "He does, but he found out under the worst circumstances. He's back to thinking I cheated on him. Not that he ever stopped."

"He doesn't just *think* it. You put it in his head and refused to deny it."

"I did today and he didn't believe me."

"Can you blame him? You left that idea to fester and rot in his mind for months."

"I know. But he's not innocent either."

"So? Are you going to talk about it or will you consider solving this a few years from now? Because he might not have the time."

My heart thunders as a gloomy halo confiscates my thoughts. "What do you mean?"

"Now that you're Lia, you should know that he killed Richard."

"I already figured that out. Didn't he do that to get me back by his side again?" Though I'm glad for it, Adrian's methods can be extreme. He really frightened the shit out of me back then.

"No, he did it because the scum Richard put his hands on you."

"Oh." A rush of something hot goes through me and for some reason, it's not disgust.

My husband said he'd protect me and he did. Even when I completely erased him.

"That's not all, Lia. Richard was the Bratva's mayoral candidate and Sergei isn't happy that he died. If he finds out it's an inside job, he'll consider it a betrayal."

"Does he…does he suspect Adrian?"

"Yes, and he put Vladimir on the task to bring him down. That mule fucker won't stop until he proves that Boss is behind it. Igor, who never forgave him for tossing Kristina aside for you, is also plotting his demise so he can put his eldest son in Boss's position."

"But...but...isn't he the most valuable asset to the brotherhood? Sergei wouldn't abandon him just like that."

"He would."

"But why? Adrian is the pillar of that stupid brotherhood. They can't simply cast him out." I'm so enraged on his behalf. He gave those assholes his youth and his life, yet they have the audacity to do this to him for someone as insignificant as Richard?

"They sure can. Richard's death allowed the Lucianos to push their candidate forward and that's a clear act of betrayal."

My heart skips a beat at the mention of Dad's last name. My biological father—the reason why Adrian approached me in the first place. "But he didn't do it to benefit the Italians."

"True, but that's what it'd look like to Sergei and everyone else."

"Shit."

"Shit, indeed, Lia. So don't waste any more time."

"I don't plan to."

Yan hesitates, running his hand through his hair as he watches me from beneath his long eyelashes.

"What is it, Yan?"

"I heard you that night, you know."

"What night?"

"When I was shot."

"Oh."

"You knew that man." He lowers his voice. "You *know* him."

"Yeah," I murmur.

"Ah, well, fuck. One more complication."

"Are you going to tell Adrian?"

"Of course not. He'll take it out on you."

"But Kolya said Adrian suspects you and thinks you got shot as a ploy."

"He has no proof to go with it and he doesn't act without that. I'll be fine. Just focus on yourself."

"Thank you. I'm so glad I have you."

"Me too. Or else my cause of death would've been boredom."

I smile, then peek at him. "Can you do me one more favor?"

"Now what?"

I suck in a deep breath. "Tell me all about the time I was Winter."

Becoming whole depends on me and me alone. Only when I put all the pieces of my life together will I be able to take the next step.

Whether it will build or destroy us, I have no clue.

NINE

Adrian

THE OVERSTIMULATION OF MY MIND STOPS ME FROM processing anything.

Or perhaps I'm processing so much that my brain cells are burning faster than I can form thoughts.

Ever since I witnessed Lia kissing her lover, I've been seeing a mist of red. Dark fucking red.

Rage red.

And I couldn't blow it by killing the fucker because she was protecting him.

Again.

She just regained her memories and stopped asking me to call her by another woman's name, but the first person she went to was him. Her lover.

Fucking again.

I slam my fist against the table and revel in the shock that reverberates through my arm. At least the pain distracts me from murderous thoughts about her.

About him.

About everyone.

It's temporary, but it's better than nothing.

The fact that she got on her knees for the first time, told me to fuck her mouth for the first time, made things even worse.

While I enjoyed the feel of her hands on me and the way I used her mouth to the point of eruption, the gratification ended at that very moment. Because now, all I keep thinking about is how she only did that to shield him. To distract me from following after him.

I knew that at the time, I did, but I had to take her mouth, had to punish her.

And the need for more is still pulsing through my veins.

Maybe this was her plan all along—seducing me so she can distract me.

"Do you want to call it a night, Boss?" Kolya asks from his position on the sofa.

Leaving the surveillance monitors, I stand up and stride to the window, releasing a heavy breath as I stare at the dark garden outside. "I want his location, Kolya."

"Yes, but watching hours upon hours of public surveillance will probably be a waste of time. He knows how to cover his tracks and always wears a mask and a hat. We only got his profile and it's impossible to get a facial identification from that."

I tap my finger against my thigh, then halt as the dots start connecting in my head. When I turn to face Kolya again, the idea forms clearly. "Black leather jacket, mask, and hat...just like the kidnapper from Igor's birthday party a week ago."

"You think it's the same person?"

"I'm almost sure of it." I stride toward him and sit by his side. "Pull up both feeds."

After a few clicks, Kolya retrieves a still image of the person who kidnapped Lia and shot Yan, then puts it side by side with the footage we hacked from the public surveillance cameras today.

The clothes are similar, but they're standard, so anyone can wear them. It's his build that gives him away. He has the same profile and the same height and broadness.

I tap the screen. "It's the same fucker."

"It is." Kolya's brows bunch. "Why would he kidnap Mrs. Volkov, though?"

"Because he couldn't find a way to talk to her. We were keeping a close eye on her, even when she was Winter, and he couldn't get close, so he had to pull that stunt."

"I still don't understand why he needed to kidnap her, shoot Yan, and risk being caught. It couldn't be just because he's her lover."

Kolya's reasoning makes sense, but if the bastard is as crazy about her as I am, he'd risk it. Though, someone of his caliber, clearly trained and with enough skill to avoid nearly all surveillance cameras, wouldn't have approached her at a party held by the *Pakhan*.

It's like he wanted to drive home a message, a 'fuck you' of sorts, to tell me that he could get to me anytime he likes.

That my system isn't bulletproof.

My system isn't bulletproof.

The thought snaps blurred lines in my head and the only other time where my system failed rushes to the front.

The assassination attempt about a year ago. The only time I couldn't find information on who tried to kill me.

The incident after which Lia's depression struck harder and she admitted to cheating on me.

"Could he be the same man who participated in the hit last summer?" I ask Kolya.

He perks up. "That's a possibility. But considering his skills, wouldn't he have done it on his own? Why would he hire a mercenary to do it on his behalf?"

"The same reason he hired the Spetsnaz that he shot and let crash down the cliff with the car. Camouflage. He probably doesn't want anything to link back to him."

"Why would he want to kill you?"

"To have Lia all for himself," I grit from between clenched teeth. "He could also be working with one of our enemies."

"I'll rearrange what we have thus far and look at it from the perspective that it's the same person in all three cases."

"He could be related to either Lazlo Luciano, the Rozettis, or one of our own."

"Like who?"

"Vladimir or Igor. Hold on." I retrieve my phone and dial the number I never wanted to call to ask for help.

Kirill picks up after two rings, sounding as smug as ever. "Adrian. What a lovely surprise. To what do I owe this honor?"

"What do you know?"

"Cutting straight to the chase, I see."

"Don't waste my time, Morozov."

"You know, in case no one told you, when asking for a favor, you're supposed to do it nicely."

"My nice phase is coming to an end and so is any agreement we might reach together."

"Jesus. You're as grumpy as an old man."

"*What do you know?*" I emphasize.

"What makes you think I know something?"

"You've been giving less than subtle hints."

"So you did catch those. Here I thought I had to take my hinting game to the next level. What do you want to learn first?"

"What do you have?"

"What if I told you I know a tidbit about your wife's past that you might not be aware of?"

I still the slow tap of my forefinger on my thigh. There's no way in hell he knows she's Lazlo's daughter. The people who are aware of that information are dead. I made sure of it.

So I hold onto my cool. "What is it?"

"Did you know that she grew up with an Italian boy?"

"An Italian boy?"

"Yes. Neighbors. I didn't think much of it at the beginning when I looked into her, but then, alarms went off in my head."

"You *looked* into her?"

"Of course I did. Vladimir, Igor, and Sergei did, too. You bring a woman out of nowhere and announce she's your wife and baby mama and think we'll just nod our heads? You don't make mistakes, Adrian, so no matter how much you try to convince everyone that you only married her for an accidental pregnancy, I don't believe it. I'm sure it was all part of a master plan. Now, where was I? Right. The Italian. Even though it seemed normal, when I looked further into him and his parents, I found nothing."

"Nothing?"

"Absolute nada. No normal citizen would cover their tracks that meticulously, would they?"

"No."

"Exactly."

"What's his name?"

"Luca."

"Last name?"

"Brown. Luca Brown. Ring any bells?"

"No."

He clicks his tongue. "To me neither. But I'll find that motherfucker. No one hides from me."

"Keep me posted."

"My, my, Adrian. Aren't you full of love today?"

"Just do as you're told."

"And I'll get something in return?"

"Yes."

"Fantastic. Love doing business with you."

I stare at my phone, then focus on Kolya. "Why didn't you tell me she had an Italian neighbor in your first screening of her?"

"Didn't seem like it mattered at the time. They were both kids and many in New York have Italian neighbors. I didn't feel like I needed to go more in-depth."

He's right. It shouldn't have mattered. But after what Kirill mentioned, I have a suspicion that this Luca is even more involved than I ever thought.

There's only one other person who can tell me the details, even if I have to punish them out of her.

"Let's call it a night, Kolya." I stand up and my second-in-command follows.

"Boris sent me a text earlier and I didn't want to disturb you."

"About?"

"Mrs. Volkov went to the guest house to visit Yan."

I clench a fist. "You didn't want to disturb me or were you protecting the little fuck?"

He releases a long sigh. "Both."

"He knows something, Kolya. He was there and he's hiding it from me."

"I know."

"You finally agree?"

"Yes. He wouldn't tell me either but it's obvious. He's protecting Mrs. Volkov."

"From me?"

"Yes, sir. You know he's still mad about how you drove her to the edge of that cliff."

"So now you're on his side?"

"I'm on *your* side. And to do that, I have to tell you things as they are. That's how it's been for the past three decades."

I jam a finger into his chest. "Find out what he's hiding or I'm torturing him the same day he can get on his feet."

With that, I leave the office and head upstairs. I don't bother with dinner, having no appetite whatsoever.

It's ten in the evening, so Lia must be in Jeremy's room. I

go there, bent on carrying her out and extracting the answers from her skin.

The raging need for more that I've felt since I painted her mouth with my cum returns with a vengeance.

Surprisingly, when I get to Malysh's room, he's the only one sleeping there. I close the door quietly and set out for our bedroom.

Don't tell me she's still with Yan? If that's the case, I will—

My murderous thoughts and feet screech to a halt in the doorway.

The only light comes from red candles that sit on every surface—the vanity, the nightstands, and even the chairs. The sheets that I didn't even know we had are red and the scent of roses wafts in the air.

A tray of food is on the vanity, surrounded by more candles and roses.

The setting is similar to last night, but the only difference is the woman standing in the middle of the room, wearing just a bathrobe and lighting more candles.

"Oh." She lifts her head. "You weren't supposed to be back for another half hour. I didn't even put on makeup—"

I charge toward her and grab her by the arm. The lighter falls from her hand to the chair and she faces me, her lips parted and her skin flushed.

For a moment, I want to believe that she's doing this for me.

For *us*.

But why would she when she never has before?

There's only one way to find out the truth.

TEN

Lia

WHEN I PLOTTED THIS, I HAD ONE THOUGHT IN mind—get to Adrian.

I didn't care whether I got his anger or his wrath, as long as he expressed it instead of bottling all his emotions inside as usual.

To ensure I had everything prepared, I brought out the candles, the sheets, and the lingerie I bought a year ago but never had the courage to use. I had to hide them at the back of the closet as if they were some sort of disgrace.

Back then, I was more afraid of the idea of him and didn't want to fully give in to my feelings or to him.

A part of me still battles that. Still whispers in a corner of my head that Adrian is a monster and there's nothing that will change it.

However, that part is what made me lose my mind, because I denied something I wanted so much, and in doing that, I screwed up my head.

So now, as he holds me by the arm, the dark gray pools of his eyes shining with malice, I don't run away.

I stare.

I fall.

I just stay in the moment.

Which isn't so hard since Adrian is able to confiscate my entire attention by merely being there.

Goosebumps erupt on my flesh from where he's gripping me. The shadow on his sharp cheekbones gives him a darkened, lethal edge.

He's such a handsome man with a quiet beauty that creeps up on you out of nowhere and a physical perfection that gets better with time. I might have been a bit infatuated with him for years.

Okay, a *lot*.

"What do you think you're doing, Lia?"

I love the sound of my name on his lips. In fact, I love it so much that I may have leaned closer merely to hear it clearer in the tenor of his voice.

Snap out of it, Lia.

"Just dinner," I say with nonchalance.

"This doesn't look like *just dinner* to me."

"You're the one who called me earlier wanting a date, remember?"

"Who said I want it anymore?"

I ignore how his words sting, especially since we've never really had a date before, but I tamp it down. "Well, I want a date."

"If by a date, you mean you'll either answer my questions or I will get your ass red, then fine, Lia. Let's have a date."

"And they say romance is dead."

"Drop the sarcasm. It doesn't suit you."

"I think it suits me just fine."

"Lia…" he warns. "Don't talk back to me or your ass will pay the price."

A jolt of excitement goes up my spine and I feign

indifference, trying hard not to rub my thighs together. "The dinner is getting cold."

"What are you playing at? Are you going to seduce me in order to ask for something later? To get out so you can meet the fucker, maybe?"

"No." I shake my head. "I never cheated on you, Adrian. I swear."

He grabs me by a fistful of my hair and I wince as he tugs backward. "So this is your new game? Denial?"

I hold onto his wrist, not to remove it, but to touch him, to establish a connection with him so that whatever vulnerable thread exists between us doesn't break.

"How about I treat you the same, Lia? Should I bring in a mistress, too? I'll tie you to the bed and fuck her right in front of you while you watch. Is that what you want?"

"No!" Tears fill my eyes and a green-eyed monster rears his head from the depths of my soul.

I have no doubt he'd do it just to teach me a lesson, to hurt me as much as I hurt him, and I don't think I would ever survive the sight of Adrian touching another woman.

It'd break me to the point of no return.

"Why not? You sent your lookalike in my direction, so isn't that what you expected to happen? For me to fuck her?"

Bitter tears slide down my cheeks and I clamp my lips together to prevent them from trembling.

"Answer me, Lia."

I choke on a sob before I speak. "I wasn't thinking straight back then."

"You weren't thinking, but you obviously thought hard enough about having her take your place. Did you imagine her in my bed? Did you like that image?"

"No...no! No!" I dig my fingers into his skin. "Don't torture me like this."

"You mean, like the way you've been torturing me for months?"

"I didn't cheat on you and I'd never be able to. Not when you own every part of me."

"I own every part of you?" His eyes darken to a frightening hue.

I nod, though it isn't very noticeable with the hold he has on my hair.

"Let's prove it then."

He hauls me to the bed, kicking away the carefully situated pillows I put there.

I don't protest as he forces me to my back on the mattress. Instead, a spark of twisted excitement rushes through me like never before.

Adrian's hand bunches the robe and he rips it off me. I haven't been able to change into anything sexy or get fixed up.

My nakedness is completely visible to him and I revel in his darkened gaze, in the promise there.

I have that effect on him. It's not another woman who breaks his frigid façade and yanks out the man inside, it's me.

Only me.

My husband straddles me and grabs both of my wrists in one hand, then slams them over my head, using the sash of my robe to tie them to the bedpost. My heart shivers with each of his sure, methodical movements.

He's melting me piece by piece, and there's no way in hell I'll be able to resist him.

Not that I want to.

If anything, I need this side of him. I need the unrestrained pleasure and the unstoppable passion.

I need him to not hold back.

Usually, he proceeds to punish or fuck me when my hands are tied.

Not this time.

Adrian gets off me, reaches for the nightstand, and retrieves some pieces of rope. Before I can decipher what he's doing, he heads to the foot of the bed and ties one of my ankles to the post, then does the same to the other so that I'm spread-eagle for his view.

A foreign sense of arousal shoots through me at the position. I'm completely naked, tied, and the only one who's able to save me from this is the same one who put me in it.

My husband stands across from me, in direct view of my pussy, as he unbuttons his shirt. The hard ridges of his chest are revealed with each button until the material is hanging open. He rips it off his body and throws it beside him.

I get an unrestricted view of his naked chest and the full sleeve tattoos that always get my nerves in a bunch.

His abdomen muscles ripple and I want to clench my thighs together, but I'm unable to due to my position.

Adrian removes his belt, but not his pants, then loops the leather around his strong veiny hand as he walks to the side of the bed.

Or more like, he stalks like a giant cat with his sights set on a prey to devour. A thousand shivers explode on my skin and the torturous anticipation makes my tongue stick to the roof of my mouth.

"What are you going to do to me?"

His ash eyes feast on my nakedness as he speaks with veiled nonchalance. "What do you think I'll do?"

"Punish me?"

"Cheaters deserve more than mere punishments."

"I'm not a cheater."

His belt whooshes in the air before it comes down on my hardening nipples. I shriek, the sound echoing in the silence as a searing pain explodes in my sensitive peaks.

Holy. Shit.

"With every lie out of your mouth, I'll whip you."

"I am *not* a cheater."

He slaps my breasts again and I wail, but this time the

sting doesn't stay at the surface level, instead getting deeper and darker to reach the sick, twisted part of me that only Adrian can touch.

A sob wrenches from my throat and I choke on it. "I'm not…ahhh—"

My voice is cut off when he whips me again. I buck off the bed, but the ropes bring me right back down, preventing my escape. My nipples are blood red and pink welts spread across my breasts.

Adrian glides the tip of his belt over a tight bud and I arch my back. A jolt of pleasure rips through me and settles at the base of my stomach. Equal amount of pleasure and pain rush through me all at once. I'm delirious, sobbing and begging for more.

"Did he touch these nipples, Lia?"

"No…I swear…"

"Who do these nipples belong to?"

"You," I let out a strangled murmur.

His belt comes down on them again. "I didn't hear that."

"You!" I cry out.

"Correct." His belt glides down the hollow of my stomach and I brace myself, sucking in a breath and sniffling through my tears that leave hot streaks on my cheeks and neck.

Adrian has the ability to turn me into a mess with a mere touch. It's insane how much he turns my body against me, then makes me enjoy his depravity.

Crave it, even.

"When did you start your affair, Lia?"

"I didn't…there was no affair…ahhh…" My voice ends on a cry when his belt meets my stomach.

"Let's try again. *When?*"

"I never…never…"

Slap!

I arch off the bed, my eyes filled with tears until my vision is blurry, but I meet his gaze head-on. "You can whip me to death, but I won't tell a lie…I never looked at any man but you."

"Never looked at any man but me?" *Slap!* "Then who was the man you were kissing, Lia?" *Slap!* "Who the fuck was he?"

I'm wailing and bawling by the time he finishes. Any sound I make is broken by the force of my sobs. My thighs are shaking, my nipples are throbbing, and a bizarre state of painful arousal takes hold of my entire being.

"Adrian…please…stop…"

"You're the only one who can make this stop by giving me what I want. Stop fucking protecting him."

"I'm…I'm not protecting him."

"Is that why you refuse to tell me who he is?"

"It's because he's dangerous …I…I don't want you hurt."

He laughs, the sound harsh, humorless, and tugs on my heartstrings. "You've already done that plenty, Lenochka."

"You hurt me, too…" I whimper between my sniffles. "You crushed me when I learned you only married me to use me against my father."

His belt pauses at the valley of my legs. "Did I ever use you?"

"You could have. I was living in damn anxiety expecting you to do it at any time."

"Answer the question. Did I fucking *use* you, Lia?"

"No…"

"No, I didn't. I *wouldn't*. If I'd planned to, I wouldn't have married you. In fact, I got rid of every fucking member of the Rozettis who knew about your existence and then hid you from your father. Including the bastard you saw me kill that first day in your apartment's parking garage. He was following you and I finished him."

My jaw falls open and even though it's hard to focus on his

words with the amount of pain and constant arousal plaguing my body, I let them filter into my conscious.

"You...you were following me?"

"For a few months before I met you, yes. So if I'd wanted to use you to get close to Lazlo, I would've done so around that time."

"Why didn't you?"

"Because you became fucking mine."

"Why didn't you tell me that when I first confronted you? Why did you have to hurt me until I had to hurt you back?"

"Someone from the outside helped you and you said he was your lover."

"He's not..."

His belt comes down on my pussy and I gasp, my mouth remaining open.

"Don't lie to me, Lia."

"He's not!"

Slap!

"Ahhh...*please*...I believe what you said just now. I trust that you didn't intend to use me, I really do. Now you have to believe me...please...please..."

Because if he doesn't, we'll be caught in a vicious, toxic cycle that will destroy us both.

"Why should I? You insisted on cheating, remember?"

"Adrian...take it as if I'm begging you. Don't do this to us."

"Do what?"

"Kill us again."

Hard lines etch his features and I can tell he's on the edge of something—what, I don't know.

He glides the belt between my legs, across the sensitive flesh of my thigh, but he doesn't whip me. If anything, his touch is soothing, taking away the pain and replacing it with carnal bliss. One that beats beneath my skin and connects with my bones.

I pull on the bindings at my wrists and ankles, but that only tightens them around my tender flesh.

"Give me something, Lia."

"S-something about what?"

"About him. If he's not your lover, then you shouldn't be protecting him."

I suck in a sharp breath as his belt glides up and down the wetness of my pussy. Luca has never helped me since I got involved with Adrian. In fact, he used me and I turned a blind eye to it because he reminded me of Grandma and my childhood.

If it were up to me, I would've kept him and Adrian as far away from each other as possible. But knowing my husband's closed off nature, he'll continue to torture me and himself until he gets the answers he needs.

Since he's going to get them, anyway, why should I deny him?

"Luca," I whisper. "His name is Luca and he was my childhood friend. We lived in the same neighborhood when Grandma was alive and went to the same school."

If he appreciates the information, he doesn't show it. His expression is as blank as his demeanor. "Why did you have to meet him in secret?"

"Because he runs with the wrong crowd."

"What crowd?"

"I don't know. I kept away from his life because it's dangerous."

"But you ended up in mine." There's a softer edge in his tone and I nearly cry with gratefulness.

"You said it yourself. I didn't have a choice."

"And if you did have a choice?"

A sob of relief leaves me. "I'd choose this, Adrian. I would choose *you*."

He closes his eyes for a brief second, grunting. When he opens them again, he rasps, "Fuck, Lenochka."

"Yes, please."

"Yes, please, what? Fuck you? Whip you? Own you?"

"Any... All..." I struggle against my bindings to no avail. *"Please."*

He throws the belt away and undoes his trousers as he settles between my spread legs. I'm so wet that I feel it dripping between my thighs and onto the mattress.

"You want me to fuck that tight cunt of yours until you scream, Lenochka?"

"Yes..."

He grabs me by my hips and I arch into his touch. The stimulation from his belt has left me turned on to the point of oblivion so that even the slightest blissful flicker of touch will be enough to detonate me.

"You'll scream for me, Lia."

"I will...ohhh..." my word ends on a moan as he plunges inside me with the delicious ruthlessness that I'm used to from him.

My body bucks off the bed as he thrusts inside me with increasing intensity. His rough handling leaves me gasping, sobbing, and bawling.

It leaves me feeling alive.

The welts from his belt spark bursts of pain into my nipples and stomach. It mixes with the pleasure, coalescing in my belly and core.

His punishments have a curious overpowering effect that make me delirious and beg for more.

I will always want more with Adrian, even more than he can give me.

Like his heart.

His soul.

It's only fair after he confiscated mine. He's holding them in the palm of his hand, whether he'll squash them or revive them, no one knows.

But I continue holding onto the hope that the six years we've spent together mean something.

They have to.

Adrian drives all the way into me, hitting my sweet spot before he pulls out, then powers in again.

I fall apart with no safety line.

And at this moment, I don't want one.

I'm tied down, completely and utterly helpless, and yet I haven't felt this free in such a long time.

The orgasm comes with a sudden blast that I don't feel until it hits me. There's no warning, no hazard sign.

Just…freedom.

"Adrian… Oh, yes…yes…"

"Fuck, Lia," he grunts as his movements turn harder and longer. "Say my name again."

"Adrian…"

"Say that you're mine."

"I'm yours…yours…"

He grunts and comes inside me then, his hot cum filling me.

My husband collapses on top of me and I expect him to take a moment to catch his breath, but instead, his lips find mine.

Adrian is kissing me.

I know he did it when I thought I was Winter, but this one is different. This one is meant for me. His tongue meets mine, and I kiss him with abandon, letting him devour me whole.

So what if nothing is left at the end? I know he'll be there for me.

He'll pick me up again.

He'll kiss me again.

After I told him I cheated on him, Adrian stopped kissing me, and that killed me slowly. Now that he's back to it, that must mean he believes me, right?

When he pulls back slightly, I'm panting, but my eyes are drooping. I could fall asleep kissing him, letting him explore me all night long.

"Don't fall asleep, Lenochka. We haven't even gotten started yet."

ELEVEN

Lia

WHEN I WAKE UP, MY HEART SINKS.

Adrian isn't here.

Judging by the darkness outside, it's still night. Is he going back to leaving my side right after sex like I'm his whore?

I thought he finally believed me. I thought he trusted me—or at least has started to.

Turns out, that's not the case.

But if he thought I would cower away and cry myself to sleep while he spends the night in his office, he thought wrong. I'm not going to budge from his side until he fully opens up to me.

I'm about to push away the covers when my phone vibrates on the nightstand. I pick it up and check the text.

Unknown Number: You had to go and force my hand, Duchess. Now you'll bear the consequences. I told Adrian you helped me in his assassination attempt. Rest in peace.

No!

No...

I stumble to a standing position, reading and rereading the text message. If Adrian thinks I helped Luca, he'll never forgive me. I've barely managed to reach through his frigid exterior.

Sliding on a robe, I sprint to the door, but my feet come to a halt when it opens and Adrian appears on the threshold. His face is a blank mask, devoid of emotions.

"It's not what you think… I can explain…"

"Explain what? That you wanted me dead?" He pulls out a gun and I step backward.

He grabs me by the wrist and shoves the gun in my hand, then points it at his chest. "Do it then. Finish the job, Lenochka."

My hands shake, sweat covering my palms. "No…no…I don't want you dead. I love you. I'm in love with you, have been for years."

"If you loved me, you wouldn't have plotted my assassination. Go ahead then. Pull the trigger."

"No…"

"It's a mere pull of the trigger and you'll be rid of me."

"No."

"Shoot!"

"No!"

A *bang* echoes in the air and I shriek so loud, my ears pop.

I startle awake in warm arms. Strong, protective arms that surround me in a cocoon.

Adrian.

He's holding me in a sitting position in the middle of the bed, his palm slowly stroking my sweat-damp hair away from my face.

My shaky fingers feel up his chest and down his tattooed bicep to his forearm, mechanically searching for any injury.

"I'm fine, Lia. It was just a nightmare."

I still, staring up at him. "A nightmare?"

"Yes. You're fine." His lips find the top of my head and they brush over my hair, creating a buzz of comfort, of…safety.

My head rests on his chest as I catch my breath, burrowing into the hard ridges of his muscles, using him as my nook, my anchor.

My husband.

After he fucked me until my voice turned hoarse and no more sounds or orgasms were left in me, I don't remember much.

He must've untied me and cleaned me up at some point, or I wouldn't have been in this position.

"Are you hungry?"

"No." I lean my head back but don't leave the cocoon as I stare at him. It's night outside and some of the candles are still lit, their red hues casting a warm glow on his face.

I love his face.

I love how he's more beautiful than a Greek god and just as lethal.

But most of all, I love how his hard granite features only soften around me. As if no one in the world is worthy of his gentle side but me—and Jer.

While he continues to hold me, Adrian reaches back to the nightstand and retrieves a bottle of water, removes the top, and places it at my lips.

"I'm not thirsty."

"You must be. Drink up or you'll dehydrate."

I attempt to take the bottle, but he keeps it out of reach.

"I can drink on my own," I grumble.

"I know."

"If you want me to drink water from your hand, all you have to do is say so."

"I don't want you to drink water from my hand." After he takes a swig, he grabs my jaw. His mouth meets mine and he pours the water into it. He nibbles my lip, then his teeth tug on it and he sucks it inside his hot, wet mouth.

By the time he finishes, I'm hyperventilating, my jaw open and my throat dryer than before he gave me the water.

Holy. Shit. Can I drink that way for the rest of my life?

"Go on. Drink, Lia."

"From your lips?" I ask like an idiot.

Adrian's mouth twitches in a smile as he motions at my hand. That's when I realize he already placed the bottle between my fingers.

"Though if you prefer my lips, I can arrange it."

"That's not what I meant," I blurt out, then gulp half the bottle down in one go to soothe my dry throat and the embarrassment heating my cheeks.

"Slower." He pulls the bottle away. "Or you'll choke."

I stare up at him, my heart squeezing behind my ribcage. I've known him for six years. Six whole years, but seeing him this close never gets dull.

He never gets dull.

"How did you find me back then?" I ask in a low voice.

"Back when?"

"That…night at the cliff. Rai's guard was fast, but you still found us in no time."

"I tracked you."

"Tracked me…wait a second. You have a tracker on me?"

He taps my cheek. "Dental."

I try to pull away, but Adrian's hold keeps me glued in place. "Since when?"

"Soon after I married you."

"Oh my God. Were you ever planning on telling me?"

"I just did."

"Wow. You're…you're…"

"Impossible?"

"I was going to say a jerk. I can't believe you've been tracking me all along." Though I shouldn't be surprised and it did save my life, but the fact remains that he's been doing it secretly.

"It's for your safety."

"Are you sure it's not for your controlling nature?"

"Perhaps a little."

"A lot." I glare at him. "What else have you done?"

"Where should I start?"

"Let's go back to the beginning. You said you watched me for months before showing up at my apartment building."

"I did."

"I can't believe I never noticed you."

"You couldn't have even if you tried. If I didn't show myself that day, you wouldn't have known I existed."

"Why did you show yourself?"

"To kill those Rozettis guards who were watching you."

"But you could've disappeared after."

He strokes my shoulder blade, his eyes darkening as if he's taking a trip to the past. "Not after I saw that delicious fear in your eyes, no. I had to explore it…and you."

"You're such a sadist."

"If you say so."

"And before then? Did you make it your mission to watch me?"

"Correct."

"Did you attend my ballet performances?"

"Yes."

"And yet, you said you weren't a stalker."

"Stalker or not didn't matter. I was on a mission at the time to learn your habits, know your life, and eventually become a part of it so I could ask you a few questions about Lazlo. Turned out, you knew nothing and even believed the cover-up surname was yours."

"Sorry I was useless," I mock.

"I'm not."

"Really? I thought I ruined your plan."

"You did. You shredded my patterns apart and dug

yourself a place in the middle of them. You tore through my original plan and I had to come up with another drastic one to get close to Lazlo without getting you involved."

"I assume it worked?"

"It did."

"Then why isn't he helping you to not be suspected by Sergei?"

His jaw clenches. "I see Yan's mouth is getting loose."

My hand wraps around his tattooed bicep as I implore. "We're on the same side. I just want to help. If I were to talk to my father, would that—"

"No."

"You didn't even let me finish."

"You don't have to. The answer is no."

"But—"

"No, Lia. I didn't keep you away all this time to bring you in now."

"We're husband and wife. We're supposed to do this together."

"It's because we're husband and wife that I'm protecting you. This subject is closed for discussion."

"You're a dictator."

"Back to the labels, I see."

"Well, you are one."

"And you only figured it out now, Lenochka? If I weren't, I wouldn't have been able to bring you in from the streets."

I pause, staring down. "You...scared me back then."

"I had to so you'd know there was no way out."

"I...was also attracted to you."

"Hmm. You were?"

"So much so that I secretly hated your wife. I wanted to claw her eyes out."

"You were jealous of yourself?"

I hide my face in his chest as I nod.

"Look at me, Lia."

I shake my head, too embarrassed to stare at him.

Adrian grabs my chin and lifts it up so I'm once again held prisoner in the storm brewing in his eyes. It's tamer now, softer, but I have no doubt it'll erupt any second if need be.

"What else did you feel?" he asks.

"Envious, mostly. I wanted you and Jeremy for myself more than anything."

"You had us."

"Not during that first month. But you eventually brought me home. Thank you and I'm sorry."

"For what?"

"For lying to you and for earlier. I didn't mean to use Jeremy to make you commit to the vacation. Kolya said you didn't react well to that."

"First Yan is on your side and now Kolya? Are Boris and Ogla next?"

"They just want what's best for you."

"Uh-huh."

I squeeze his bicep tighter. "Was your mother that bad?"

"I told you she was a villain."

"I'm sorry."

"I'm sure she's more than sorry. She had an ending that fits your Disney movies."

"What type of ending?"

"She only ever wanted my father and power, and she died with a bullet to the head because of them. It happened when I was ten."

"Oh, Adrian…" My heart aches for him as if the pain is mine. He might not have been close to his mother, but she was still the woman who gave birth to him and raised him. Her death must've affected him in a way.

No wonder he grew up to be an emotional vault. It must be hard for him to feel after everything that happened in his childhood.

"She's in the past. Both of my parents are."

"How did your father die?"

"There was a hit against the previous *Pakhan*, Nikolai, and he protected him with his body."

I gulp. "Did he have to?"

"Not really, but it's expected of us to protect our *Pakhan*."

"Don't do it."

"What?"

"Don't protect him with your life."

"I won't. I have a family, remember?"

"Didn't stop your father."

"I'm not him, Lenochka. Never."

I hug him tight, burrowing my face in his chest. I'll make sure he's not his father.

Even if it's the last thing I do.

TWELVE

Lia

THE NEXT DAY, SOMETHING KEEPS NAGGING AT ME.
I try ignoring it and pretend that it doesn't exist, but my feet lead me back here, anyway.

What's the point of burying my head in the sand? It only made my state worse and managed to push me off that cliff where I could've lost everything.

And I did, in a way.

I temporarily lost Jeremy and Adrian. I lost the life I'd been fighting tooth and nail to protect. I don't care what I have to do to never end up on another literal—or metaphorical—cliff again.

You're stronger than this, Lia.

My hand trembles on the doorknob as I slowly turn it and crack the door. But instead of going inside, I remain at the threshold, staring at the small opening through which a patch of the white wall is visible. The beeping sound of the machine beats down my chest and through my bones.

I'd hoped Boris would stop me from going into the guest house, or that Kolya would magically appear by my side and tell me in his monotone voice that "the boss ordered me to stay away."

None of that happened.

Instead, Boris stepped aside, not bothering to stop me. After the heart-to-heart I had with Adrian last night, I can tell he's giving me more leeway. He's not the type of man who gives second chances, as Yan likes to remind me, so I'm grateful that he's trying, that he's taking a different path that doesn't include punishing or bestowing me with his neglectful silent treatment.

I'm not an idiot. I know that Adrian's newfound trust is fragile at best. If I show any sign of siding with Luca—or anyone aside from him—his wrath will be the most dangerous I've ever witnessed.

And because he's trying, in his own way, I need to do the same. In order to get rid of my visceral nightmares, I have to take care of the source. Namely, the woman lying in bed.

Since it's nighttime, there's a soft light in her plain room that looks right out of a hospital. The nurse probably keeps the light on for when she comes to check on her. I noticed her leaving the building earlier and that's when I gathered my courage and came here right after I put Jeremy to bed.

I leave the door ajar as I approach the bed on which Winter sleeps. Her eyes are closed this time, but her skin is less pale, a bit flushed, as if blood is pumping harder in her veins.

One of her frail hands lies on her stomach and the other is by her side, an IV tube punctures her skin and is attached to a bag hung above her head.

I stare at the door to make sure it's open and I'm not trapped here with her. She might be comatose, but she scares me. Maybe not like when I thought she was Lia and I'd stolen her husband, but the ominous feeling is still there.

It's probably my stupid guilt.

"I'm so sorry, Winter," I whisper. "I shouldn't have gotten you involved in this life. I shouldn't have cut your free wings and forced you into this bed. I'm so…so sorry."

I want to say more, to apologize more and make amends, but what's the point? She's motionless while I'm healthy.

Well…almost healthy.

After all, I paid for the sin I committed by living as her and losing my family, even if only for a while. Adrian also said that my abdomen scar is from when I fell from the cliff, not a birth scar as I believed in my other identity. I felt Winter's loss so viscerally because deep down, I missed Jeremy to the point of madness.

I flop onto a chair by her bedside. "I'm sorry I put you through this, Winter."

"She put herself through this."

I lift my head to find my husband leaning against the door-frame, his arms folded over his developed chest and his long legs crossed at the ankles. He's in black pants, a white shirt, and an open dark brown cashmere coat that reaches his knees.

He's always dressed so simple yet so elegant.

He must've just finished working, because his office door was closed when I passed it earlier.

"You scared me," I murmur.

"Then you shouldn't have come here."

"I can't keep avoiding her forever while we live under the same roof."

"You're not living under the same roof."

"Fine. Same property."

"Then I can move her away."

"Away…where?" I sound as spooked as I feel, probably because I know what life means in Adrian's dictionary—nothing.

"Anywhere but here."

"No. She's like this because of us. We need to take responsibility."

"Responsibility for what? Did you force her to switch places with you?"

"Of course not."

"Then I'm taking no responsibility for a choice she made on her own."

"Did hitting her head also happen because of a choice she made?"

"Yes. She tried to run away, tripped, and cracked her head."

"Really?" I frown. I thought he'd caused her to be like this somehow.

"If I'd hurt her, I wouldn't be ashamed to admit it. She took your place and that alone is punishable by death according to me."

"Is there anything that's not punishable by death according to you?"

"Not really."

"Death is supposed to be the last possible resort, not the first."

"Not to me. I don't believe in second chances, Lenochka."

"But you…gave me one. Right?"

"You're the exception."

I get what he's saying without him having to voice it aloud. This is the only chance he'll give me, so I better use it well.

Not that I didn't know already.

"How did you know I was here?" I opt to change the subject. "Let me guess, Boris or Kolya."

"Kolya."

I scoff. "What a perfect right-hand man. You spend more time with him than with anyone else, you know. If you swung in the other direction, he would've been your model wife."

"Are you jealous of my second-in-command, Lia?"

"Of course not!"

"If you say so."

"Stop it, Adrian." A small smile lifts my lips, but he keeps his signature blank expression.

"What? I'm agreeing with you."

"You're teasing me."

"Hmm. Is that so?"

"There. You're doing it again."

"Am I?"

"Yes!"

Adrian pushes off the door and stalks toward me. I suck in a deep breath, my heart hammering in my ears. Now that he's getting closer, I'm caught in that trance that's exclusive to him. The one where he's the only thing I can breathe or feel.

This isn't healthy, is it? I'm not supposed to hang on to every breath out of his sinfully proportioned mouth. I shouldn't be burning up from the inside out because of the simple fact that he's approaching me.

Why did I have to go and fall in love with him? It would've been easier if I didn't have feelings for him.

Or if, at least, all I felt toward him was fear.

As he stops beside me, I just want to throw myself in his arms and burrow my face in his chest.

His large palm engulfs my slender shoulder and I freeze in place, my heart beating so violently in my chest, I'm surprised it doesn't break free from my ribcage.

His hand still in place, he glides his fingers up my neck, unhurriedly, deliberately until my harsh breathing is louder than the beeping of the machine.

"Did you know that red creeps up your delicate throat and ears when you're flustered or lying?" He leans over, his voice dripping with seduction. "Or when you're turned on."

"Adrian…" I mean to scold, but his name comes out as a whisper.

"There. It's happening again." He glides his finger over the pulse point in my neck. "I assume you're aroused, Lenochka?"

"Do you enjoy driving me out of my element?"

"Yes."

"Why?"

"Because I'm the only one who does it."

"You're so arrogant."

"And you're so fond of labels."

"I told you. I'm just giving things their names." I focus back on Winter because if I allow myself to be sucked into Adrian's orbit, I won't be able to escape at all. It's impossible to ignore his hand on my shoulder or the slow up and down motion of his fingers. "So?"

"So what?"

"What are we going to do about Winter?"

"I can keep searching for her family. Though from Kolya's report, she doesn't have one. Or as I said, I can transfer her."

"Don't do that. The nurse can keep taking care of her here. Don't you think we owe her that much?"

"No. As I mentioned, no one forced her to come here."

"You can be so heartless sometimes."

"You mean logical."

"*Heartless.*" I stare at Winter. "She was so happy when she thought she could live a rich person's life."

Adrian's movement pauses and his hand remains inert on my shoulder. "And you were so ready to give up your life for her."

There's no accusation in his quiet tone, but it couldn't have been clearer if he pointed a finger at me.

Letting my hands rest in my lap, I stare at them. "I never wanted to give up my life. I was just...trapped."

"Trapped," he repeats in that infuriating way he uses to get on my nerves.

"Yes, Adrian. *Trapped.* As in, with no way out. But you wouldn't know what that term means, not when everything you want magically comes true."

"Believe me, there's no magic involved. I forged my way through, and while I didn't give a fuck about who got destroyed in the process, I didn't walk all over you. I didn't step on you and continue my path as if you were nothing."

I glance up at him, at the menacingly beautiful face and merciless gray eyes. "Do you really believe that? Do you honestly think you didn't walk all over me?"

"Yes. If I had, you wouldn't be sitting in front of me right now."

"Then should I be thankful that I didn't end up like Winter?"

"That's not what I said."

"That's what you *mean*."

"That's what you want me to mean, Lia. Don't project your misconceptions on me."

I release a long breath in a last-ditch attempt to calm my nerves. As if feeling my distress, Adrian strokes my shoulder. "Don't compare yourself to anyone else, is that understood?"

"You say that as if you weren't fooled by Winter."

"I wasn't. One look into her eyes and I figured out she wasn't you."

"That simple?"

"That simple."

I don't know why that rips a small sigh out of me. The fact that he could've replaced me with her ate me alive back then. "Does that mean you wouldn't have...you know..."

"Fucked her?"

My cheeks heat as I stare at my hands and nod once.

"What do you think?"

"You have a crazy sex drive...so...it could happen." The words burn in my throat on their way out.

"Having a crazy sex drive doesn't mean I'd stick it anywhere, Lenochka."

My head snaps up until I'm once again trapped in his stormy eyes. "No?"

"No. You're not just my wife, the mother of my son, and completely and utterly mine, but you're also the only woman

I've wanted since the first time you begged me to fuck you when you were drunk."

"Back then…I wanted you…"

"Since when?"

"Since the first time I saw you."

"I thought you were scared of me."

"I was, but it didn't stop me from wanting you."

"Hmm. You're a masochist."

"Shut up. You made me a masochist."

"I couldn't have made you into one if the traits weren't there from the get-go. I only nurtured them a little, maybe whipped them into submission at some point."

"Perverted sadist," I mutter under my breath.

"I never denied that."

"When did you learn that you…prefer it rough and twisted?"

"Early on. Around my late teens."

"Do you think your upbringing had something to do with it?"

"Probably."

"I'm sorry."

"Why should you be? If it weren't for my upbringing, we wouldn't have been compatible, Lenochka."

"I disagree."

"Is that so?"

I stand up, forcing him to release me as I wrap my arms around his waist. "I think we're the most compatible we could ever be."

"What gave you that idea?"

"First of all, we gave birth to the most beautiful angel alive and no one but us could be Jeremy's parents. Second, you know my body better than I ever would and…you saved me from myself. Not to mention, you didn't mistake me for another woman. You get extra points for that."

"Extra points, huh?"

"Uh-huh."

"Do I get to use them tonight?"

I grin. "Absolutely."

Adrian lifts me in his arms and I squeal as I snuggle into his hold. In my utter delight, I catch a glimpse of Winter's open eyes glaring at me.

I blink once, but her eyes are closed.

Holy shit.

As Adrian carries me out of her room, my nails dig into his shoulder as I keep staring at her, expecting her to open her eyes.

She doesn't.

But I'm sure I saw them open a second ago.

Or was it a hallucination?

THIRTEEN

Lia

"Y OU DIDN'T HAVE TO COME WITH US," I SAY AS WE walk through the mall.

I want to buy a few things because I realized just how boring my old wardrobe is. I also want to get Jeremy a new coat in preparation for our small family vacation.

Adrian said he'd take care of it, so I have no clue where we're going. That doesn't stop me from being excited about our first getaway as a family, though.

It took six years, but it's finally happening.

After learning about the scrutiny my husband is under, I want him to step away from work for a while to clear his head. He doesn't agree, but he'll eventually change his mind.

When I told him about wanting to go shopping, he insisted on coming too. Kolya and Boris follow us, and even though they're keeping a short distance, we're drawing attention wherever we go.

Jeremy seems oblivious to all of it as he trots between us, one hand in his father's and the other in mine. It's strange how my little angel is lively and bright despite being born in such a dark world.

And it's that light that's kept me going.

Adrian tilts his head to the side. "I'm not allowed to come along?"

"That's not what I said."

"Then what?"

I narrow my eyes at him slightly. I'm well aware he doesn't trust me and probably thinks I'll meet Luca as I did a week ago. But I guess, even if he started to believe me, he wouldn't give me free rein this soon.

I puff out a breath. "Don't you have work?"

"Not today, no." He strokes Jeremy's hand. "Aren't you happy I came along, Malysh?"

"Yes, Papa!"

Adrian's attention slides back to me. "See?"

So now it's his turn to use Jeremy against me. It's not that I don't want him with us, it's his reason for joining that sits wrong with me.

He's keeping an eye on my every move because he doesn't trust me.

Ever since I divulged Luca's name, he's been asking me all sorts of questions about him. His last name, family details, and everything in between. Surprisingly, I didn't have any trouble answering those. However, I couldn't tell him about the other part. The 'I agreed to spy on you for Luca' part.

We're barely getting out of a sensitive phase and falling into some sort of understanding. I can't just ruin it.

Adrian kisses and hugs me again. He doesn't look at me like he wants to hate-fuck me, then throw me away.

And I want to hold onto what we have for as long as I can. But Yan is right—I'll tell him all about it.

Soon.

We go into several shops and I buy some jeans and try on a few low-cut dresses that Adrian shakes his head at. When I come out of the dressing room in a short red dress with a deep décolletage, Adrian glares.

"You're beautiful, Mommy," Jeremy says from his position next to his father.

"Thank you, my angel. At least you have the sense to say that." I run my hand over the soft material, glaring back at Adrian.

"You are beautiful, but you're not going outside like that."

"I used to be in ballet, remember? We wore shorter outfits."

"But you're not anymore and this is no ballet performance. You won't be wearing a short dress."

I scrunch my nose, then mutter under my breath, "I bet you didn't think they were short when you were stalking me."

"I heard that," he says as I turn around and head to the changing room.

Of course, he did. It's like he has superpowers when it comes to these types of things.

Still, I grin at his tone and the way his gaze keeps following me even as I walk away.

At the checkout, I slip a few dresses between my other purchases behind Adrian's back. He only hands her his card and doesn't care for what's in the bags.

Outside the boutique, Boris offers to take the bags for me. I tell him I'm fine, but Adrian practically yanks them from my hand and shoves them at his guard.

He's impossible sometimes.

We get chocolate milkshakes and sit on a bench. Or more like, Jeremy and I do. Adrian just watches us with rare satisfaction as we slurp in unison. Soon after, Jeremy says he has to use the bathroom and Adrian takes him, leaving both Kolya and Boris with me outside.

I stare at them. "Aren't you tired of standing all day?"

"We're fine," Kolya grunts.

"You're really as grumpy as Yan says."

He lets out a sound that resembles a scoff but doesn't say anything.

"I feel bad for leaving him at home." I sigh. "Do you think he's all right?"

"The doctor said he's healing and he's moving, so it should be fine."

"Maybe I'll buy him something…"

"Please don't." Kolya stares at the bathroom door.

"Yeah, don't," Boris agrees. "Unless you want to witness his murder at Boss's hands."

I roll my eyes and continue slurping from my milkshake.

"Lia?"

My head turns to the side at the familiar voice. Stephanie, the choreographer from New York City Ballet, walks toward me at a brisk pace.

Boris gets between her and me, his frame shadowing her petite body.

I stand up. "It's okay, Boris. Let her through."

He begrudgingly moves and she joins me, her gaze wary as she observes the two guards. I can't help the smile that moves to my lips at the sight of her. "Hey, Steph."

"Hey, girl!" She hugs me and I do the same before we pull back and sit down. "Look at you, alive and well. I thought you left the country."

"No, still here."

"Married, too." She points at my finger.

"Yeah. I also have a five-year-old son."

"Whoa. You changed, Lia. If Philippe were to see you, he'd be weeping. He always said you were his only muse and nothing would change that. He was depressed after…what happened."

I smile a little. "Have you guys been well?"

"You know, the usual."

"I saw *Giselle*'s posters. I wish you guys all the best."

"Thanks. You can come if you want to…" she backpedals. "Or not. No pressure."

"I'll think about it."

Thinking about ballet still hurts, but I believe I'm at a point in my life where I'm able to move on, even if not entirely.

"You'll love the male lead for this one."

I laugh. "What? Ryan no longer leads?"

She frowns. "Ryan stopped leading six years ago. Since you."

"What?"

"He disappeared the day you broke your leg, Lia. No one knows where he is."

"Really?"

"We searched everywhere for him and his family even filed a missing person report, but the police couldn't find a trace of the man."

Oh.

"So he disappeared after my accident?"

"Yes. At first, we thought he felt guilty, but when we couldn't reach him, something seemed off. It's Ryan, after all. He wouldn't blow a performance, no matter how guilty he felt."

The arrogant Ryan. The selfish Ryan.

The…Ryan who had a strike with Adrian.

Oh. My. God.

He couldn't have.

"We have Joel lead now and he's a darling. He made Hannah shrink her bitch behavior a little. She's been trying and failing to get to your level. Not to be biased or anything, but you'll always be my and Phil's favorite. I know life goes on and all, but it's simply not the same without you."

I smile at her, and she goes on and on about how Philippe is making her life hell and how he's become a grumpy old man.

However, all I can think about is the information she just gave me.

The fact that Ryan disappeared six years ago.

And that my husband is most likely behind it.

FOURTEEN

Adrian

"STAY THERE, PAPA."

"I will."

"You don't have to come inside. I'm a grown-up."

"You are, Malysh."

My son grins as his feet dangle from the toilet. I'm in his direct view while remaining outside the stall as he instructed.

"I don't call Mommy anymore," he says. "I can do it on my own."

"That's a good boy."

"That's right. I am. I'm gonna be big as you and protect Mommy when I grow up."

"And what am I going to do then?"

"It's okay. You can protect her too."

Too. As in he's being benevolent by allowing me into her life. The little rascal is taking after Yan, I swear.

My phone vibrates and I think it's Kolya, but the very familiar number gives me pause. I do a long sweep of the empty bathroom, then march to the entrance and lock it.

"Where are you, Papa?"

"Right here." I go back in front of Jeremy's stall, but keep enough distance so that he doesn't focus on my phone call.

"Volkov."

There's a pause on the other end, the sound of a long stream of water before his signature smooth voice comes through, "Morozov."

"Did you get the information?"

"No."

"Then why are you wasting my time?"

I hear a gurgling before Kirill's strained tone filters through, "This is also important. Hold on…" He switches to English, speaking to someone else. "Hi, I think we understand each other better now. So why don't you tell me the name?"

Intelligible noises fill his end of the phone before there's a distinctive plop into water. "Wrong answer, motherfucker." He goes back to Russian. "So… Where was I?"

"Are you torturing someone, Morozov?"

"Waterboarding, to be more specific. This cunt has something of mine. But that's not what's important, Vladimir is."

"Vladimir?"

"My intel tells me he's getting close to solving Richard's murder."

I tap my finger against my thigh and smile at Jeremy when he grins.

I've been keeping Vladimir in the background, considering everything that's happened. But if he's been getting close, then I need to deal with this accordingly.

Having Sergei suspect me is the worst thing that could occur at a time like this, especially since I know he'll demand retribution.

"How about you tell the *Pakhan* what happened?" Kirill asks ever so casually as more gurgles come from his end. "He's always been benevolent with you."

"Is this the only reason you called?"

"The only reason? What's more important than…I don't know, your fucking life?"

I'm starting to learn there's a lot. And in order to protect that, I need to remain safe and sound.

"Get me the information we agreed on." And with that, I hang up.

Ever since I heard the information Lia gave me about Luca, the fact that he was her childhood neighbor and friend, my men and I have been extensively checking him out. This doesn't only confirm Kirill's suspicions, but it also raises mine.

It was never a coincidence. The fact that he's on her trail and has stayed there for all these years. The fact that he takes risks to meet her. He knows who she is and her relation to Lazlo Luciano.

He can't be a part of the Lucianos unless he's plotting a coup against their Don. Everyone knows Lazlo thirsts for his own offspring, but he never left his wife, even when she didn't give him any children. His clan tries to act as if she's at fault, but he's still with her out of respect and duty. However, in my extensive research on him, I found out he had a surgery decades ago, one that rendered him infertile.

Everyone in the crime world knows that his brothers will inherit his fortune once he passes, but considering their bond, any of the Lucianos would be thrilled to discover the existence of another member of their family—Lazlo's daughter, no less. So Luca couldn't have been working for them.

That just leaves the possibility that he's in an Italian warring clan. And the only one who knows about Lia, and went to great lengths to keep her hidden from Lazlo, are the Rozettis.

Now, the question is, his position. Most of that family is wiped away and the other is in hiding like rats. I've been actively killing all the older guards who knew about Lia's existence so they don't go after her.

Is that why Luca wants me dead? He probably also has plans for Lia once I'm gone. Plans that I'll thwart the moment I find him. It's a matter of time before I fucking end his life so that he and his family will stop disturbing hers.

Jeremy trots out of the stall and refuses when I try to help him wash his hands.

He gives me the stink eye. "I'm a grown-up."

"Of course you are. I'm just going to lift you and you'll wash your hands, all right?"

He nods. I hold his small body as he lathers his hands with a lot of soap, then grins at the bubbles. I can't help the smile that stretches across my lips at how he finds the smallest things joyful.

I was a sad fucking kid and I'm grateful my son's fate isn't the same.

By the time he finishes washing his hands, he squirms.

"I can walk on my own, Papa."

Apparently, my son is at the stage where he wants to do everything himself and would judge anyone who'd commit the mistake of trying to help him.

Shaking my head, I put him to his feet and take his hand in mine.

As soon as we leave the bathroom, I can sense the change in the atmosphere without having to look twice. Jeremy releases my hand and runs to Lia before slamming into her legs.

She smiles at him, but her sharp glare falls on me.

I narrow my eyes. *What's wrong with her now?*

She stands up with a force that shakes her tiny frame, takes Jeremy's hand, and starts walking in the direction of the exit.

What the fuck? I thought she was the one who wanted to come here.

Boris follows her as Kolya falls in step beside me. "Mrs. Volkov ran into an old friend, sir."

"An old friend?"

"The choreographer from the ballet. Stephanie."

The image forms clearly in my head and I whisper, "Fuck."

"Stephanie told her about Ryan's disappearance and Mrs. Volkov froze. I believe she knows, sir."

"Of course she does." Lia is smart enough to connect the dots and figure out exactly what happened.

"What do you intend to do?"

"Let me deal with her."

I didn't want Lia to find out under the current circumstances, but it's long overdue. She would've figured it out sooner or later.

It's not that I purposely tried to hide it, but the conditions weren't right at the time. Judging from the way Lia glared at me, they still aren't.

But there's one thing my dear wife seems to forget.

She once labeled me her villain, and that's the most accurate label she's ever given me.

As is true with any villain, right or wrong is never black or white.

It's always gray.

FIFTEEN

Lia

BY THE TIME WE REACH HOME, I'M FUMING.

No, that's an understatement.

I feel as if my emotions have reached the boiling point and will now spill over, leaving only havoc behind.

Not only am I sure my husband is behind my ex-colleague's disappearance, but he also never thought about mentioning it to me. I wish I was being paranoid or distrustful or that I was merely assuming the worst about the situation.

I wish what I'm thinking was tied to my insecurities and painful memories.

But I've known Adrian for six years. And those six years started with me witnessing him finish a life. A life that he ended because the Italian men were watching me.

So no, I'm not paranoid to assume that he hurt Ryan somehow, that he's the reason a lead dancer who was extremely disciplined when it came to work, disappeared without a trace.

Jeremy fell asleep on Adrian's lap on the ride back and it took everything in me not to snap at my husband while his men were present.

After we get inside, Adrian carries Jeremy to his room. I go straight to the bedroom and keep the door open so that I can watch in case he decides to go to his office and ignore me.

I remove my coat and throw it on a nearby chair as I pace the length of the room. My body is burning with pent-up frustration to the level that even the air feels suffocating.

Soon enough, Adrian walks in and closes the door behind him. Before the click has barely echoed in the air, I'm in his face. "Is there something you want to tell me?"

He turns away, simultaneously removing his coat. Oblivious to the change of atmosphere, he takes his time with the task, unhurriedly sliding it down his arms and hanging it up as if he has all the time in the world. Even his expression is neutral, unperturbed. "Something, like what?"

"Like, I don't know, an incident that happened about six years ago?"

"A lot happened around six years ago, Lenochka. I met you, fucked you for the first time, put a baby in you, and married you. You'll have to specify."

"Ryan," I grind out. "Is that specific enough for you?"

A shadow crossing his features is the only change in his demeanor before his composed expression returns as he unbuttons the cuffs of his shirt and rolls them over his defined forearms. "Ryan who?"

"Are you going to pretend you don't even know him?"

"I've met a few Ryans in my life."

"My co-lead, Ryan."

"Former co-lead."

"So you do remember him."

"Yes. What about him?"

"What did you do to him, Adrian?"

"Why ask a question you already know the answer to?"

I stagger backward, my jaw nearly hitting the ground. "You're…you're not even going to try to deny it?"

"Why would I?"

"You killed someone!"

"He was neither the first nor the last."

"No…no, Adrian! He's not like the criminals you've killed. He was a dancer with a bright future ahead of him and you… you just ended it as if it never existed."

"Just like he ended your career."

I gasp, covering my mouth with my trembling hands as the clash of what he's said ripples through me like an aftershock. The complete apathy he speaks with renders me speechless, unable to gather my scattering thoughts and put them into words.

Having lived more than half a decade with him, I should've been used to his cold, unfeeling side by now. I should've considered his aloofness normal. But I guess someone like me will never be able to overlook that side of him, and I sure as hell will never understand it.

I let my hands fall to my sides as I hold on to a quivering thread of logic. "I jumped earlier than I was supposed to. It was an accident, not Ryan's fault."

"Yes, it was. Yan witnessed it and I saw it on the footage. Kolya and Boris did, too. That fucker could've caught you but chose not to."

"And you saw all that through some footage?"

"Correct, because, unlike you, I read the worst in people before the good. In fact, I only see their bad side, and that blond bastard deserved every bullet I emptied into his body."

My lips shake and nausea assaults me at the sadistic undertone in his voice. The tone that implies he enjoyed every second of killing Ryan and is not the least bit remorseful about it.

"You don't even see what you did wrong, do you?" I whisper.

"I just told you he was the reason behind the end of your career and you're saying I'm wrong?"

"Yes, Adrian! You're wrong because you fixed something ugly with something way uglier. Did you think I'd be thankful that you killed someone? Or that I'd be flattered that you did it for me?"

"I didn't expect you to be, no. That's why I never told you."

"What else haven't you told me? Is there a line of other bodies you've killed for me buried somewhere?"

Adrian's in my face in a split-second, his hand shooting out for me before I can make an escape. He imprisons my chin between his thumb and forefinger, forcing me to stare up at him. "So what if there are? What if there fucking are? You labeled me a killer, a devil, a monster, a stalker, a fucking *villain*. This is what villains do, Lia. We kill for our end goals, and we do it often. So get your head out of the clouds and stop pretending you're not part of this, part of *me*."

"You can chastise me all you want, but you won't twist my morals. I'll never get behind murdering people."

"I don't give a fuck whether you get behind it or not, but you will *not* question me when I make a decision with the intention of protecting you."

"A decision like killing Ryan?" I bite out.

"Like *torturing* and killing Ryan, yes."

"T-torturing?"

"He didn't have the privilege to die fast so I—"

"Stop! I don't want to hear the details."

"You brought this up, so you'll hear all about how I cut his precious legs and stomped all over them. How I took a knife to his flesh and severed the tendons while he wailed and begged and pissed himself."

"I said stop!" My voice chokes as the gruesome images fill my head.

"That's what I do, Lia. I can't stop when it comes to you. If I had a chance to go back in time, I would've ended his miserable life that day in the club when he dared to put his fucking hands on you. If I had, you wouldn't have lost ballet."

"But I lost it, Adrian. I'd already *lost* it. Did killing Ryan bring it back?"

"No, but it was a small price to pay. He deserved to die for driving you to stand on that windowsill with the intent of finishing your life."

"You drove me to stand on a cliff ready to finish my life, too. Do you deserve to die for that?"

I regret the words as soon as I say them. *Shit.* I'm so pissed at him that I didn't filter my thoughts. That's not what I meant to say, it came out wrong, but before I can retract them, Adrian speaks with chilling quietness. "Probably. But I can't die, because that will leave you and our son unprotected."

"It's not...I..."

He flattens his thumb against my lips, putting a halt to any words I can form. "Shhh. You've angered me enough for one day. You don't want me to punish you more than what I'm already planning."

My thighs clench at the promise of his punishment for me. My body doesn't recognize the anger I still feel toward Adrian and his actions. Or maybe it does and it couldn't care less, having grown accustomed to my husband's cold-heartedness. He'll never change, no matter what I do. He's just wired differently and he doesn't give a fuck about how that looks in the eyes of others.

Even mine.

In fact, he's willing to go the extra mile to mold me to his ways. But that will never happen. Because I killed someone, and even though he was a criminal, that incident messed with my head so much, I'm surprised I was able to survive it. *Barely.*

Adrian removes his hand. "Strip."

"W-what?"

"You heard me."

"But why...?" It's the first time he's ever asked me to strip. Usually, he's the one who does that, taking pleasure in yanking my clothes off my body and ripping my panties.

"Don't ask questions. When I tell you to strip, you fucking strip, Lia."

I flinch at the hard edge in his authoritative tone, but it's not out of fear—at least, not entirely. My panties are soaked with arousal at the command in his voice and my hands instinctively go to the back of my dress. I don't know if it's the intrusive way he's watching me or the unknown that's waiting for me, but my hand is unsteady on the zipper as I awkwardly slide it down.

I let the dress pool around my feet and remain in my underwear. This is far from the first time I've been in this type of position in front of Adrian, but the novelty of how it started causes my nerves and anticipation to simultaneously escalate with each passing second.

He steps back, crossing his developed arms over his chest, and his muscles stretch beneath his shirt. "All of it."

I hastily unhook my bra, letting it join the dress. My nipples instantly peak, and it's less to do with the cold air and more because of his heated, dark gaze. He looks on the verge of either devouring or spanking me.

Or maybe devouring me *while* spanking me.

A shiver crawls its way up my spine as I hook my fingers in either side of my panties and slide them down my legs so they're piled with the rest of my clothes.

By the time I stand again, a noticeable tremor is racking my body. What the hell? Why does it feel like my first time with him?

Or ever, actually. Because I don't remember being this nervous or turned on the first time I had sex.

The fact that he's only watching, not attempting to touch me, adds a different type of anticipation, one that coils at the base of my stomach and spreads all the way to my core.

"Now what?" I ask in a small, breathy voice that surprises even me.

He shakes his head once. "You don't get to ask that. In fact, you don't get to ask anything. This is your punishment, so if I tell you to stand like that until tomorrow, that's exactly what you'll do."

He wouldn't be so cruel as to do that.

Though…he did say I angered him, so maybe that's exactly his plan.

A weird sense of apprehension engulfs me and I attempt to grab my arm with my hand, but Adrian shakes his head again. "Drop it."

I do, trembling as I remain completely exposed. Everything is visible to him from my abdomen scar to the older leg scar to the few stretch marks I have due to pregnancy.

Sometimes, I feel self-conscious about my body, especially since the end of my career. I'm no longer the toned, thin dancer with athletic legs and slim figure. Though I haven't gained much weight, I'm not as fit as I was six years ago.

However, Adrian has never looked at me any differently. Not only has the hunger persisted in his gaze, but it also seems to intensify every time he touches me sexually.

It's been years, six *long* years, filled with all sorts of things that should've turned him off, but he's never looked at me differently from how he does right now.

With raw lust.

With a furious need to touch me.

I guess that's how I've always looked at him, too, even when I haven't wanted to show it. But for me, the arousal comes hand in hand with my feelings for him. I've wanted him more ever since I realized how irrevocably in love with him I am.

"Turn around and walk to the bed," he commands.

I do so, adding a gentle sway to my hips as I feel his wild gaze on my back and ass. I can sense his need for ownership even without him having to say it.

"Get on your knees at the foot of it, face against the mattress and ass in the air."

I suck a deep breath into my starved lungs and drop into

position. He didn't even touch me, but the friction of the duvet against my breasts makes me stifle a moan.

Adrian's presence behind me is as real as air, impossible to ignore or live without.

The sound of him unbuckling his pants echoes in the silence of the room and I dig my fingers into the mattress when I turn around to watch.

"Eyes ahead, Lia."

I comply even as I release a frustrated breath. Why is he the only one who gets to watch?

Dictator.

"Grab your ass cheeks and spread them. Show me that tight hole."

I choke on my own breath for a second, my fingers trembling as I obey the command. God. He's so full of perverted orders today. The fact that he's never told me to do this before adds more stimulation to my already slick core.

And he hasn't even touched me.

I'm pulling on my ass cheeks, fully aware that my back hole and the juices coating my pussy are in his direct line of view.

"You need to learn a lesson on not questioning my decisions, Lia."

"But—"

"Shhh. If you're going to open your mouth to disagree, it's better if you keep it shut."

I feel him kneeling behind me, his warmth radiating down my back and exposed flesh. "I'll start with your ass and then your pussy before I whip you, and then I'll go back to the beginning and do it all over again."

My breathing crackles and my thighs quiver at the image he's painted in my head.

"It's been a long time since I fucked your tight ass, hasn't it?"

I nod into the mattress.

"Use your words."

"Yes…"

"How long?"

"Three months." *Since before I thought I was Winter.*

"You've been counting, my Lenochka?"

I can feel the blood rising to my ears, nearly bursting them. "Yes."

"Mmm. You miss being fucked in the ass until you scream, don't you?"

I swallow.

"Answer."

"Yes…I do."

"Tell me to fuck you."

"Fuck me, Adrian." I don't even hesitate, the words falling from my mouth so naturally.

"But that means you'll enjoy it when I want to punish you."

"P-please…"

"Maybe we can come to a compromise then." He shifts behind me. "Don't move."

I don't, my heart thumping with increased intensity as he repositions himself. A cool liquid covers my back hole and before I can focus on the lube, Adrian grabs me by the hip and slams inside me in one go.

I gasp, my nails digging into my ass with the force of his thrust.

Holy. Shit.

I can feel him buried so deep in me, his cock pulling at my hole with a savageness that actually hurts.

"I told you. This is supposed to be a punishment." His hot, dark whisper assaults my ear as he drives into me with ferocious vigor. My upper body slides back and forth on the bed with each urgent move.

I attempt to grab the mattress for balance, but Adrian's voice stops me. "Don't even think about releasing that ass. Keep holding it for me."

He pulls out slowly, almost halfway, then rams back inside in sync with my scream. I try to wiggle, but he slaps my ass, wrenching a throaty mewl out of me.

"Move again and I'll turn this ass red while I fuck it, Lia."

His words spark against my flesh and rattle into my bones. And the only thought I have is that maybe I want that.

Maybe his depravity matches mine after all.

Otherwise? Why is my pussy dripping wet at the promise of his brutal punishment?

The pain soon mixes with pleasure as he shoves back in, his hips rotating to hit a deeper place with each thrust.

His free hand finds my swollen clit and he works it with masterful twists and strokes that leave me panting, begging, and unable to breathe properly.

It's unbelievable how much of a hold he has on my body, how he can levitate me to a state of complete abandon in a matter of minutes.

But I guess it's not only my body that he's able to possess in this exhilarating yet frightening way.

It's also my heart and my soul.

It didn't even matter when I thought I was a different person. I fell in love with him all the same and I'm starting to think there's no way out for me after all.

"Understand this, Lia. I would kill for you over and over again if I have to, and you will never, *ever* question that." His thrusts are longer, harsher, as if he's driving the point home with them.

I don't last. I can't. With the double assault on my ass and clit, I come apart with a hoarse cry, calling his name like a sacred chant.

Shit.

Maybe I am as defective as he is, because I'm orgasming while he's promising to kill for me in the future. That he'll never stop killing for me.

That he's indeed a monster.

My monster.

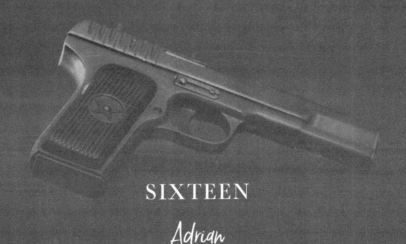

SIXTEEN

Adrian

IF THE THERAPIST HATED ME BEFORE, SHE MUST LOATHE me now.

It's evident from the way she keeps staring at me from beneath her gold-rimmed glasses whenever I accompany Lia to her sessions.

She's been having extensive therapy since I found her at the park. And because I don't trust anyone else to keep my wife safe, I've been driving her to the shrink's office and then I wait until she's finished.

Today, however, Dr. Taylor is standing in the doorway of her office and buttons her suit jacket as we approach. "Would you like to join us today, Mr. Volkov?"

"Why would I?"

Lia stares at me with a hopeful expression. She's wearing a flowery dress and has gathered her hair in a ponytail, which highlights her soft complexion. Even her rose scent is stronger than usual today. "I…asked for this. You can be with me when I talk. Dr. Taylor says it can help since you play a big role in my life."

"Let's go then." I intertwine my fingers with hers and we step inside. What? I'm not going to miss a chance of witnessing Lia talk about everything that's happened.

I'm well aware that Dr. Taylor is helping her. Not only has Lia slowly emerged from her cocoon, but she also hasn't had any hallucinations or any of those visceral nightmares lately.

After she found out about Ryan's death a few days ago, I thought she'd direct her disapproval inward and let it rot inside her, but she spoke her mind. And that night, she didn't have any nightmares.

Lia and I sit on the brown leather sofa across from the therapist's chair. Her office is entirely white, from the walls, to the desk, to the frames of the few nature paintings. The only break in color is the brown of the sofa and Dr. Taylor's chair. The scent of vanilla fills the space, but that might be coming from the therapist herself.

After she grabs a notepad, she starts asking Lia about her week, and my wife is surprisingly responsive. I focus on the joyous inflections in her voice as she talks about Jeremy learning new words and how we went shopping a few days ago.

She pauses for a few seconds, her expression falling and so does her voice. "Dr. Taylor, if I learn that my husband did something bad for my sake, how am I supposed to react?"

The therapist's expression remains calm as she asks in a soothing tone, "How does it make you feel?"

"Bad. I don't want him to have done it. But at the same, I understand why he did. Or more specifically, I know that his nature is different from mine and his brain isn't wired like the rest of us, so for him, that decision was logical."

I stare at her, then at how her hand trembles in mine. It took courage for her to admit to the fact that, in a way, she empathizes with me. Even if it goes against her core principles.

The therapist jots a few notes on her pad and clears her throat as she slides her attention to me. "What do you think of what Lia said, Mr. Volkov?"

I face Lia as I speak. "I think you're brave for seeing my side, even if you didn't have to."

"But we're husband and wife. I'm supposed to see your side…just like you're supposed to see mine, Adrian."

I know what she's getting at. Lia wants me to see how much she loathes the mafia part of my life. The hunting, killing, and torturing. And while I do understand her hate, there's no escaping the reality of our lives.

If anything, leaving the Bratva would mean I'd lose its protection. We'd be vulnerable and on the run. And that's not a fate I'd inflict on her and our son.

But in order to keep her and shield her mind, I need to stop being forceful with her fragile mentality. I'll wait until she rebuilds herself and stand with her every step of the way.

One day, she'll realize that the world we live in doesn't matter.

We're the only ones who do.

SEVENTEEN

Lia

A WEEK LATER, WE GO ON VACATION.

This isn't the place I had in mind when I suggested a retreat. In fact, it's probably the last location I would've ever thought about.

But here we are.

In Russia.

I should've known that Adrian's unpredictable nature would strike again.

He took us on a private flight to a house with a redbrick roof in the countryside with a smaller cottage situated beside it. It's surrounded by miles of land, covered by snow that's formed layer upon layer over other layers. Trees line the property, casting a cozy feel on the driveway that leads to the house. When Kolya drove us here, we barely saw any other houses on the way.

It's not a surprise that Adrian wouldn't take us to a place full of people. He's too paranoid about security to ever do that, and in a way, I prefer less crowded areas, too. I never liked the outside world too much, even before I married him.

If I thought New York was cold, Russia is fucking freezing.

We're talking temperatures below zero. The only way I'm able to cross the distance from the car to the house is because Adrian carries an excited Jeremy with one arm and holds me close with the other.

Yan, Boris, Kolya, and two other guards escorted us. Yan insisted on coming, saying his injury is completely fine, and even though Kolya was against it, Adrian surprisingly allowed it. My friend said it's because his boss wants to keep a closer eye on him.

As soon as we're inside, I release a relieved breath. Warmth instantly seeps into my bones and chases away the merciless cold from outside. I honestly have great respect for people who survive such harsh winters year in and year out.

The place is fully heated and seems to have been already prepared for us. It's small, cozy, and has a cottage-like feel to it. The dark wood flooring seems to be heated as well. A living area with large, mismatched sofas is just inside the entrance and across from what I assume is the kitchen. There are narrow wood stairs that lead to the second floor, where I'm guessing the bedrooms are located.

Adrian puts Jeremy down and our son sprints in different directions before he gawks at the snow from the glass door that opens up to the balcony. "Mommy! Can we make a snowman?"

The mere thought of going back into that cold makes me shudder.

"Not now, Malysh." Adrian smiles at him. "There's a storm coming tonight."

"Then tomorrow?" Jer asks hopefully.

"Yes."

"And you'll join us, Papa?"

"I will."

"Yay!" He jumps up and down, then runs straight to Adrian's leg.

Kolya and Boris bring our bags inside and nod as they're about to leave.

"Where are you going?" I ask.

"The other cottage, Mrs. Volkov," Kolya says.

"To stand guard," Boris elaborates.

"Hell no! You're not standing guard in this freezing cold."

Adrian glares down at me and I glare right back. "What? Surely you're not making them go outside when there's a storm coming. They'll freeze to death."

"They will not," he says with slight exasperation.

"Of course they will. Have you seen all the snow?"

"I have and so did they. We're Russians, and we can handle the cold."

"No."

"No?" he repeats with clear skepticism, as if he doesn't believe I just told him no in front of his men.

"Yes, no. This is supposed to be a vacation, not a way to test their endurance in the cold. Who would even reach us here?"

"You would be surprised," Adrian says and nods at his guards, who nod back and leave.

"Come back for dinner," I call after them. "Bring Yan and the others, too."

They don't show any sign of hearing me and continue on their way. As soon as the door closes behind them, Adrian towers over me, his face a mask of coldness that mirrors the outside. He speaks low enough that Jeremy—who's preoccupied with running his toy soldier across the windowsill—doesn't hear. "Don't ever, and I mean *ever*, defy me in front of my men again unless you're in the mood to be punished in their presence."

"I didn't mean it that way," I shoot back in the same tone. "But I'll not stand by as you torture them."

"Feeling too attached to them, Lia?"

"Of course I do. I've known those men for six years, Adrian, and despite them being an extension of you, I've gotten used to them and I don't wish any of them harm."

"Careful, Lenochka," he grinds out. "You're tempting me to get rid of them."

"You're impossible, did you know that?"

"Not impossible, no. I'm merely possessive and have no control when it comes to you. I don't like it when you speak of any other man."

"How…am I even supposed to reply to that?"

"You're not. Just don't put any man before me."

"I can't just stop talking to or about other men."

"Yes, you can." He pauses. "Within reason."

"You don't even know the right definition of reason, Mr. Volkov."

His lips twitch a little. "I can conjure it. Under the right circumstances."

The sight of his smile always gets me in a better mood, no matter the subject, and I find myself mirroring it even as I shake my head.

"Mommy!" Jeremy tugs on my coat. "Did you bring my war zone?"

"I did."

"Let's build it!"

I groan and Adrian's smile widens.

"Seems that your mother still hasn't learned how to assemble your war zone, Malysh."

"Hey, that's not true!" I poke him. "Not everyone is good at that stuff."

"Malysh and I are." He lifts a grinning Jeremy in his arms. "Isn't that right?"

"Yes, Papa!"

He taps our son's nose and he giggles. "Should we teach your mommy?"

"I don't think she'll ever learn, Papa."

"Jer! You little traitor."

He gives me a coy smile. "It's okay, Mommy. You tell stories better than Papa."

I place a hand at my hip. "I do a lot of things better than your papa."

"*Really?*" Adrian's voice drips with rare amusement. "Like what?"

"Like bathing Jer."

"Papa does it well, too."

"But I'm better."

"No, Mommy. You're the same."

"I gave birth to you, Jer. Your papa didn't." I smirk at Adrian. *Beat that, mister.*

"But you did it together." Jeremy frowns. "That's why I have Mommy and Papa."

"He just did something easy and I'm the one who was pregnant with you for nine months, then gave birth to you."

"Something easy?" Adrian drawls.

"Shut up," I whisper-hiss.

Jeremy stares between us, eyes widening like whenever he figures out something. "If it's easy, do it again and give me a baby sister."

"It's not *that* easy," I blurt.

"But you just said it is, Mommy. Can't you do it again? I want a baby sister." He pulls on Adrian's coat. "Papa, please?"

"We'll see, Malysh."

"Yay!"

"We will?" I murmur.

"Why?" Adrian asks. "You don't want to?"

"It's not that I don't want to. It's just…I never thought about it." Well, that's a lie. I have and I've often wondered why he's never insisted on having another child or why he didn't comment when I went back on birth control after Jeremy's birth.

But I thought he only needed one heir and didn't want to deal with another child.

"You can start now," he says ever so casually, then addresses Jeremy. "Let's build that war zone, Malysh."

"Yes, Papa!"

I follow them into the living room, removing my coat on the way. Now that he's planted the idea of another pregnancy in my mind, it's the only thing I can think about.

Do I want another child?

The answer to that is so muddled by other facts, starting with who Adrian is and the many secrets that I'm still keeping from him. I'll need to sort those out before I can even think about bringing another innocent existence into the equation.

Both father and son get busy building the war zone and I barely help. I really don't like anything that has to do with assembling. My mind is simply not wired that way. However, I love being a part of this little family and having the privilege of watching Adrian and Jeremy up close and witnessing their bond.

It's a subtle one, only visible when they're doing an activity together, like right now. They're both quiet and they understand each other without talking sometimes.

While Adrian is too busy to have a lot of time for Jeremy, he's there when it matters. And our son is such an understanding angel. He never bothers Adrian or demands things from him. However, he always looks up to him and my husband is never too busy to look back.

The view of Adrian in his casual shirt and pants, muscles relaxed and face serene while holding Jer on his lap, is an experience. I love watching him this way, out of his office and away from his mafia business, and just…a father.

I could watch him like this for an eternity, even though I'm slightly jealous of the effortless connection he has with our son.

"Can you please give me that piece, Mommy?" Jeremy points at the one beside me.

I pass it to him and he grins, snuggling in Adrian's lap. I continue observing them for a bit, fingering the Lego container. "Why did you bring us to Russia of all places?"

Adrian remains in his element, assembling a few pieces together. "Jeremy needed to come here sooner or later."

"Any particular reason?"

"He's Russian and needs more contact with his roots." He turns Jeremy to face him. "Malysh, this is where your grandfather and ancestors were born. We come from Yaroslavl and have many generations. You're the last member."

Our son's eyes widen. "I am?"

"Yes, you are."

"Thank you, Papa."

"He's American-born," I say.

"Doesn't make him American."

I roll my eyes but choose to probe instead of focusing on that. "Is that what your parents did to you, too?"

"Did what?"

"Bring you to Russia."

His movements falter on a Lego piece and then he snaps it in place. "My father often brought me here, especially for Christmas."

"How about your mother?"

"Not before she married my father."

"Did you…come here with your stepmother?"

He nods once and I can see the shadow that darkens his expression whenever his past is brought up. "Remember when you asked me what the map of Russia tattoo means?"

I nod frantically. "You said it's because of a vacation you were never able to have."

"Yes. I was supposed to come here with Aunt Annika, but she passed away before I had the chance."

"Is that why you brought us here?"

"Probably." The word is quiet, low, as if it weighs on him.

I wrap my arm around his bicep and lean my head against the hard ridge of his muscles. "We'd never leave you, Adrian."

He stares down at me with molten gray eyes. "Really?"

"I promise," I murmur, then brush a quick kiss on his cheek.

Just when I pull back, he captures my lips in a slow, all-consuming kiss that steals my breath and apparently my logic, because for a brief second, I forget Jeremy is there.

I place a hand on his chest and push him away. He releases my lips with a low growl.

Jeremy stares at us with a grin, and even as my cheeks burn, I can't help but grin back.

Because this moment? This peace? It feels like the beginning of our happiness.

If only the ghosts from the past don't catch up to us.

EIGHTEEN

Lia

OUR VACATION IS SURPRISINGLY…WARM.

Despite the freezing weather and the ice storms, the days we spend in the Russian countryside are so full of fire. And strangely, that isn't entirely due to the lash of Adrian's punishments at night or how he lights my body on fire every chance he gets.

It's the fact that we're spending uninterrupted time together and with our son. The fact that no work is keeping him from us. The fact that we built a snowman together before Jeremy and I ganged up on Adrian in a snowball fight.

We lost, by the way, and it was the best loss I've ever experienced. Jer and I ended up laughing until we snorted as Adrian buried us under his merciless snowballs.

I love seeing my husband carefree, without the endless weight that's usually furrowing his features or making him overanalyze everything.

Ever since we stepped foot in Russia a week ago, he seems to have left all his burdens back in the States and is giving me the one thing I've always wanted—him.

I often fantasized about stealing him away from his work and demanding that he choose me over his endless Bratva responsibilities. But I've stopped due to my stupid pride.

And fear.

I was too afraid of Adrian's nature to ever embrace him fully.

In truth, I still am.

I don't think I will ever not be scared of him. There will always be that slight tinge of terror about how dangerous he is and how monstrous he can get to ensure his goals are met. However, I'm strong and mature enough to ignore that fear and focus on what he is.

Who he is.

The man who showed me a different world, one where I'm cared for and I come before anything else.

The man who fought for me when I didn't have the will to fight for myself.

The man who saved me, even when he tortured me. Who took my hand when I thought there was no hope left for me.

The man who gave me the most precious gift in the form of Jeremy and nurtured him with me. He provided me light, even when he himself was always used to the darkness.

And to have him all to myself these last couple of days has been more exhilarating than anything I've experienced in recent memory.

I know he keeps himself updated by talking to his guards, especially Kolya, in hushed tones, but he doesn't let it occupy his days and nights.

Jeremy and I do.

We have movie nights and lazy mornings. We cook together and mess up the kitchen before Adrian shoos me away so he can clean it. We take walks together whenever it's not snowing hard, and Adrian is even teaching Jeremy how to ski.

At night, after we put our son to sleep, Adrian worships

my body or makes up some sort of punishment just so he can satisfy his sadistic tendencies—and my masochistic ones.

But today, there's a change of plans.

After Jeremy is in bed, I invite the guards over so we can play Scrabble. Something that Adrian isn't very happy about, and he says that there's no way in hell all the guards will come over and we'll stay unprotected.

So Yan shoos the two younger guards outside, filling their hands with snacks.

I expect Kolya and Boris to scold him, but they just sit on the sofa across from me and Adrian. After Yan finishes his mission of getting rid of the younger guards, he settles on the chair on my right.

Tightening the wool scarf that's draped over my shoulders, I angle my neck to soak in the warmth from the fireplace. Although the house is fully heated, I feel like a kitten in the cozy setting.

I prepared countless snacks and placed a case of beer on the table beside the Scrabble board Jeremy found in his exploration of the house.

Adrian loops an arm around my shoulder, his fingers digging into my skin. It's not strong enough to hurt, but it's firm enough to imply he's not pleased with my idea of spending the evening playing with his guards.

His lips brush against the shell of my ear as he whispers in hot words, "Tell them you're feeling unwell and go up to the bedroom. *Now.*"

"No," I hiss.

"If you don't, I'll whip you hard, then fuck you just as hard so that you won't be able to move tomorrow."

"It'd be worth it," I murmur, even as my core throbs at the promise.

It's official. Adrian has ruined me beyond repair.

"I feel bad for them," I tell Yan, who opens a bottle of beer and drinks from it, releasing a sigh of contentment. Kolya and Boris are dressed in army fatigues and Adrian is in his formal attire, but my friend is wearing a casual shirt and pants with a jacket.

I'm just glad he's well enough to move and even drink now. I also saw him running with Adrian and the guards during their morning workouts. And yeah, these crazy people actually run in the snow when it's below zero degrees.

"They'll survive." Yan throws up a dismissive hand. "The cold will make men out of them. They're lucky they weren't in the Special Forces."

"Was is that brutal?" I ask.

"Brutal?" Yan scoffs. "Try deadly. Try, we're the fucking chosen ones for getting out of that training alive. Remember dragging kilos of tires in fucking freezing Siberia, Borya?"

Boris's stoic face falters for a second as he nods, and even Kolya's lips twist, probably recalling the same circumstances.

"Seems the cold hasn't made a man out of you, Yan," Adrian says with nonchalance, then takes a sip of beer.

"How can you say that, Boss? I was second in my unit."

Adrian raises a brow. "Not first."

"Not everyone is a perfectionist freak like you and Kolya."

I stare at Adrian. Yan told me he was in Special Forces before, but he never mentioned rank. "You were first?"

"Unlike Yan."

"He's all bark and no bite," Kolya agrees with his boss, opening a bottle of beer.

"Oh, fuck you, Kolya." Yan's temper rises. "Rank isn't important, skill is. What do you say, Boris?"

"I was first in my unit, too." Boris throws a nut into his mouth. "Pay respect."

"To being first." Kolya shows a rare smirk and raises his bottle of beer.

My husband and Boris mimic him, drinking while Yan

tightens his hold on his bottle, glaring at them before he sighs heavily.

"It seems you're the only loser here, Yan." Kolya smiles.

The younger guard flips him off under the table and I can't help but smile. These men are all ruthless, coming from dangerous backgrounds that allowed them to not only survive Special Forces, but to also excel at it, and although they might be competitive about it, they feel like a family.

A fucked-up one, no doubt, but at the same time, it's very loyal and protective.

A family I want to belong to.

"I'm going to make you eat your words by the end of to-night, Kolya." Yan bunches up his sleeves. "There are five of us. How are we going to do this?"

"I'm not playing," Adrian announces.

"Come on." I nudge him. "Don't be a fun-ruiner."

"If I play, I'll win every round and ruin your actual fun."

"He's right." Yan rolls his eyes. "Don't be fooled by the si-lent façade. Boss is competitive to a fault and makes sure to win at everything."

"Except shipping you back to the Spetsnaz." Adrian sips his beer. "Though that can be arranged rather swiftly now that we're here."

Yan winces. "You didn't forget about that?"

"Never. Now, play. I will be the judge."

Yan clears his throat. "Lia and me against Kolya and Boris."

"No." Adrian objects.

"Why not?" I ask.

"It'd be boring. You and Kolya against Boris and Yan would be more entertaining."

Or more like, he's doing everything in his power to keep me from pairing up with Yan. But whatever, Adrian will always be Adrian.

"Hold on." Yan stands up. "Let me get some real drinks."

I frown, not understanding the meaning behind his words as he disappears in the direction of the kitchen. A minute later, he reappears with a bottle of vodka and glasses.

Boris and Kolya grunt in approval. *Right.* Of course, beer isn't a real drink for them.

The three of them definitely fit the stereotype of how much Russians love their vodka. Adrian usually prefers cognac, but he does push the beer out of the way when vodka is in sight.

At first, I'm too much of a wimp to try straight vodka. They don't even mix it in a cocktail or drink it diluted. However, after Boris delivers a knockout in the first round, I chug down an entire glass to cool off my wounded pride. It burns my throat and I cough a few times, hitting my chest to make it go away.

"Take it easy," Adrian whispers in my ear, his fingers drawing circles on my shoulder.

"I'm fine." I point at Boris. "You're going down. You, too, Yan."

My friend lifts his chin. "I'm sorry to say this, but you'll be collateral damage, because Kolya's destruction is my mission tonight."

"It's the other way around." Kolya's usual calm falters as he assembles his tiles in front of him.

Once again, Boris and Yan take the lead. I swear, Boris is like an encyclopedia that keeps coming up with the right words.

I take another sip of my vodka, mouthing at Kolya to give me a six-letter word that starts with *R*, but he comes up empty.

"Royal," I exclaim.

Boris stares at me with an unusual smugness. "That's five letters."

"Royalty."

"That's seven." Yan chugs down his drink. "Give up, already, and pass."

I don't have the correct letters to spell any form of royal, anyway. With my two blank tiles and a load of vowels, I'm just punching in the dark for ideas.

Adrian drapes my scarf up over my shoulders and whispers in my ear, discreetly enough that no one notices him, "Regius."

I don't want to cheat, I really don't, but with my blanks, I can make it work, and the way Boris is smirking and Yan keeps taunting us is getting on my nerves. So I stoop low and align the tiles in place after the *R*.

"That's cheating, Mrs. Volkov," Boris fixes me with a stare.

"Are you accusing me of being a cheater?" There's a slight slur at the end of my words.

"Boss told you that word."

"No, he didn't."

"He didn't," Kolya says at the same time.

"Wait a minute!" Yan slams his glass on the table. "You're supposed to be impartial, Boss."

"I have been," Adrian says ever so casually with a perfect poker face that betrays nothing.

"You obviously haven't." Yan motions between the two of us.

My husband remains as collected as always. "You have proof?"

"Well...no."

"Do you, Boris?" When the other guard shakes his head, Adrian continues, "Then your accusations are null and void. Proceed."

They both grumble but pick up their pieces as Kolya smirks. I grin up at Adrian, murmuring, "I didn't know you were a cheater."

"I'm not, usually," he whispers back against my cheek.

"You just did."

"Only for you, Lenochka."

We win that round, but Boris and Yan end up crushing us in the next one so hard, my pride is wounded.

As a result, I end up drinking more vodka than should be allowed and telling Yan he and I aren't friends anymore while acting like a sore loser toward Boris.

At some point, Adrian pulls the glass of vodka from my hand. "That's enough drinking for one night."

"Nooo, I'm okaaay. Oops. *Fiiiine.* I mean, I'm totally fine. I know, I know. That word shouuuld be out of my vocabulary by now. You haaate it." I slap my hand against his cheek, staring up at the peaceful look in his gray eyes. "Did you know, you're sooo beautiful?"

"That's our cue to go." Boris's legs are unsteady as he stands. "It was lovely to win against you, Kolya. Mrs. Volkov."

I point a finger at him. "I'll get a rematch and beat you."

"Wait. What?" Yan shakes his head, eyes half-drooping. The two of us drank the most tonight. "It's over? I was just getting started on kicking Kolya's grumpy ass."

"Get up." Kolya grabs him by his good arm and he sways. "And it'll be a lifetime before you kick my ass."

Yan punches him in the chest, and though it doesn't seem hard, Kolya staggers a little. "I'll break through that ice one day, you have my fucking word."

Kolya pushes him in front of himself, nods at us, then singlehandedly hauls Yan out, refusing Boris's aid.

"They left." I motion at the door after it closes behind them. "But I'm not done playing."

"I am more than done." Adrian lifts my chin, his long fingers creating delicious friction against my skin. "No one gets to see you drunk but me."

"I'm not drunk." I hiccup and giggle, hiding the sound with the back of my hand. "Oops. Maybe a little."

"A little?"

"Okay, a looot." I nuzzle my cheek against his hand and sigh. "You're so warm."

"I am?"

"Yes, even when you're cold. Even when you give me the silent treatment, you're so caring and warm. That's one thing I don't want you to change."

"What else do you not want me to change?"

"Hmm. The way you look at me."

"And how do I look at you?"

"Like you want to tie me down and fuck me."

"I *do* want to tie you down and fuck you."

I giggle as arousal tingles between my legs. "All the time?"

"If I can help it." His voice drops to a seductive range.

"What if you can't? What if I become old and wrinkly and sex isn't the same anymore?"

"I'll find a way."

"What if something happens and I can't have sex altogether?" I don't know why I'm asking these questions, but for some reason, I feel vulnerable and the only way to fight it is to poke at the weight perching on my chest.

Adrian's fingers glide over the ridge of my nose, then trace a path to my cheek as if he's engraving me into some corner of his head. "If something happens to you, it won't push me away. If anything, it'll bring me closer, Lenochka. Sex plays a part of who we are, and I love how you submit to my dominance, but it's not the reason why I've been married to you for six years."

"What is then?"

"You."

"Just me?"

"Just you."

I gulp, feeling moisture glistening in my eyes. A strange rush of emotions overwhelm me until it's hard to breathe, let alone think. It's two words. *Just you.* But it's like he reached inside himself, ripped a part out, and offered it to me in the palm of his hand.

"Don't ever change, okay?" I whisper.

"Lia, what did I say about that word?"

"Oops. Does that mean you'll punish me now?"

"Oh, I'll do more than punish you."

My heart skips a beat when I glance at him. "What?" I ask, my voice breathy and sultry.

"I'd rather show you."

I squeal as he sweeps me off the floor and into his arms, and then I break into a fit of laughter.

Happiness.

I've never dared to dream about it before, but this must be what it feels like to be happy, and now, I'm finally daring to experience it to its fullest.

Please let it stay this way forever.

NINETEEN

Adrian

LIA GRABS ON TO ME WITH HER DELICATE FINGERS AS I carry her to the bedroom.

I, on the other hand? I'm thinking of ways to punish and fuck her after she's kept me waiting all night long.

There's no way in hell I'm letting my guards near her in the future. This one time was enough. In fact, it's more than I would have preferred.

If it were up to me, she'd have no contact with them at all. A certain dark obsession takes hold of me whenever she talks, let alone smiles, at other men—even if they're my own guards. It provokes the beast inside me who's ready to come out and slaughter any man in her vicinity so that I'm the only one she ever gives her attention to.

I kick the wooden door shut behind me and Lia digs her tiny hands into my shirt, giggling as she squirms. Her cheeks are rosy and her eyelids have drooped from drinking. Another side of her that I don't want anyone else to witness.

She looks so beautiful, flushed and with the blue of her

eyes softening. There's no trace of the sadness that seems to have haunted her life.

If anything, she appears a bit…mischievous. A trait that she rarely shows, if ever.

Lia has always been the soft, elegant type who keeps her emotions to herself. She said she hates my silent treatment, but she doesn't realize that she often uses the same tactic herself. In fact, she was the one who pulled away first and refused to let me in no matter how much I coaxed her.

She always used to see the worst in me, and as a response, I resorted to forceful methods in order to keep her. To some extent, it was because that's all I know, but I also did it because the thought of her leaving me turned me into a fucking beast.

But she hasn't seemed to have those thoughts about escaping since the day I found her at the park. Actually, she feels closer, especially since we came to Russia.

She was right. I brought her here as a twisted pay of homage to the trip I never got the chance to take with Aunt Annika. However, it turned out to be so much more for our family. Even if, deep down, I'm still torn apart about her infidelity.

Despite being naturally distrustful, a strong part of me believes she didn't cheat on me; however, there's also the wary part.

The part that was cut in half when she confirmed having a lover.

The part that believes this is all a sham and that, sooner or later, she'll go back to trying to escape.

That if given the choice, she won't look twice before she leaves.

I thought I'd gotten used to people leaving when I was a child. First Aunt Annika, then Mom, then my father. But the idea of Lia joining them strikes a completely different chord.

One that keeps me awake at night, racking my brain to find a solution.

"Let me down," she slurs.

"Why?"

"Stop asking questions for once. Trust me."

I raise a brow even as I put her to her feet. She stumbles and I grab her elbow to steady her.

Lia wraps both of her hands around mine and sighs deeply as she sways on her feet. "I love your hands. They're so strong and masculine. You even have veins in them."

"Is that so?"

"Mmm-hmm. But do you know what I love the most about them?"

"What?"

"How rough they are while still being caring." She flattens my palm on her beating heart. "See how much I love it?"

A deep groan escapes my chest as I feel her erratic heartbeat and watch how her cheeks redden to a bright crimson. Lia isn't the type who lowers her guard or touches me freely. It's probably the alcohol, but I revel in every moment of her losing her inhibitions.

The night wasn't a complete waste after all.

Not only do I get to witness this side of her, but I also get to hear her honesty. She's never allowed herself to get drunk around me after that first time in the restaurant. It's like she's scared about letting go in my company.

Because she didn't trust me even when she wanted me. Even when she sought my affection.

And I didn't permit her to get drunk when she thought she was Winter, because she wasn't herself and wouldn't have been choosing to do it freely.

She did tonight, though.

My wife willingly chose to show me this part of her.

Lia releases my hand, but I keep it against her breastbone, basking in the feel of her erratic breathing.

She unbuttons my shirt, her touch unsteady but

determined until she reveals my chest. Her palms flatten on my pectoral muscles and they flex beneath her tender touch. Her throat works with a swallow as she slides her hands down my abdomen, her dainty fingers pausing on my skin every so often until she finds my belt and undoes it.

Her movements are shaky and awkward at best, but I don't try to help her, curious where she's taking this.

My wife lowers herself to her knees in front of me as her trembling hands slide down my pants and boxer briefs.

A growl spills from my lips and a carnal sense of lust hardens my dick.

The only time Lia has ever sucked me was in that alley, and that was only because she initiated it. While I have constantly thought about making her take my dick at the back of her pretty throat, I've never acted on it, because I needed her to want it. I wished her to get on her knees for me, not because she had to, but because she wanted to.

Like now.

She frees my cock, her tiny hands wrapping around it and her tongue darts out to lick her lips.

My fingers dig into her dark hair as I groan deep in my throat. "Fuck, Lenochka."

"You like this?" She stares up at me with her huge eyes, still stroking me up and down.

"What do you think?"

"I think you do." She swirls her tongue around the crown, lapping at the droplets of precum. "Mmm. I love your taste."

Holy fuck.

It's the first time she's talked dirty and it's a strange turn-on.

"Why haven't you fucked my mouth before, Adrian?"

"For the same reason that you've never gotten on your knees before, Lenochka."

"And that is?"

"You didn't want it."

She shakes her head with a frown etched deep between her brows. "Of course I did. I just didn't express it. There hasn't been a day when I didn't want you. Not even when I thought I hated you."

I'm on the verge of coming then and there, even before she opens her mouth and takes me to the back of her throat.

Her words are the strongest aphrodisiac that's ever hit me. The knowledge that she's had me on her mind, probably as much as I've had her on mine, swells a dark corner of my heart with strange warmth.

Lia tries to suck me hard, even with her half-drooping eyelids and wobbly knees. My hand fists in her hair and when I thrust to the back of her throat, she loosens her grip, allowing me to use her mouth, to drive in and out of her wet heat.

My wife gags, tears welling in her eyes and drool rolling down her chin. I love this sight of her, the submission in her gaze and in her posture, even while she's choking on my dick. She doesn't fight me, doesn't try to push me away as I confiscate her air.

This is why Lia has always been special to me. She takes the lash of my punishments and comes back for more. It's like she trusts I'd never hurt her beyond repair and that I'll only satisfy her.

My roughness matches her softness.

I pull out of her wet heat, allowing her to breathe. She sucks in audibly, her cheeks streaking with fresh tears, but immediately opens her lips, sticking her tongue out slightly.

Fuck me.

Gripping her hair tighter, I pound inside, my rhythm increasing. "You can't get enough, Lenochka?"

"Mmm," she sputters around my hard dick.

"You like having your mouth fucked by me?"

She nods frantically and reaches a hand beneath her dress, touching herself as if to show me just how she likes it.

"Are you wet because I'm using your mouth this roughly?"

"Mmm." Her movements quicken underneath her dress and so do my thrusts.

I pull out of her with an animalistic groan, even though my dick is so hard, it's fucking painful.

Lia licks her lips, her fingers pausing as disappointment etches across her delicate features. "Why did you stop?"

I grab her, lift her up, and throw her on the bed. She lands on her back with a delighted squeal as I yank her skirt to her waist.

She bites her lower lip, lust and something similar to adoration shining in her eyes. "Is it time for my punishment?"

"I have something else in mind." I don't bother with removing her panties and, instead, rip them against her swollen pussy. She makes this startled, seductive sound whenever I do that and I had made it my mission to hear it whenever possible.

Lia opens her legs and I slide inside her with an ease I've never experienced before. She arches off the bed, the soles of her feet digging into the backs of my thighs.

My pace remains slow, unhurried, as I drive into her tight heat. She's always felt like home, the one I think about going back to whenever I'm away from it.

"Oh, Adrian…" Her lips remain parted with no more words coming out, only moans, while I take my time powering into her body with deep, long thrusts. I roll my hips, letting her feel every stroke, every touch.

Every sliver of connection.

My hands are all over her, squeezing, grabbing. My lips find her tender ones, kissing her with the same rhythm of my thrusts, then I'm sucking on her neck, finding my way to her shirt and removing it with one hand so I can feast on her tight nipples.

"Adrian…oh, God…" She pants, holding on to me while she throbs around me, then cries out, her muscles milking me as she comes undone.

Her soft moans and sexy, throaty sounds echo in the air, luring my own orgasm. The rush is hard and potent and it takes everything I have to make it last.

I come inside her the longest I ever have, my blood rushing to where we're connected. My groans reverberate around us as spurts of my cum fill her and drip all over her cunt.

My wife is the only woman who's ever made me feel out of my mind with an animalistic sense of pleasure. One so carnal, I don't ever want it to end.

But it's not only pleasure that beats under my skin whenever I'm inside her.

It's something deeper, darker, and would freak her out if I ever found the words to voice it.

Lia wraps her arms around my neck and smashes her lips to mine, kissing me with a desperation that flows in my blood and reaches into my fucking bones.

"I love you," she whispers against my mouth, her breath stuttering. "I love you so much, Adrian."

I groan, her words hardening my dick all over again as if I didn't just empty myself inside her.

Before I can act on that or sort out my own words, she smiles a little, her breathing evening out and her lids closing. Then a tear escapes one as she falls asleep. I kiss it away, tasting the salt and her unsaid words.

I pull her to me and she snuggles into my hold, sighing when I cover us both.

We sleep wrapped around one another so tight, she's the only thing I breathe. She smells of roses and sex and belonging.

Lia is the only person I've ever wanted to belong to me, no matter how illogical and impossible that is.

∽

A tap on the door pulls me from sleep's clutches.

I check the clock on the nightstand to find it's only six in the morning. Lia is sprawled all over my chest, breathing against my skin.

Another knock comes before Kolya's voice surges through. "Emergency, Boss."

Sleep immediately leaves my brain as I slowly ease my wife to her back and cover her. Kolya isn't the type who would call a situation an emergency unless things are indeed getting out of control.

I pull on a pair of pants and a shirt, which I don't bother buttoning as I step out of the room, closing the door behind me.

My second-in-command stands in the hallway, his eyes bloodshot and a frown etched between his brows. He's in barely put together army fatigues, which means he was also urged out of sleep.

"What is it, Kolya?"

"Sergei is demanding your immediate return."

"What for?"

"Vladimir." Kolya runs an agitated hand through his blond hair. "He brought forward evidence that you're behind Richard's death."

"What type of evidence?"

"I don't know, but it's strong enough that Sergei and the others are livid. They've been calling me non-stop the past hour since they couldn't get a hold of you."

If they're putting their weight into this, it's definitely serious.

"Prepare to leave."

"Boss, no. You have to stall until you find something to counter their accusations. Staying here for a bit longer will placate their anger."

"Or make it worse. Sergei will think I'm guilty."

"You *are* guilty, Boss. You shouldn't have killed Richard."

"He touched Lia. I would kill him a thousand times over if I got the chance to repeat it."

He runs his hand through his hair again. "There's something else."

"What now?"

"Mrs. Volkov might not be what we've thought all along."

"What is that supposed to mean?"

"Since Yan was drunk last night, I managed to make him talk."

"About?"

"The night she was kidnapped. Boss…Yan heard it all. She knew the man, and from the information we gathered, he was indeed Luca Brown."

"I suspected as much. But why would that make Lia not who we thought she might be?"

"According to Yan, Luca told her she had one mission."

"What mission?"

"He didn't mention that, but here's the thing, Boss. If my speculations are correct, it has something to do with your assassination attempt at Mikhail's party last year. Since Luca hired that Spetsnaz he killed and threw off the cliff a few weeks ago, all evidence points to the likelihood that he also hired the mercenary we found dead at the party."

Kolya's words strike me like a lightning bolt and I have to take a moment to steady my breathing. "What does Lia have to do with any of that?"

"Mrs. Volkov was the one who pulled you down right before the gun went off. I didn't think about it much at the time, just figured she had a quick reflex. However, the facts are that she saw something before you or I or even Damien and Kirill did, and she couldn't actually have quicker reflexes than the four of us or Kirill and Damien's guards. I believe that the only way she could've managed to pull you down that fast is because she knew about the hit beforehand."

Even though I'm hearing him and I've somehow come to the same conclusion myself, I don't want to believe it. "Yan could've lied."

"Not when he's drunk. He begged me not to say a word, said he believes she didn't mean to and must have had her reasons. But what reasons could those be?"

"Kolya…" I grind out. "You're saying that my fucking wife had a hand in my attempted assassination."

"And that's why it's the only attempted assassination we haven't been able to solve. You're too blinded by her to see it."

"Shut up."

"She betrayed you, Boss. All evidence points at her."

"I said, shut the fuck up." I raise my fist and punch him in the face. He staggers backward, blood exploding from his lip.

My senior guard straightens in front of me again and for the first time since we were growing up, he grabs me by the collar of my shirt, his voice rising. "Wake up, Adrian. You're a traitor to the Bratva because of her and if you don't use your brain, you'll be executed by Sergei. I don't give a fuck if you kill me, but I will not allow you to die now after how far you've come."

I breathe so harshly, my pulse roars in my ears. My chest aches to the point that it's about to explode, because I know, deep down, that Kolya is right.

And this might as well be the end.

TWENTY

Lia

PAIN LODGES AT THE BACK OF MY HEAD WHEN I OPEN my eyes.

Moisture clings to my lashes as I blink tears away. Was I crying? But from what?

I cradle my temples while I try to recall the nightmare I just had and why I'm on the verge of bawling my eyes out.

My teeth chatter and I decide not to ponder over the nightmare. Instead, I hold on to last night's memories.

A tender ache blossoms between my legs, but it's the delicious type, the type that brings a smile to my lips. I remember each and every one of Adrian's touches, the way he was considerate, passionate, but also slow, taking his time in owning my body.

While Adrian has the best aftercare, last night was the first time he's been that affectionate during the act itself. As if he wanted to engrave himself beneath my skin and stay there. Not that he needs to. He seeped through my bloodstream like a potent potion long ago.

One thing's for sure, something changed between us last night, because, in a way, I feel closer to him now more than ever.

But it hurt to confess my feelings for the second time and get silence again.

I try convincing myself that I'm used to this, that I'm already aware of Adrian's inability to have those feelings, that his care and attentiveness are enough.

But I guess I'm too greedy to settle for that.

I'm too greedy for the touch I felt yesterday, for how he held me, kissed me, and worshipped every inch of my body as if it were the first and last time he'd be with me.

The hangover headache is worth it.

Though I would've preferred he be by my side this morning. Did he perhaps go to train with Kolya and the others as usual? Or maybe Jeremy tried to barge into the bedroom and Adrian decided to have breakfast with him.

I take my time waking up, trying not to trigger my already blinding headache. When I straighten to get out of bed, I startle when I notice Adrian sitting on a chair by the door. He's wearing a white shirt and black pants, his elbows on his knees and his hands forming a steeple at his chin.

I smile, but it vanishes as I stare into the soulless depths of his ashen eyes. They're dark, cold, and absolutely savage, like that day he killed that man right in front of me.

The only difference is they're now focused on me. He was probably watching me like that the whole time I was sleeping.

A strange apprehension grips me by the throat as I pull the covers to my chin, feeling like I need every barrier possible right now. "Adrian…? What's wrong—"

"I'm going to ask you some questions and you'll answer," he cuts me off, his calm like a thousand needles pricking into my skin at the same time. "Lie and it'll be the last you'll utter."

My heart thrums violently in my chest and my breathing shatters into fragmented pieces. Adrian has only been this cold to me when he thought I was cheating on him. But I thought he believed me for a few weeks now.

I thought we'd started a new page.

"Do you remember Mikhail's last birthday party, Lia?"

Oh, God.

Oh, no.

Why is he asking about that? Did he figure it out? Of course, he did. Adrian isn't an idiot. He wouldn't have brought up that day if he didn't have a purpose behind it.

My lips feel dry and chapped as I speak. "I…can explain."

"I didn't ask if you could explain, I asked if you remember Mikhail's last birthday. Answer the fucking question."

Moisture gathers in my eyes when I murmur, "I do."

"You saved me that day because you magically happened to notice the mercenary." He stands up and I shrink against the headboard. "See, I don't believe in magic, Lia, but I chose to at that moment. I chose to believe in a coincidence, in a statistical fluke that you saw the assassin before Kirill, Damien, Kolya or I could."

A tear escapes my lid. "Adrian…please…"

"Were you planning to kill me from the beginning, Lia? Is that what you and Luca agreed on?"

"No, no, I swear. I didn't…didn't…want to kill you…"

"But you planned it?"

"No…"

"I said not to lie to me." He stops by my side, glaring down on me. "I said it would be your fucking last."

I grab his wrist with both hands, and even though my skin is cold, I need to establish some sort of a connection between us. To hold on to the hope that we knew each other for years and that it should mean something. "He only asked me to keep an eye on you, saying he'd tell me about my parents' deaths in return. But I stopped. I swear, I never wanted to hurt you."

"You only meant to kill me. Fucking betray *me*." He grabs me by the wrist and yanks me off the bed.

I squeak as I stumble and nearly fall to my knees. His hold

is harsh and unforgiving, with the intention of inflicting pain. "That's not true…please…please…hear me out. I know you're angry but…"

"Angry? I'm not angry, Lia. I'm enraged, disappointed, in *pain* right fucking here." He taps the center of his chest. "All I've ever done is protect you, even when you could've been a huge disadvantage for me. I married you instead of using you as a pawn when I knew Sergei would have my head if he learned of your origins. Even when I was fully aware that Igor would plot my demise if he figured out I abandoned and humiliated his daughter, a Russian, one of my *own*, to marry an Italian. But what did you give me in return? You *betrayed* me, you took the training I gave you and fucking stabbed me in the back with it."

"No…" I'm sobbing, salty tears the only thing I can taste. "No, I didn't…"

"There's only one punishment for betrayal, Lia."

I suck in a sharp, shattered breath, shaking my head over and over. "Adrian, please, I know…I know I shouldn't have talked to Luca, but he was the only friend I thought I had. I realize now that he was just using me. Back then…back then…I was too lonely, too scared, and I needed someone when you were being too harsh and distant."

"So you chose a lover?"

"I told you he was never my lover! You think I could ever think about another man after meeting you?"

"You obviously did since you plotted my death. I'm curious, what did you plan to do after I was dead, start anew with him?"

I shake my head violently until my neck aches. The thought of Adrian dead brings fresh tears to my eyes.

"Fucking answer me, Lia! Did you sit down and plot the perfect way to kill me?"

"I would never plot to kill you, not even when you hurt

me, not even when I thought I hated you." I push at him with all my might. "I killed for you, you fucking idiot! I killed the man Luca brought that day, because the thought of him hurting you made me lose my damn mind! That's why my depression hit hard afterward, that's why I was like a zombie to the point I couldn't pay attention to my own son! Killing a man, even if he was a criminal, hit me hard and I couldn't survive it. But do you know what the worst part is? If it were to protect you, I'd repeat it in a heartbeat."

Adrian doesn't say anything, his chest rising and falling with alarming speed. We watch each other for several long seconds, my sniffles and his harsh breaths filling the air.

"You were the one who killed him?" His voice is low but firm.

"Yes, and I removed the bullet so you wouldn't know it was me."

"Why didn't you tell me?"

"Because of the exact way you're acting right now. I knew you wouldn't believe me, that you'd think I'd betrayed you. I never have, Adrian, I swear. I couldn't even if I wanted to."

"Why not?"

"Because I *love* you," my voice cracks with the wrecking force of my sobs. "I'm *in love* with you, and that means I would rather hurt myself and jump off a cliff instead of causing you any pain."

"Fuck, Lia." He closes his eyes, sucking in a deep breath, then pushes me to a sitting position on the bed. "Tell me everything."

"Does…does that mean you believe me?"

"Tell me everything," he repeats. "Don't leave any fucking detail out."

I wrap the covers around me as I recite what happened in the last six years, starting with when Luca approached me about keeping an eye on Adrian, then on to our meetings in the shelter's bathroom, and I even tell him about the crumbs of information I shared with Luca.

It's useless to keep anything from Adrian at this point, not when he seems to be on the verge of throwing it all away.

"So you've been meeting him regularly," he says with deceptive calm after I'm done. "Behind my back."

"It meant nothing. I promise."

"How could it mean nothing when you did it religiously?"

"I told you, I just needed a friend. After…after I killed that man, I pulled away from Luca. That day at the park, I told him we no longer had any sort of relationship and that we should each go our separate ways. He forced that kiss on me because I was no longer on his side."

"Should I be grateful for that? Should I be fucking grateful that you stopped meeting the man who's been planning to kill me, Lia?"

"No…that's not what I meant…"

"If I hadn't found out, would you have taken your secret to the grave or would you have rekindled your relationship with Luca and come after me again?"

"No, never! I…I wanted to tell you all about it but couldn't muster the courage. You…you can be so scary sometimes and I didn't want us to lose what we have."

"Well, congratulations. We already did."

My heart falls to the bottom of my stomach. The room spins around, and although I'm sitting, it feels as if I will fall in a heap on the ground. "W-what?"

"Get dressed."

"Why?"

"Get fucking dressed."

I jerk to a standing position, letting the covers fall to the floor as I head to the closet. My hands are clammy, shaking, and tears won't stop escaping my lids, blurring my vision and rolling down my cheeks and neck.

Due to my state, it takes me some time to put on my underwear and a black wool dress.

My husband watches my every move with his cold expression. I want to ask him what he meant by his words, I want to beg for another chance, but the fear of his cold shoulder and rejection keeps my quivering lips shut.

As soon as I put on my coat, he grabs me by the arm and drags me out of the room and down the stairs. I'm unable to keep up with his long strides and end up stumbling and nearly falling a couple of times.

"Adrian..." My voice cracks. "Whatever it is you're planning to do, don't... Please...don't..."

He yanks the front door open and I grit my teeth when the freezing air hits me and saturates to my bones.

The sky is gloomy, nearly invisible as heavy snow falls and blurs the horizon.

I'm still begging and pleading while Adrian drags me in the direction of the forest. Our feet form holes in the thick layers of snow as we go on and on until the house disappears from view.

"Adrian...Adrian..."

He yanks me in front of him and I stumble before falling on my knees, face-first into the snow. I lift my head to stare at his closed off expression.

"Sergei found out that I killed Richard and he will demand retribution for such betrayal." His voice is more frigid than the merciless snowstorm.

"You...you...don't mean..."

"There's only one punishment for traitors, Lia." He retrieves his gun from the back of his pants. "Death."

TWENTY-ONE

Lia

SIX YEARS.

It took six years for me to find myself in this position again.

I stare at the muzzle of the gun. And not just any gun—Adrian's.

He's not pointing it at me. At the moment, it's in his hand by his side, but I know exactly what's coming.

What he plans to do.

My lips part, allowing my salty tears to seep into my mouth, but I'm not crying because of death. I was ready for that the day my career ended, and I only stayed alive due to Adrian and the gift he gave me in the form of Jeremy.

The reason why I can't stop the flow of tears or the pain that's splitting my chest in half is because of the hurt on his beautiful face, taking refuge in his hypnotizing eyes. The fact that he thinks I betrayed him or that I would ever wish him harm.

"I trusted you, Lia, even more than I trusted myself. You were the light I wasn't allowed to have and I did everything I could to protect it and not let it burn out. You were the only purity I saw in the world and I did my hardest not to tarnish it. In my own fucked-up way, I wanted to preserve you, to go against my nature and keep you, but I should've known it was only a pipe dream."

"You did. You protected me, you…gave me a reason to live after I thought everything was over. I always called you a monster, but it took forgetting you to realize you're the monster I need. So…please…please give me another chance. Give *us* another chance, for Jeremy, for our family. I…don't care if you punish me for an eternity as long as you're with me. Please…"

Snow sticks to his shoulders and dark hair as he stares down at me with lips twisted in what seems like pain. "I can't."

"Adrian…"

He grabs me by the arm, hauling me to my feet and slamming the front of my body against his. His lips find my parted ones and I sob against them as he devours me, his tongue plunging inside to feast on everything I have to offer and then some.

My husband kisses me with a desperation that matches mine and passion that awakens my own. He robs me of thoughts until he's the only thing present, as if I'm existing for him, for the way he kisses me like it's his first and last.

I choke on my tears, fingers digging into his shirt when his arm wraps around my waist. He lifts me off the ground so that I'm suspended except for his hold on me.

He throws the gun away and flings me against a tree trunk while his tongue is still hooked around mine, swirling and devouring. He uses his other hand to pull my dress and coat up.

A sting of cold hits my bare skin and I hiss, but my fingers move of their own accord, undoing his pants with an urgency I've never experienced before.

I want him with a desperation that leaves me breathless.

I need to have him, to not lose him, and if that has to happen only through sex, then so be it.

My lips never leave his while I free his hard cock and guide him to my aching core. My legs wrap around his waist in a steel embrace as he slides my panties to the side and drives inside me in one savage go.

I gasp in his mouth, kissing him with renewed energy, my arms hugging his neck and gripping the short hairs at his nape. He powers into me, one hand gripping the tree behind my back for balance and the other cupping my jaw, tilting my head up so he can kiss me deeper, confiscating more of my breaths.

My back slides up and down the harsh surface of the tree as he powers into me with deep, raw thrusts that match the merciless strokes of his tongue.

Scorching heat flows in my veins despite the freezing weather, the snow, and the white that nearly buries us. I'm anchored in the moment, in life, by Adrian's strong, protective hold.

The thought of losing him fills me with a void so large, I hear its echo in my aching chest. I hold on to him tighter, kiss him faster while my tears burn my skin and soaks his.

We come together, my orgasm detonating inside me with chilling force as his cum warms my core.

He pulls back from my mouth, and I release his lips with a low whimper. At least he was with me while fucking me, but now, he's not.

Now, we have to touch the ground after levitating.

I hug his neck tighter, burying my face into his skin and inhaling his woodsy scent into my lungs.

He pulls out of me, forcing me to release my legs from around his waist as he smooths my dress and coat down. His strong palm lands on my hip to keep me steady since I'm currently dangling from his neck, my feet not touching the ground.

"Let me go, Lia." The order is quiet, not as firm as usual.

I furiously shake my head against his neck.

"You'll freeze to death."

"I don't care. Freezing to death is better than whatever you're planning."

"Look at me."

"No…"

"Lenochka, look at me."

I can't resist him when he calls me by that nickname or when he lowers his voice to that coaxing range.

Not releasing him, I pull back so I can stare at him through my blurry vision. Adrian wipes my tears with the pad of his thumb even as fresh ones fall. "When I was ten, my mother betrayed my father by talking to other crime organizations behind his back. She was so power-hungry that she singlehandedly plotted a coup against the *Pakhan* at the time with the intention of making my father the number one man in the Bratva. When he found out, he chased her, forced her to her knees and shot her between the eyes right in front of me. That's how traitors are treated in the brotherhood, no matter who they are or what their rank."

I whimper, shaking all over in his hold, but it's not because of his underlying threat, it's the fact that he witnessed his mother's execution as a kid. My heart aches for him, even if he's planning to do the same to me. I guess this is what it means to love. It's to feel the pain of the one you love in spite of what he's plotting for you.

"Are you…are you going to kill me now?"

"Never." No hesitation. No second thoughts.

"I-isn't that what you're supposed to do?"

"Maybe. But like you, I'm unable to hurt you, Lenochka, even if my own life is on the line."

"What…what do you mean that your life is on the line?" I don't like the sound of that. In fact, I hate it so much that I'm shivering and quivering for a reason entirely different from the cold.

"Remember when you asked me if I ever loved you?"

I nod, fresh tears surging to my eyes.

"I didn't understand my emotions at the time, but I do now. I do love you, Lia. I always have. But my form of love isn't sweetness or softness. It's nothing noble or delicate. My love is selfish and villainous. My love is the type where I will kill people to protect you and erase others to avenge you. My love is possessive, obsessive, and knows no boundaries, not when I first met you and certainly not now."

A helpless noise tears from my throat. Even though his words are everything I've wished to hear, the circumstances he's saying them under fill me with a raw agony.

"And because my love is selfish, I will put you ahead of everything else."

"Adrian…"

Before I can organize my thoughts, he picks me up, carrying me bridal style, and heads back through the blurry snowstorm to the house. There's a car waiting outside, in front of which all the guards who came with us are standing.

Kolya stares at me with his stoic expression and Yan doesn't meet my gaze.

"Boris and Yan, you will stay here to protect Lia and Jeremy with your lives," Adrian announces. "The rest will come with me."

"Go with you where?" I whisper in a spooked voice.

He puts me to my feet, stroking my hair behind my ear. "I wish it could've been different between the two of us. I wish I were the man you deserve instead of the villain you've got."

"What are you talking about? Why are you saying things like that?"

"Raise Jeremy well. My men will be able to ensure your safety."

"Why not you? Why would your men do it?"

"I told you, Lia. The punishment of betrayal is death."

"No…no…" I grab his hand in a helpless attempt to stop him. The thought of where he's going and the fate that awaits him cause me to gasp and blubber at the same time, "Don't go to Sergei."

"If I don't, he'll come here."

"Then…then let me talk to him, let me tell him about Richard and—"

"That will get you killed."

"But—"

"No. It's final."

"Adrian, please." I dig my fingers into his arm.

He kisses the top of my head and removes my hand from around him, then heads to the car without a look back.

At first, I'm frozen in place, hot tears tingling on my cheeks. It isn't until he's driving away that I snap out of it.

The knowledge that he's going to his death burns me like a thousand flames in the midst of the freezing cold.

"Adrian!" I shriek, running after him. "Adrian, no! Don't leave me…don't!"

My foot gets stuck in the snow and I stumble, but I continue hobbling after the car as it slowly disappears. "No, no…"

Loud, haunted sobs echo in the air and I realize they're mine when my lungs burn with the need to catch up to him, to prevent him from walking to his own death.

"Adrian! Adrian!!" I scream at the top of my lungs. My feet give out and I fall to my knees in the middle of the snow.

I get up again, my chest quaking with the force of my cries and shrieks as I run after the car.

Strong arms grab me, preventing me from going any farther. I think I hear Yan's and Boris's voices, but I can't make out what they're saying.

All I'm focused on is the dot of black that's slowly vanishing into the white.

And with it, my life vanishes, too.

TWENTY-TWO

Adrian

A WEIGHT HAS BEEN PRESSING ON MY CHEST SINCE I left Russia.

Or more accurately, since I left Lia.

The view of her running after me, crying and screaming in the middle of the freezing snow, still plays at the back of my head on repeat.

I run a hand over my face to dispel those images. If I think of her, I won't be able to get on with my plan.

I won't be able to save her and our son.

While finding out she's been meeting with Luca behind my back was like being stabbed with a thousand blunt knives, I believed every word she said.

If it were the old me, I wouldn't have. If anything, my trust issues would have gotten the better of me and I would've taken it out on her. But that's not the case now. Not only do I trust her, but everything she said made sense, filling in the missing puzzle pieces.

After the assassination attempt, her mental health took a sharp decline and her descent to rock bottom was fast. At the time, I thought it was due to witnessing the assassination attempt since she was always stressed about that side of my life. However, knowing that she killed someone with her own hands explains how she often went into a trance.

And she did it for me.

Lia, who used to tremble in front of a gun, killed someone to protect me.

I probably shouldn't be proud of that fact, but I am.

Even if I want to strangle her accomplice with my bare hands.

"Find Luca and kill him," I tell Kolya who's sitting beside me in the back seat as Fedor and another guard occupy the front.

We're heading straight from the airport to Sergei. I haven't stopped by the house, merely calling Ogla to inform her about the course of action to take once I'm gone, just as I've spent the entire flight telling Kolya what he'll do from here on out.

"With all due respect, sir. Luca is not the problem now."

"He is. Since he's so invested in her and knows that she's Lazlo's daughter, his roots run deeper than I thought. He wants to hurt her and has manipulated her all along, which means he's most likely one of the Rozettis. He was probably assigned to keep an eye on her and he's used her ever since. Remember the guard who betrayed their secret about hiding Lia from Lazlo after we tortured him? He said that Lia is their trump card against the Lucianos and they'll use it whenever they see fit. They kidnapped her mother while she was pregnant with her and married her off to one of their own to keep her under their thumbs."

"Wouldn't Lazlo know about her mother? The pregnancy? Her grandmother?"

"She wasn't her real grandmother, Kolya. She was merely a woman who knew Rachel Gueller at some point in her life, and the Rozettis paid her well to pretend to be Lia's grandmother."

"Why couldn't it be that Lazlo knew he had a daughter somewhere and simply never paid attention to her?"

"He's heirless, Kolya. Believe me, if he knew he had an offspring somewhere, he wouldn't hesitate to bring him or her into the family."

"So now what?"

"I want Luca and anyone he works with dead. Since he knows about Lia's origins, he's a danger to her."

"You're the one who's currently in danger. You could force Lazlo's hand by telling him about her. If you bring him around, Sergei might forgive you."

"No."

"Boss."

"If Lazlo finds out about her, he'll know I duped him all along and will stop at nothing until he takes her. She's well protected away from him."

"With all due respect, she won't be protected when you're dead."

"Yes, she will be. You will make sure of it."

He releases a deep sigh, staying silent for a beat too long. "Is it worth it?"

"Is what worth it?"

"Losing everything for her?"

A small smile grazes my lips. "Absolutely."

Fedor stops the car in front of Sergei's house, then accompanies me and Kolya inside.

We pass by a huge painting of angels battling demons in the entrance. It's a piece of art that Nikolai and Sergei acquired from the black market and exhibited where it's visible to anyone who walks in.

The previous and the current *Pakhans'* display of power in even the smallest of details is intriguing. Through the painting, they subconsciously make their guests pick a side. Angels or demons. Good or evil.

I always thought myself above such mind games, but now, as I stare at the furious paranormal faces frozen in their battle cry, I can't help but feel a slight twinge of discomfort.

Another thing they hoped to accomplish by placing the painting here.

Sergei's senior guard stops Kolya and Igor at the bottom of the stairs and speaks in gruff Russian, "Only Volkov is allowed upstairs."

Kolya steps beside me. "I'm going with him."

"*Only* Volkov," the guard repeats, pulling his gun out.

Kolya reaches into his holster, to bring out his own weapon, no doubt, but I shake my head at him. I follow Sergei's guard up the stairs toward his office, but before I go inside, the guard steps between me and the door. "Your gun."

This is the first time I've been asked to leave my weapon at the door. While I figured Sergei didn't call me in for tea, if he's going as far as disarming me, this might as well be my death certificate.

I reach beneath my jacket, retrieve my gun, and give it to the guard. He searches me for any hidden weapons before he knocks on the door and opens it for me.

It takes me a moment to walk in. If it were a few years ago, I wouldn't give a fuck about being summoned, but if it were a few years ago, I wouldn't have let my system fail me. I wouldn't have been illogical.

I wouldn't have been…alive.

Because even though I performed the act of living before, I've never truly lived until Lia came into my life.

I meant what I told Kolya earlier, Lia is worth failing my system, digging my own grave, and putting myself in this unfavorable position. I would do it all over again if it means having her.

The guard follows me inside, then closes the door and stands in front of it in case I try to escape.

Not that I would.

Sergei sits in the lounge area with Igor and Vladimir across from him, their expressions as hard as granite. Four of their guards are in erect positions by the balcony.

I stop before Sergei and don't bother greeting him. "You asked for me?"

"Yes, I asked for you." Sergei grips the armrest of his chair tight. "Don't you think you have some explaining to do, Volkov?"

"What type of explaining?"

"Richard's death." Vladimir stands and stares at me. While we're about the same height, he's bulkier and has a more piercing stare. "I know you killed him."

"Proof?"

"Recordings. You probably didn't know that he secretly recorded everything that happened in his office."

He couldn't have. If he did, my hackers would've found out when they cleaned up his digital files afterward.

Unless...

"How did you find them?" I ask.

"That doesn't matter, the content does."

"How did you find them, Vladimir? If you had before now, you would've come forward with it, but I assume you got outside help. Someone sent you those files recently."

"Why the fuck does that matter?"

"*Who* sent them to you?"

"You're in no position to question me, Volkov. It's the other way around. Why don't you tell us why you killed our candidate for mayor?"

"I will if you tell me who sent you the recordings and how."

"Or I can just kill you without hearing your explanation."

"Tell him, Vladimir," Sergei says after watching the exchange silently.

The man in front of me scrunches his nose at being

ordered to do the very thing he has no desire to do. "They were emailed to me."

"By whom?"

"It was an encrypted address. I couldn't track it down."

Whoever got those recordings hacked into Richard's files right after I left and before I ordered my hackers there for a thorough cleanup. But if he had those recordings on me all along, why wait until now to use them? They could've threatened me with them or sent them to Vladimir earlier.

Unless their only aim is to get rid of me. But why now, of all times?

"The fact remains, you killed Richard, who could've become an asset to us." Igor glares at me. "Why?"

"I assume you listened to the recordings and already know why I did it."

"Say it, Adrian." Sergei's voice rises with every word. "Enlighten us with the fucking reason why you endangered the brotherhood's future in this city."

"He touched my wife and had to die."

"You know what also died with him?" Vladimir snarls in my face. "Our chances for having a mayor under our control. So tell me, Adrian, is he only dead because he touched your wife or because you're playing house with the Italians? Because, now, their candidate is mayor and guess fucking what? Lazlo is telling him to refuse our shipments."

"Watch your fucking mouth, Vladimir. Do not speak of my wife or my honor again." I stare at Sergei. "I told you my reason, *Pakhan*. If you think I'm able to betray the brotherhood after everything I've done for it, then do what you must."

"You hid it from me when you could've told me."

"No, I couldn't."

"Why not?"

"Because you would have demanded I eliminate the

reason why I made such a decision and derailed me from my logical thinking."

"I'm demanding it now. Divorce the woman who's muddying your thinking and I will overlook this incident."

"*Pakhan*," Vladimir and Igor say at the same time.

Having lived my entire life in the brotherhood and witnessed Nikolai's and Sergei's brutality, I know this isn't a chance the *Pakhan* would offer anyone.

I should accept it while bowing my head and being grateful.

However, I stand tall. "No."

Sergei rises and Vladimir steps out of the way, allowing the older man to meet my gaze with his harsher one. "Are you refusing a direct fucking order, Volkov?"

"Yes."

"Either you do as you're told or you'll face dire consequences."

"I'll face the consequences."

"You'd rather die than fucking divorce that woman?"

"I know you won't stop if I divorce her. As soon as I do, you'll have the full liberty to kill her."

"What do you care? You only married her for Jeremy."

"I will not divorce her, *Pakhan*. If you want punishment, take it from me."

"You know what the punishment of betrayal is, Volkov."

"Fully. I watched my mother being executed by my father, per your brother's orders."

"And you're telling me that you're ready to meet that fate for a nameless nobody?!" he yells, his face reddening.

"Yes."

"I'm disappointed in you, Volkov. You're supposed to be better than this." He dismisses me with a hand. "Take him out of my fucking sight until I decide how to kill him."

Igor stares at me with his usual neutrality. "If you had married my Kristina, none of this would've happened to you, and if it had, I would've pleaded your case. However, you chose a nobody and you'll end as a nobody. Georgy must be rolling in his grave."

Fuck my father and fuck Igor.

Despite everything, marrying Lia was the best decision I've made in my life.

Two guards grab me by my arms. I don't struggle as they lead me out of the office.

Probably to my last stop.

The only thought that keeps me calm is that Lia and Jeremy are safe.

TWENTY-THREE

Lia

I DON'T KNOW HOW I FIND MYSELF BACK AT THE HOUSE. Though I have an idea.

Yan and Boris must've dragged me back in while I kicked and screamed and cried.

My energy wanes as I sit down on the sofa, my limbs shaking. The heat tingles against my frozen extremities, but it can't reach inside and melt the ice that's been forming frosty layers around my heart since the moment Adrian's car vanished in the snow.

A warm cup touches my hand and I glance up to find Yan staring at me. "It's hot tea."

"I don't want hot tea." A wave of fresh tears blur my vision. "I want to go to Adrian."

"That's impossible, Lia. You'll be killed as well."

"I don't care. I'd rather die than live without him."

"How about Jeremy then? How will he survive without the both of you?"

A sob catches in my throat at the reminder of our son, at how Adrian said I should raise him well for the both of us.

No.

He'll do it with me. He has to. There's no way he'll leave me all alone after everything we've been through.

"I'm sorry." Yan sits beside me, still cradling the drink even as Boris stands across from us in his inflexible position.

"About what?" I sniffle.

"I was drunk and ended up telling Kolya about what I heard the night I was shot. That's how Boss managed to put together everything concerning you and Luca."

I shake my head. "I don't care about any of that. It would've come to light sooner or later."

"Is it true?" Boris asks.

"Is what true?"

"Did you betray Boss?"

"Boris." Yan shakes his head at his colleague.

The other guard glares at him. "*What?* He went to the *Pakhan* ready to die for her. If she betrayed him, I want to know."

"For what reason?" Yan slams the cup on the table and jerks up. "You gonna go against your boss's order and hurt her? Because you'll have to get through me first."

I grab Yan's arm and tug with the little strength I have left so he'll sit down. He complies hesitantly, and I shake my head at Boris. "It's true that I talked to Luca, but I would *never* hurt Adrian. I know you don't believe me, but I…I didn't."

Boris thins his lips but says nothing. Like Kolya, he has only ever been loyal to Adrian and always sees things from his boss's perspective. But I understand his skepticism about protecting me when he thinks I'm the reason behind this whole mess.

Focusing back on the situation at hand, I face Yan. "Surely we can do something?"

"No."

"If I talk to Sergei and tell him about what happened in the shelter…"

"If that were an option, Boss would've considered it."

"You can't possibly be suggesting that we all sit here and do nothing?"

"For the time being, that's what we will do. Kolya will bring you and Jeremy different identities and then we can go to another place—"

"No." I cut him off, jumping to my feet and glaring at both guards. "You claim to be so loyal to your boss and yet, you're content with just sitting here, waiting for news of his death."

"Believe me, Mrs. Volkov." Boris grits his teeth. "If it were up to me, I would be out there with him, dying for him if need be."

"Then why aren't you?"

"Because his last order was to protect you and Jeremy."

A whole body shudder overwhelms me and I'm shaking all over again. "I can't stay here and do nothing. I won't."

Yan sighs, his shoulders drooping. "Boss said—"

"Your damn boss left me and went to his death, Yan. His opinion doesn't matter." I pace the length of the room, my legs trembling and tears stinging my cheeks. "There must be something we can do."

An idea springs to my head and I stop, staring between Yan and Boris. "My father."

"Your father?" Yan asks.

"Lazlo Luciano. You said that his lack of cooperation with the Bratva is part of the reason why Sergei, Vladimir, and Igor are mad at Adrian."

"No, Lia."

"Yes, Yan. If I talk to him, he might help."

"Or he might lock you the fuck up. He's childless and if he finds out that he's had a daughter all along, he won't let you go. Not to mention that he'll figure out Adrian married you to get to him."

"I won't know unless I try."

"This is a bad idea."

"It's the only one we have." I stare at Boris. "What do you think?"

"I think Boss will kill us." He pauses. "But he won't be able to do that if he's dead."

Yan squares his shoulders. "I'm against this."

"Your opinion doesn't matter." I stand beside Boris. "It's two to one."

Yan points a finger at Boris. "I'll stand by when Boss gets your balls."

"I'll gladly let him if he stays alive."

Both guards glare at each other, but even with Yan's stoic expression, I know that deep down, he realizes this is our only chance to rescue Adrian.

That is, if he's still alive.

The thought of his death brings a new wave of tears to my eyes.

No. I would know if he'd died. I would've felt it in the corner of my heart with his name engraved on it. That corner has been bleeding since he left.

"Mommy?"

My attention snaps to Jeremy, who's rubbing sleep from his eyes and approaching me slowly. He's wearing his pajamas with spaceships drawn on them and his hair is disheveled.

His chin trembles as he stares up at me. "Why are you crying?"

I wipe my eyes with the back of my hands and crouch so I'm eye level with him. "It's nothing, my angel. Mommy is just a little sad, okay?"

My heart skips a beat at how I said 'okay' and I'm about to correct myself when I recall that Adrian isn't here. There's no vocabulary police to worry about and that brings a new surge of heartache.

Jer pulls the sleeve of his pajama top down his palm and

dabs it against my cheek. "It's okay, Mommy. Papa and I will make it better."

It takes everything in me not to break down then and there, because those words? They're the truest I've ever heard. Adrian and Jeremy have always made it better.

No matter how hard it's gotten, having them by my side has always helped, even when I was too blind to see it.

"Where's Papa, Mommy?"

I hug Jeremy to my chest, smoothing his hair. "He's not here, my angel, but Mommy will get him back."

TWENTY-FOUR

Lia

I'VE NEVER THOUGHT ABOUT MEETING MY FATHER before.

When Grandma told me who he is and what he does, I thought I was lucky to have never been in his path and decided to keep it that way.

I didn't even try to learn his name or dig around to find out about him. Partly because the thought of him brought back painful memories of Italy and my parents' death. Partly because I didn't want to get caught up in that type of life.

After I learned that Adrian has gotten close to me because of who my father is, it hurt so badly that I wished he'd never had me. I wished that my real father was the kind Paolo Morelli, who took care of me and my mother. I wished I had no relation to Lazlo Luciano.

Now, it's different.

Now, I'm well aware that he's possibly my last chance to keep the love of my life alive, to fight for my family and protect it.

Adrian has always been our shield, and I realize now how

much I took that for granted. I even forgot what type of horrors await us out there without him.

Now, it's my turn to save him.

"This is bad," Yan grumbles as we stand in front of Lazlo's house in one of Brooklyn's exclusive sections.

We flew here as soon as we could and it took us thirteen hours I don't have to spare. I've been trying to call Adrian, Kolya, and Fedor, but all I've gotten are their voicemails.

Yan attempted to placate me, saying that they were probably in a meeting, but I nearly had a breakdown every time I couldn't reach them. The only thing that kept me together was Jeremy.

My baby boy is back home with Boris and Ogla, who surprisingly also agreed with my plan.

Yan is the only one who didn't and has been grumbling at me all the way here, even when he insisted to tag along.

"If you hate this so much, you could've let Boris come on your behalf."

He scoffs. "No way in hell. I told Boss I would protect you with my life and that's what I intend to do. Also, don't even think about exchanging me with Boris. One, he's boring. Two, I'm younger and better to look at."

"I wasn't." I smile at him. "I'm glad you're here with me."

"You won't ever get rid of me, even if Boss throws a jealous fit and ships me back to the Spetsnaz. I'll find a way to crawl back here."

"You say that as if I would let him."

He gives me a lopsided grin. "Of course you wouldn't."

I stare up at the huge house. Its walls are tall, allowing no view inside, and several cameras blink in every corner. My father is inside this place somewhere.

It's still surreal to think that I have a living parent.

"Are you ready, Yan?"

"I'm supposed to ask you that. The Lucianos are brutal,

Lia. Lazlo and his brothers have been ruling the Italian families in New York with an iron fist and they won't hesitate to shed blood if it serves their agenda."

"You forget something, Yan. No matter how brutal they are, I'm their blood and that should count for something." *At least I hope it does.*

"We will see."

"What should we do now? Is there a bell?"

"There'll be no need for that." Yan tilts his head in the direction of a blinking camera. "They already saw us."

Sure enough, the gate creaks open with a loud, haunting sound and I jerk before I anchor myself in place.

A guard with a pointy face and a bulky frame that dwarfs his suit comes outside and stands in front of us with his shoulders squared. When he speaks, it's with a pronounced Italian accent. "Mrs. Volkov, to what do we owe this visit?"

Good. He recognizes me. Yan said they would, that no matter how much Adrian has kept me hidden and out of the limelight, everyone in the crime world makes it their mission to know about his or her family.

Squaring my shoulders, I speak in a firm tone. "I would like to meet Lazlo Luciano."

"I'm afraid that won't be possible without a personal invitation from the Don."

"He would want to meet me."

The guard remains unaffected. "Still impossible, *Signorina.*"

I step in front of him, meeting his impassiveness with a glare. "Listen to me. I came here to meet Lazlo and I will not leave until I do."

He stares at me but says nothing.

"I'm his daughter," I whisper. "Tell him I'm his illegitimate daughter with Rachel Gueller."

The guard narrows his eyes.

"What are you waiting for?" Yan spits out. "Do it."

"I do not believe you," the guard says.

"I couldn't care less whether you believe me or not, but I assure you that you will be sorry if he finds out I came here and you turned me away just because you refuse to fucking check with him."

The guard stares at us for a heartbeat before he turns around and heads inside.

"Is it done?" I whisper at Yan.

"He's probably calling him. It's all up to Lazlo now."

Only a minute passes, but it feels like an eternity until the guard comes again. "The Don will see you now."

My heart thumps as I share a look with Yan. The guard leads us inside, but before we can go into the mansion, he shakes his head at Yan. "Only the signorina."

My friend's shoulders go rigid. "I'm going with her."

The guard steps forward, glaring at him, probably ready to throw him out by force.

I touch Yan's hand and muster a courageous smile. "I'll be fine, Yan. Wait for me here."

He doesn't look convinced, but he also doesn't act stupid and cause a ruckus when we're obviously greatly outnumbered by the countless guards we spied in every corner of the property.

"Last door to the left, Signorina," the guard tells me, motioning inside.

I follow the path he showed me, walking down a long hall with several Renaissance paintings hanging on the walls. By the time I reach the door, my heartbeat is erratic and irregular.

You can do this, Lia.

After inhaling deeply, I knock on the door.

A gruff, "Come in," propels me to open it and step inside.

Soft piano music fills the place. *Chopin.*

I expected to find an office, but it's a dining room. The large table is fit for over fifty people, like one from a castle, and the chairs surrounding it are tall and gold-rimmed.

At the head of the table sits a man who appears to be in his late fifties, but his hair is completely white, even though it's thick. His physique looks fit for someone his age, with his muscles filling his suit. A scar runs diagonally down his face, across his cheeks. His eyes, though? They're the same exact color as mine—blue, mysterious. Haunted.

This is my father.

I've seen him a few times before at the Bratva's banquets, but I've never stopped to look at him, to even see the resemblance between us. I've always kept a barrier between me and that part of Adrian's life, which Lazlo belonged to.

He's all alone in the dining room. No guard or family member present. Isn't he worried that I might do something to him? Though he could easily overpower me if that were the case. And he probably has some guards hidden in invisible places.

He's cutting a piece of steak in front of him as he watches me with his piercing eyes.

I stand a few seats away, meeting his stare.

"Mrs. Volkov," he says slowly, with a distinctive Italian accent. "My guard tells me you claim to be my daughter."

"It's not a claim." I swallow down my nerves. "I am your daughter with Rachel Gueller."

"How do you know of that name?"

"She was my mother."

"Your mother's name was Morelli."

I frown.

"You thought I wouldn't do a background check on Adrian's wife when he's my closest ally in the Bratva?"

"Then you know my father was Paolo Morelli and that I was born in Italy."

"Correct. Which is why I would like to know why you claim to be my daughter."

"My mother was forced to leave the States after she got pregnant with me and married my father—stepfather."

"What are you getting at?" He continues cutting his steak but doesn't bring anything to his mouth. "Is Adrian aware of what you're doing? If he does know—"

"He won't know, because he's in danger." I approach him in fast steps, but if my sudden movements alarm Lazlo, he doesn't act on it. Instead, he observes me closely when I'm a step in front of him. "I'm not sure what else to tell you to make you believe me, and I'm probably wasting my time, but know this, my mother was happy in Italy and with my stepfather, but sometimes, I saw her crying alone. Sometimes, she would hug me and tell me she wished it was different. The day those men came and killed her and Papa, I wished it was different, too. I know someone hid me and smuggled me to the States, but I have no idea who it was or why they did it. All I'm certain of is that it had something to do with you and the Rozettis and that Luca could've been working with them…"

I trail off when he releases the utensils and reaches a hand toward me. I'm about to flinch back when Lazlo wraps his fingers around the pendant that's peeking out from my coat.

His eyes widen as he runs the pads of his fingers across the surface with infinite caution. "How did you get this?"

"Mom gave it to me."

"I gave it to Rachel. She said it was a precious gift and she'd hand it down to our child if we had one." He stares at me with what seems like awe. "You…are my daughter."

"I believe so, yes."

"And I never knew you existed."

"I think someone tried hard to make it so you wouldn't."

"Or some *people*." His expression tightens. "Did you mention a Luca?"

"You know him?"

"Luca Rozetti."

"His last name is Brown."

"It's fucking Rozetti. He and his family have tried every

trick under the sun to destroy me, but I never thought they would go so low as to hide you from me." He stands and strokes my face. "My daughter. My blood."

I swallow at the tone of his voice, at the way his eyes soften as if he's finding a long-lost treasure.

"I should've found you sooner. If I had known Rachel had you, I would've followed her." He taps the scar on his cheek. "I should've sensed something was wrong when she gave me this."

"Mom did?"

"Yes, though it was a bit of an accident. She didn't take my engagement to my current wife well and held a knife so I'd leave her alone. I was trying to disarm her when she cut me. That was the last time I saw her."

"How come you...didn't hurt her for it?"

"I hurt her enough by choosing another woman over her. You, however, I didn't know about. If I had, it would've been different."

"Would you have married my mother?"

"No. But I would've raised you."

"That must be why she chose to stay away."

I can tell he doesn't like my response, but he doesn't press the issue.

"How did you know?" He pauses, narrowing his eyes. "Did Adrian figure it out and kept you from me?"

"No, no he didn't."

"Then who told you?"

"Luca."

"Filthy Rozetti." He curses under his breath in Italian.

"What's your problem with them, anyway?"

"We always have territory wars. However, they made the mistake of killing my father, so, in turn, we're killing all of them."

Typical.

His expression softens as he tightens his hold on my

hand. "I'm happy you came, Lia. You are a gift that I've finally received."

"If I'm a gift, then please help me."

"Anything."

"My husband, Adrian. He was taken by Sergei because they believe he killed Richard Green in order to help you and betray the Bratva. You're the only one who can rectify the misunderstanding."

"I do not get involved in the Bratva's internal affairs and they do not allow outsiders in."

"You said you'd help me with anything."

"Not when it comes to Bratva business. Besides, I don't believe it was by mere chance that Adrian ended up marrying you. He knew about your relation to me for years yet chose to keep it a secret, and for that alone, I will not help him."

"He's my husband and the father of my son. If you don't help him, then you can forget you ever had a daughter."

"Are you threatening me, Lia?"

"If that's what it takes. I don't want to threaten you, and I really want us to be different and for me to get to know you, so please, *please* help him. Help *me*."

"You will allow me a chance to get to know you?"

"Yes, I will."

He grunts. "I will try, though don't get your hopes up. Sergei doesn't like it when anyone gets involved in his internal affairs."

A huge smile stretches my lips. "I have a plan."

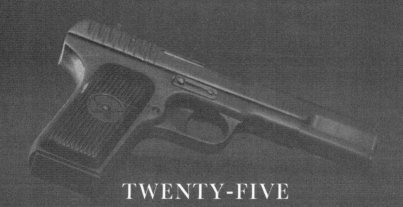

TWENTY-FIVE

Adrian

IT'S STRANGE HOW MUCH SOMEONE THINKS WHEN THERE'S nothing else to do.

I'm sitting on the freezing floor with my back leaning against the equally cold wall. My legs are bent and my hands lie limply on top of my knees.

My brain has been in a constant state of overdrive ever since Sergei locked me up in his basement—or rather, his torture chamber.

I know what he's doing. By putting me in a cold room with torture devices laid out on the table, he's showcasing what he could do to me before my death.

Vladimir already made his intentions known by punching me a few times until he busted my lip and bruised my chest. He said it was only an introduction until he got permission to get rid of me.

However, there's something neither he nor Sergei seem to understand.

I couldn't give a fuck about being tortured or killed.

Inflicting that type of fate on countless people myself fully prepared me to accept it once it comes.

But that was before I married Lia. At some point, protecting her became my life's priority and I survived if not for anything, then for that purpose alone. Now that it's impossible for me to live, I can't stop thinking about how her life will be after I'm gone.

I know Kolya, Yan, Boris, Ogla, and the others will do their best to make sure she and Jeremy are well taken care of. Not only do I come from a rich family, but I've always invested in various ventures to grow those assets. I have enough fortune that will sustain them for generations to come and they would never have to worry about money.

But that still doesn't put me at ease, probably because I thought that I'd always be there for them. That I'd spend the rest of my life shielding them from the world.

I shouldn't have made assumptions. I don't usually, but it won't be the first time I've gone against my principles and normal courses of action because of Lia.

It started when I didn't use her as soon as I knew she was Lazlo's daughter and then chose to keep her instead. It continued when I broke off my perfectly logical engagement in order to marry her. After that, all my decisions were made with the sole purpose of protecting her, keeping her closer, and chaining her to me, even if it meant hurting her in the process.

Now that I'll be gone, the thought of leaving her all alone hurts more than I thought it would.

It hurts to the point that I'm considering other options to resolve the current situation. If I go with what Sergei wants and divorce her, I can hide her in a place he can't find. I'll be able to visit her often…

No.

He would make it his mission to finish her life. Besides, I'd go out of my fucking mind if she wasn't in my sight at all times. I'd always think something has happened to her and that she's hurt, or worse, fucking dead.

But isn't that better than not knowing how she's doing at all? I could come up with ways to defy Sergei, to flee if I have to. Go to another corner of the world where it's only Lia, Jeremy, and me.

The brotherhood is all I've known since I was a boy. The only home I had, even after my parents' deaths. When my father was shot dead in one of Nikolai's assassination attempts, I was already desensitized at that point and didn't think twice about him. Because I still had a place I belonged to—the Bratva.

But I'm ready to throw it all away if it means keeping Lia safe and with me.

Releasing a deep breath, I stagger to my feet. I'm about to knock on the door and demand to speak to Sergei when it opens.

Vladimir and Kirill appear on the threshold. The bulky man stares down at me with a snarl in his lips while Kirill is smirking.

That should be a good sign.

Vladimir has never really liked me, mainly because he believes I'm treated better than the rest of the brothers and because he thinks I want to hurt his beloved Rai, the previous *Pakhan*'s granddaughter, whom he made an oath to protect.

Kirill, however, has often been on my side, even when he manipulated his way into finding out my secrets so he could use them to force my hand.

"Come out," Vladimir says. "The *Pakhan* wants to see you."

I go outside and squint at the morning sun glaring from the long windows.

"Why, Adrian." Kirill wraps an arm around my shoulder. "I leave you for a moment and you get yourself beaten up by our brute, Vladimir?"

The latter grunts. "He deserved it."

"No one deserves your punches," Kirill says with absolute nonchalance, then whispers, "You have surprises."

"What are you talking about?"

Kirill raises a brow. "You mean to tell me you didn't plot the entire situation?"

"What situation?"

Kirill frowns. "I know you planned it, so don't even pretend you're not aware of it."

Before I can ask what the fuck he's insinuating, Vladimir opens the dining room door. If Sergei is bringing me here, he must've organized an internal meeting for the brotherhood.

Sure enough, everyone is present. Igor, Mikhail, Damien, Rai, and Kyle. Their senior guards are all here and so is Kolya. He stands near my chair that's been left empty on Sergei's right.

Vladimir and Kirill take their usual seats. Unsure whether or not I'm allowed to sit on the *Pakhan*'s table anymore, I remain standing.

"You look like shit, Adrian," Damien says while chewing on a pastry. "That's a first."

Rai places her cup of coffee down and speaks in a reproachable tone. "You shouldn't have hit him, Vlad."

"I'd do it again. He fucking betrayed us."

"Now." Kirill smiles. "Betrayal is a strong word, Vladimir. He only had a lapse of judgment, a very rare one at that, which should be taken into consideration."

"He still put another organization's best interest before the brotherhood's." Igor glares at me. He never forgave me for choosing Lia over his daughter and he probably never will.

"Not intentionally, though." Mikhail frowns, his confusion clear. "Right, Volkov?"

Damien scoffs. "Do any of you actually believe that Adrian would do anything without a prior plan? He plots everything and has control freak issues. Even I can figure out that much."

"I believe it." Kyle takes Rai's hand in his and kisses her knuckles. He's lean, too pretty for his own good, and British.

"If someone touched my wife, I would slaughter them with my bare hands, even if they were the damn president."

At least he understands.

Vladimir glares at Kyle, then at me. "That doesn't give him the right to endanger the brotherhood's affairs."

"And be secretive about it," Igor says.

"We can just choose a punishment and get it over with," Mikhail suggests.

Damien raises his hand. "*Pakhan*, me! I want to punch Adrian's face a few times."

Kirill throws a napkin at him. "Shut the fuck up, Orlov."

"*What?* Vladimir did it, why can't I?"

"Don't you have anything to say?" Rai stares at me. "You should explain."

"I already did to the *Pakhan*. I have no further explanations to offer."

"You should," Kirill grinds out. "Make it count."

"I killed Richard because he assaulted my wife and would've raped her if she didn't defend herself. I would do it all over again if I got the chance. If you consider that betrayal, you can go ahead and punish me for it. I have nothing left to say on the matter."

Sergei stares at me. "I should kill you."

"Do it, *Pakhan*," Vladimir says.

"*Pakhan*," Kirill speaks in a placating tone. "He had a convincing reason."

"One he hid from us until we found out on our own," Igor counters.

"I planned to kill you to set an example," Sergei continues. "But I had a curious visit late at night."

"From whom?" Mikhail asks.

Vladimir clicks his tongue.

"Lazlo Luciano and his underboss." Sergei interlaces his fingers on the table. "He said we'd share his new mayor and he would even give us an in with the cartels he signed with, but he had one condition."

"*What?*" Damien stuffs his face with a cupcake. "Don't leave us in suspense, *Pakhan*."

"He'll only deal with *Adrian*."

While I asked Lazlo to help me in the past, I knew he wouldn't do it so readily, and certainly not with his under-boss present. Nicolo Luciano is too cautious and has always questioned any move before Lazlo could take it. The younger brother wouldn't agree to share their power with us when they secretly planned to push us aside after they're done with squashing the other Italian families.

The timing is too perfect, too…convenient. As if Lazlo had a major push.

It can't be.

I narrow my eyes on Kolya and he lowers his head. *The fuck?*

"If it were any other person or any other circumstances, you would've had a bullet in your head right about now. But we need the Italians and the cartels, and you will make sure they're under our control." Sergei stands. "This doesn't mean you get out of any punishment. I'll think of something fitting of your betrayal."

I nod. "Am I free to go now?"

"Yes. This is your first and only strike, Volkov."

With another nod, I turn around and step out of the dining room. Kolya follows after me, and Fedor, who was smoking in a corner away from all of the other guards, joins us, stubbing out his cigarette on the way.

I rein in my temper until we're in the car and we're moving off Sergei's house. I face Kolya who's sitting beside me in the backseat. "What the fuck happened?"

"Lazlo came to meet Sergei."

"That's not what I'm asking. How *the fuck* was he

convinced? The answer will determine whether or not you remain alive, Kolya."

"I assume Mrs. Volkov met with him."

"You *assume?*"

"I saw the tracker moving when we were on the plane. Kill me if you like, but I had to turn a blind eye because I knew that was the only possible way to keep you alive. Thankfully, it worked."

Fuck!

I grab him by the collar. "At the expense of disclosing Lia's origins. At the expense of dragging her into all of this. Now, Lazlo will never let her go."

"Who cares? She's your wife and she did the right thing by going to Lazlo. If she hadn't, Sergei would've put a bullet in your head. You won't be able to protect her if you're buried six feet under, Boss."

I release him with a harsh shove, my knuckles burning with the need to drive my fist through a wall.

Or a person.

The reality of the doomed situation slams into me with a violence that bleeds through my veins.

I am alive. I am. But at what price?

Because from now on, it'll be impossible to keep Lia out of the limelight.

TWENTY-SIX

Lia

I HAVEN'T BEEN ABLE TO SLEEP.

Every time I try to, thoughts about Adrian's state flood my mind. Is he safe? Is he hurt?

And those thoughts kept me up all night, even after my father called and said he spoke with Sergei. Adrian still hasn't shown up and Yan can't reach Kolya or Fedor.

All night long, either I hugged Jeremy or I paced his room. I couldn't go back to the master bedroom, not when Adrian isn't there. Besides, my insides have been twisting with a weird feeling.

As if something is sitting wrong and I should fix it.

But what?

It must be about Adrian's predicament, though aside from my meeting with Lazlo, I have no clue what else I can do. Yan and Boris—and even Ogla—are forbidding me from visiting Sergei, saying that it will do more harm than good.

If Adrian doesn't come home today, I'm going to the *Pakhan*'s house. I have to do something aside from sitting around waiting for a bomb to drop.

It can't be as terrifying as meeting my father, the Don himself, after thirty years of never knowing him. But even if it is scary, I'm ready to face whatever life throws my way.

I'm ready to fight.

To kick.

To claw.

A potent rush of energy has been whirling inside me since the moment I realized I have no choice but to step up in order to save our family.

It might not have started in the most conventional way and we're not perfect by any means, but it's still *our* family.

Mine and Adrian's.

I cover a sleeping Jeremy to his chin and stand up. It's early morning already and surely Yan has heard something about Adrian.

After putting on my coat, I head outside and make my way to the guest house. My feet come to a halt when I spot a shadow at the window up ahead.

At first, I think I'm imagining things again. That my mind is playing a sick game on me after leaving me alone for weeks. Is it the stress? Is that why I'm seeing people who shouldn't be there?

The shadow, Winter, disappears from the window. I grab my wrist and dig my nails into the skin, and my lips part when pain explodes on the assaulted spot.

You know what? I'm done thinking I'm crazy. My mind does it just fine without me contributing to it, too.

I release my wrist and march to the guest house. One of the guards greets me at the entrance and I nod back as I breeze past him.

Taking the stairs two at a time, I struggle to keep my breath under control. When I reach Winter's room, my heart is beating so loud, I can hear it in my ears.

I barge inside, and unlike what I witnessed less than a

minute ago, Winter is in bed, the machines beeping in a moderate rhythm as she sleeps. The erratic sound of my harsh breathing spooks the shit out of me as I sense invisible hands closing around my throat.

Keeping my voice calm, I say, "Open your eyes. I saw you."

No movement.

It's as if she's a statue. But I know what I saw and it wasn't my imagination. I'm better now, I don't hallucinate or let my mind take complete control of my life.

"Winter…I don't know why you're pretending to be comatose, but it's better if you wake up and tell me."

Nothing.

I yank the sheet off her body, but she remains the same, almost like the dead.

If I want to get to her, I need to use something that will provoke her.

"We're throwing you out, Winter. We're done giving you a roof over your head and injecting nourishment into your bloodstream when you mean nothing to us. Either a charity organization will take care of you or they'll just leave you to die."

The heartbeat on the monitor escalates. Yes, it's affecting her. Now, all I have to do is continue until she cracks, even if I mean none of the words.

"If you don't open your eyes and tell me why you're pretending to be comatose, I'll make sure this is the last day you're alive—"

A loud shriek echoes in the air as she springs forward, pulling a syringe from under her pillow. I flinch back, but she jumps on me, causing the IV tube to be yanked from her arm.

We both crash to the ground and she straddles me, placing the syringe to my neck. Her chest rises and falls so hard, it's almost unnatural. Her eyes, the same color as mine, are shifty, wide, practically crazed.

"You couldn't just leave me alone, you bitch?" she snarls.

The needle of the syringe brushes against my neck and I swallow thickly before I smooth out my voice. "Why…why did you pretend to be comatose?"

"Because your damn husband said he'd torture me for answers as soon as I opened my eyes." She breathes harshly. "And this whole fucking house is filled with guards and people, so I couldn't simply leave. If he'd found out I woke up, he would've killed me."

Oh.

She must've been anxious all along, biding her time and pretending that she was asleep. But on the bright side, I wasn't imagining things when I saw her through the window the other time or when she looked at me the other day.

I'm not crazy.

"It's okay, Winter. I'll help you out."

"You just said you'd kill me."

"That was only so you would drop the act."

"How do I know you won't hand me over to your mobster husband?"

"I'd never do that. I brought you into this mess and I'll get you out. I promise."

"I don't believe you…" Her lips quiver. "Everyone here wants me dead."

"That's not true, Winter. I mean you no harm."

"Is that why you sent me, knowing that your husband would recognize me right away and try to shoot me?"

"I didn't know that…though, I should've. I was so desperate that I wanted to believe he would be fooled, even if that was logically impossible. I'm so sorry."

"He'll kill me." Her hands shake on the needle.

"I won't let him. You have my word. In fact, I'll let you walk out of the door right now."

"You…will?"

I nod. "So please drop the syringe."

She stares at me as if she wants to believe me, but at the same time, she doesn't trust me.

I remain still, coaxing her with my gaze, hoping she'll let go. Winter isn't a bad person, but she's homeless, so she doesn't trust easily and she has every right not to, considering how life kicked her while she was already down.

It takes her long moments before she pulls the needle away from my neck and slowly stands up. I do the same so that we're facing one another.

"Thank you," I say.

"Get me out of here."

I open my mouth to agree when the door opens.

My lips part when none other than Adrian comes inside.

He pulls out his gun and Winter jumps back. I run in front of her as the shot goes off.

TWENTY-SEVEN

Lia

I DON'T THINK TWICE AS I JUMP IN FRONT OF WINTER. Because I have no doubt that Adrian won't hesitate to kill her if he sees that she's posing a danger to me.

When the shot echoes in the air, I close my eyes, ready for the sting of pain.

Nothing comes.

My frantic gaze goes to Winter as I face her. Aside from the shaking and her pale skin, it doesn't look as if she's been hit either.

Strong arms hug me from behind, whirling me around, and I stare up at Adrian. His brow is furrowed and there's dried blood on his lips. He's rugged, hurt, and not his usual composed self, but he's alive.

He's back.

Oh, God. He's back and he's alive.

"Do you have a fucking death wish, Lia?" He shakes me, threat and what seems like pain creases his brows. "Why did you get in the way of the bullet? If I hadn't changed the direction at the last second, you would've been shot."

"I…I couldn't let you harm Winter."

"She has a fucking syringe."

"She wasn't going to hurt me."

Kolya strides inside and snatches the syringe from her hand. She doesn't fight, not that she could, and lets him confiscate her weapon. Tears roll down her cheeks as Adrian's second-in-command yanks her arms behind her back, imprisoning her wrists with one hand.

"I didn't mean to… Please don't hurt me." She shakes her head, eyes meeting mine. "Lia, please."

I pull myself from Adrian's hold and face them. "Kolya, let her go."

He doesn't make a move, his gaze meeting his boss's. So I direct my attention to my husband.

"Adrian…tell him to let her go."

His critical gaze studies Winter closely, obviously trying to figure out why she's awake. "Not until I make sure she's not a danger."

"She isn't."

"You don't know that." My husband pulls me to his side with a firm hand around my waist and addresses Kolya. "Keep a close eye on her until further notice."

He turns to leave, then throws over his shoulder, "And tell Yan and Boris to plan their fucking funerals."

And with that, he drags me out of the room and the guest house. I squirm, trying to get away, but Adrian's firm grip prevents me from doing anything significant.

When we walk inside the house, he releases me because of my constant wiggling about.

I plant my feet on the floor and place a hand at my hip. "What is the matter with you? Winter didn't do anything wrong."

"She thought she could take your place. That's enough to be considered wrong in my dictionary."

"*I* did it. *I'm* the one who convinced her, so if you want to punish someone, punish me."

"Oh, I will punish you, Lia, and it has nothing to do with Winter." He grabs me by the elbow. "What the fuck are you doing here? You should've stayed in Russia as I ordered you to."

"And wait patiently for news of your death?" I jab a finger at his chest. "I would never do that. I won't sit still when I can help you."

"Help me by exposing yourself to Lazlo? Do you think he'll leave you alone now?"

"I don't care about any of that. The only thing I could think about was getting you back alive." My voice cracks and the tears I resisted last night barge into my eyes. "How could you do that to me? How could you leave me behind as if I mean nothing?"

"Nothing?" His jaw and voice tighten. "If you meant nothing, I wouldn't have walked toward death for you."

"Who asked you to walk toward death for me? Since when are you a hero? You're a villain, so act like one and take responsibility for your actions."

"My actions?"

"You made me addicted to you and unable to function unless I get my fix, so don't you dare think you can leave and expect me to let you go without a fight." Tears cascade down my cheeks and my throat closes from the straining force behind my words.

"Lenochka…" He extends a hand to me and I step out of his reach.

"Don't Lenochka me. I'm mad at you right now. Do you have any idea of the number of scenarios that went through my head when I ran after the car and couldn't catch up? I thought it was the last time I'd see you, that I'd be widowed, that Jer would be orphaned. You would've killed me right along with you and ended the life you spent a lot of time and effort to save. Just what were you hoping for? That I'd get over you and pick up the pieces of my life as if you were never in it?"

"With time, yes. Isn't that what you wanted all along? A life away from me?"

"Idiot. Fucking *idiot*. You think I can live away from you when you're the one who gave meaning to my life?" I sniffle. "I only said those words because of my fears and never once meant them."

His usually savage eyes soften, despite the map of bruises on his face. "No?"

"No! What about you, then? Did you really want me to move on? What if I found myself another man, huh?"

All softness disappears and his eyes rage with an intense gray as he clenches his jaw. "Kolya would kill him."

"He couldn't possibly kill all of them."

"He could."

"Then I would meet them behind Kolya's back."

"Lia…" he warns.

"What, Adrian? *What*? You're the one who wanted me to move on."

"Fuck that." He wraps an arm around my waist and pulls me to him, flattening my front against his hard chest as he breathes harshly. "You think I would ever want you with another man? That's like gutting myself with my own hands. You're mine and I only ever want you to stay mine, not someone else's."

"Then don't say you'll leave me again. You're my last stop and I plan to stay, not move on."

"You're my last stop, too."

My heart flutters and my stomach churns at the tenderness and determination in his tone. We remain like that for a few seconds, soaking each other's existences. I want to hug him and bawl in his chest like that time at the hospital after my career ended.

It's been long years, but I still look back at that memory as the moment I started falling in love with him. Ballet was the only thing that made sense in my life and when I lost it, I was aimless and without purpose. Everything felt useless and empty.

He was the exception.

Not only did he slowly fill the hollow gaps, but he also disallowed me from running away. He became my shield and continued to even when I scratched the armor and attempted to destroy it.

A deep sigh leaves him. "You have to keep in mind that it'll only get worse now."

I blink, pulling myself out of my reverie. "Worse how?"

"Lazlo will obviously think that I hid your existence from him on purpose. Sergei and everyone in the brotherhood will keep a closer eye on both of us. And there's still that fucker, Luca, and no one knows where he's hiding."

My palm lies on his chest and I stroke it lightly. I don't want to stop touching him, feeling him, making sure he's indeed here and not dead. "It can only get worse for so long before it gets better."

He caresses my cheek with the tips of his fingers. "I wouldn't be so optimistic if I were you, Lenochka."

"I am. Everything you mentioned is scary, but none of it terrifies me as much as the thought of losing you. As long as we're together, I can get through anything."

"Is that so?"

"Absolutely." I run my fingers over the cut in his lip and frown. "Does it hurt much?"

"Not as much as the thought of never seeing you again or leaving you unprotected."

"Then don't *ever* think about that again. I mean it, Adrian. You couldn't get rid of me even if you tried. We took vows and I intend to keep them."

"I thought you didn't like those vows."

"Who says I don't?"

He raises a brow. "The fact that you begged me not to marry you."

"I hated the way you forced me into it without talking to me about it while I was still mourning the end of my career, but I've never regretted marrying you. It was supposed to happen sooner or later."

"Just as I told you. You're finally coming back to my words."

"Shut up." I get on my tiptoes and he lowers his head so I can brush my lips against his.

Tears still cling to my lids, but they're happy tears. *Relief* tears.

Because unlike yesterday, I can finally breathe. I finally have the air that I've been deprived of since the moment he left me behind in that snowstorm.

Now, I have my oxygen back.

And I intend to keep it that way, even if I have to resort to ways Adrian wouldn't approve of.

What my husband doesn't know is that he isn't the only one bent on protecting me. I'd do the same.

With my life, if I have to.

TWENTY-NINE

Lia

AFTER I GO TO CONSOLE WINTER AND MAKE SURE she's comfortable—and without Kolya being her guard from hell, I spend the rest of the day with Adrian and Jeremy.

Our son asks why his papa is hurt and I tell him that he was hit by bad guys. My husband raised his brows at that but didn't say anything.

In the evening, however, Adrian leaves me to put Jeremy to sleep and heads into his office. I know exactly what he'll do and I will not sit still and allow it to happen.

So as soon as Jer falls asleep, I go to his office and step inside without knocking on the door. Sure enough, Adrian is sitting behind his desk as Kolya, Boris, and Yan stand in a line, their postures rigid.

"What are you doing here, Lia?" My husband doesn't hide his displeasure at my barging in. He never likes me in the vicinity of his men, outside of necessity.

While I enjoyed Yan's company in the past, I've made it my mission to stay away from Adrian's business. I can count the number of times I've been inside his office, and most of them had something to do with sex.

I've gone to great lengths to keep from getting mixed up in the mafia world, but I should've known that it would catch up to me sooner rather than later. Maybe staying away has been the wrong choice. I should have known that my origins would play a part in my life.

Squaring my shoulders, I step to Adrian's desk, sort of like a front line to the men standing behind me. "I know what you plan to do and I won't allow it."

Adrian taps his forefinger on the wooden surface a few times before he stops. "What do you think I'll do?"

"You'll punish Yan and Boris for bringing me home. It wasn't their fault. I insisted."

"Fine," he says dismissively. "Now you can go."

"Not until you give me your word that you won't hurt them."

"Lia…" A muscle tics in his jaw and he seems to be reining in his temper. "This isn't your place."

"Yes, it is. I'm your wife and that gives me the right to make decisions as much as you. If I hadn't convinced Yan and Boris to go along with my plan, you wouldn't be sitting in that chair."

"They defied direct orders and showed insubordination."

"For your sake!"

"And that put you in danger."

"It's all right," Yan says with a smile in his voice from behind me. "We were prepared for this."

"We can take it," Boris agrees.

"Well, I can't. I won't allow you guys to be punished for something I started." I stare at Adrian. "So?"

He forms a steeple with his fingers at his sharp jaw, his face and voice still closed off. "So what?"

"Are you going to promise not to hurt them or should I stay here all night until you do?"

"Lia…"

I flop on the chair in front of his desk and fold my arms. "I guess I'm staying then. Don't mind me. Continue with your business."

Adrian narrows his eyes on me and I stare back, unblinking. We remain like that for what seems like minutes, both of us refusing to back down. If it were the me from the past, I would've cowered from his intense unforgiving stare by now. I would've wanted to end the conflict and escape his brutal harshness.

But losing my identity and living as a completely different person taught me to find my inner strength. To reach inside the untouched parts of me and revive them. Besides, I'm done giving Adrian full reign over our lives after he used that privilege to choose death.

He married me despite the past and my mental issues, despite whose daughter I am, and now, he'll learn what that actually means and the consequences that come with it.

"Get out." His voice gains an edge.

"Give me your word first."

"Lia."

"Adrian."

"You do realize that I won't let this slide, do you not?"

A sudden shiver shoots down my spine at the veiled promise behind his words. I was well prepared to be punished for defying him, but hearing it has a completely different effect.

However, that doesn't deter me from the reason why I'm here. "I don't care."

My husband thins his lips before he releases a breath. "Fine."

"Fine, what?"

"I won't hurt them."

"Do I have your word?"

"You do. You also have my word that you'll pay for this little show."

I stand up and flip my hair over my shoulder, then place

a hand on his desk and lean forward so my face is mere inches away from his and he can get a view of my cleavage. "Fine with me."

His eyes heat, turning wild, and I step back before he pulls me onto the table and fucks me right here and now.

I don't leave right away, though. "Oh, also. I'm letting Winter go."

"No."

"Why not? She didn't do anything."

"She's your lookalike. I can't have her walking around without supervision. If I do, others will use her for their benefit."

"Others like who?"

"Like *Luca*."

I swallow at the edge in his tone. "Okay, then. I mean, fine. But we can't keep her locked up. She's innocent."

"She'll have to stay that way."

"Until when?"

"Until I decide where to ship her."

"You're not *shipping* her anywhere. She's a person, not some cattle."

"I will *ship* her if I deem it necessary."

I widen my stance, glaring at him. I love this man, I really do, but he's so apathetic sometimes, it drives me insane. Well, he's apathetic most of the time. The moments he's not are few and far between.

Why couldn't I love someone normal?

Oh, right. Because I'm nowhere near normal myself.

"I'll spend time with her." I turn and leave before he can say anything.

I go to the kitchen, heat the soup and the ham casserole Ogla made for dinner, put them and an apple on a tray, and go outside.

Fedor and another guard greet me at the entrance of the guest house, but they don't dare to stop me. They all look at me different since Adrian was let go by Sergei. Even Kolya, who seemed to hate me before they left Russia, thanked me as soon as they got back.

It's like I gained their respect or something.

Yan was always on my side, but everyone else was blindly loyal to Adrian. I guess they must realize how foolish his decision was and that they could've really lost him.

I could've really lost him.

That thought makes me want to cry again, but I suck in a deep breath, refusing to go down that path.

I find Winter in her room, sitting on her bed with her knees hugged to her chest. She lifts her head upon seeing me and hope shines bright in her blue eyes.

"Am I free to go now?"

I sit on the chair beside the bed and place the tray on the nightstand. "I'm afraid not."

"But you promised."

"And I will keep that promise, but not now, Winter. Your resemblance to me puts you in immediate danger. There are people who want to hurt me and wouldn't hesitate to accomplish that through you."

She hugs her knees tighter, her knuckles whitening. "I...I can't spend all of my days cooped up in here. I feel like I'm going insane."

"You can stay with me and Jeremy. We're not really that fun, but we're better than nothing."

She tilts her head to the side, looking at me with undivided interest. "Why are you doing all of this?"

"This?"

"Helping me."

"Because I know how it feels like to be alone, and how your head can torture itself and you."

"Thank you," she whispers. "You shouldn't care about someone like me."

"What type of nonsense is that? Everyone deserves to be cared for." I uncover the food. "Come on, eat."

She reaches out a hesitant hand, then grasps the bowl of soup, not bothering with the spoon as she drinks straight from it, finishing it in a few seconds. But she takes her time with the ham casserole, eating slowly.

"Can I ask you something?" she asks between bites.

"Sure."

"Do you still want to escape your husband?"

"No," I say and mean it.

"Why not?"

"I never wanted to leave him in the first place. I was just… at a point where I was lost, and I thought leaving him was the right choice. It took a lot to recognize that wasn't true and to finally see where my actual priorities lie."

"That's nice." She smiles a little. "I wish I knew where my priorities are, aside from my next meal."

"You'll get there. I'll help you."

"You…will?"

"Definitely. Everyone deserves a second chance." I pick up the apple and start to cut it. "Tell me more about yourself."

We spend a good part of the night talking. Winter tells me about her upbringing and how tough life was and that until she met me, she constantly thought about committing suicide but didn't have the courage to go through with it.

My heart breaks for her and all the shit she went through despite her young age. I end up talking about ballet and everything that went down with it.

Winter hugs me when I get to the part about my broken tibia. Although I thought I was over that part of my life, tears spring to my eyes at the reminder and I have to take deep breaths to stop myself from crying.

I suggest that she see Dr. Taylor since she helped me tremendously with therapy after I got back to being Lia.

I reluctantly leave her when she yawns, promising her that she'll be able to at least go with me and Jer to the garden tomorrow.

In the main house, I place the empty tray on the kitchen counter and load the plates in the dishwasher.

"I'll take care of it."

I jump, placing a hand to my chest at Ogla's monotone voice. "You scared me. Make a noise, would you?"

The older woman stares at me with her signature snobbish expression.

Ignoring her comment, I continue putting everything in the dishwasher, then press the On button. Ogla watches my every movement with hawk attention, with both her palms placed on her stomach, but doesn't say a word or attempt to leave.

It's the first time she's willingly spent more time than needed with me. She's usually ready to leave me behind and get on with her business.

I lean against the counter, crossing my arms over my chest. "If you have something to say, go ahead, say it and spare us the suspense. If this is about Winter and how Adrian intends to keep her locked—"

"Thank you."

If my jaw could hit the floor, it would right about now. "What did you just say? I think I'm hearing things."

"Thank you for bringing Boss back. You're the only one who could've done something like that."

I swallow to not choke on my own spit, then clear my throat. "I...I did what any wife would've done for her husband."

"No, you went beyond that." She pauses. "At first, I thought you were the wrong choice for him."

I narrow my eyes on her. "You preferred Kristina, didn't you?"

"Yes."

"Wow. Your honesty is cutting."

"She was the most logical choice for him while you were… well, uninterested mostly, so I thought maybe he'd made a grave mistake. However, over the years, I've realized that you might be the most fitting for him."

"Why?"

"Because you accept him the way he is. Not even his parents did that."

My interest piques and I straighten a little. "You've been here since the time his parents were alive, right?"

"True."

"Since his stepmother?"

"Yes."

"How was his relationship with her?"

"Like yours and Jeremy's, without the singing and dancing."

"He missed out." I grin, then soften my voice. "What about him and his mother?"

"Not good. She only ever used him against his father."

"And his father allowed that?"

"Not when he was around, but he couldn't stop her when he wasn't."

"At least his relationship with his father was good."

"Not exactly. The late Mr. Volkov had…many expectations of Boss when he was just a boy."

"I can't believe how cruel his parents were. But I guess that's what shaped him into who he is today."

"Yes. Since his mother's death, Boss has been an adult trapped in a child's body, and he's kept closing off more the older he's gotten." The harsh lines around her eyes soften for the first time since I met her. "Until you."

"M-me?"

"He went out of his way to do things for you. Before you came along, he never even had meals at regular times, no matter how much Kolya and I nagged about it. Then he asked me to prepare lunch boxes so he could take them to you. After that, he at least started eating dinner. And ever since he married you, he makes the time to eat breakfast and lunch with you, too."

"I didn't know that."

"There are a lot of things that you've changed about him."

I inch closer, hungry for more. "Such as?"

"Feelings. He used to make it his mission to smother them, but you bring them out. At one point, most of them were anger, though."

"Well, he made me mad, too."

Her lips move in what resembles a smile, but it doesn't quite go there. "I'm sure he did."

"Thank you, Ogla."

"Whatever for?"

"Being there for this family. For him."

"I'm the one who's supposed to thank you for saving his life, even if there will be a price to pay."

"A price to pay?"

"Sergei and Lazlo won't let this slide. Surely you know this."

I do. That's why I have to do something about it before they do.

Offense is the best defense.

Getting Adrian on board is going to be the hardest thing about this plan, though.

But then again, I have my wifely charms to use. Adrian's guard is down slightly when he's inside me or after he's fucked me, and I'm not above using that to my advantage.

TWENTY-NINE

Lia

A FEW DAYS LATER, I INSIST ON TAKING WINTER TO see Dr. Taylor.

Of course, the tyrant, Adrian, doesn't like it and even says that my safety is in jeopardy, especially if anyone who's watching figures out that I have a look-alike.

So I made sure Winter and I dressed differently and I even helped her bleach her hair to a shiny blonde. It's strange how a mere factor such as hair color can change so much about a person. When I stand beside her and we look in the mirror, there's much less of a resemblance between us.

In fact, I'm a bit shorter than Winter and my dark hair softly frames my face. The blue of my eyes stands out in a sparkling, almost demure kind of way. I've never had a piercing stare or even a convincing glare. Winter, on the other hand, has her hair in a ponytail, which brings out her cheekbones that I spent some time highlighting with makeup. Her eyes are also a raging blue, but until now, that all seemed to be hidden under the surface.

I'm almost sure she's bottling something inside. I can tell

by her distant glances and how she escapes into her mind sometimes. If there's anyone who understands what it means to be lost, it's me.

And I'll do everything in my power to make sure she doesn't come close to having a meltdown like I did at the top of that cliff.

I link my arm with hers and smile at her in the mirror. "Ready?"

"To go outside, yes. To see the shrink? I don't know."

"I won't coerce you if you're not ready. Unless you take that step yourself, no one can help you. But I do want to be there for you if you'll let me."

She fingers the collar of her coat—my coat. I make a mental note to take her shopping for her own clothes so that she won't be forced to wear mine. "You don't have to do this, Lia. I'm thankful for just…being treated as if I'm normal."

"You are normal. If anyone tells you otherwise, I won't let them get away with it."

She smiles a little, then nods. "Okay. I'm ready."

We step out of Winter's room in the safe house. Once we're downstairs, she physically jerks further into my side, her body stiffening.

The reason behind her reaction stands by the exit.

Yan is oblivious to his surroundings as he takes a drag of his cigarette with one hand and checks the magazine of his gun with the other. Daylight slips through the ajar door and casts a harsh shadow across his face. Yan might be beautiful, but he can actually look scary when he's being serious. Especially to those who don't know him.

I pat Winter's hand to placate her. She's usually afraid of Adrian and all of his men, but she only ever gets this urge to hide whenever Yan is in sight. Wait…did something happen between them behind my back? He couldn't have hurt her, right?

No. My friend wouldn't do that.

I clear my throat and Yan raises his head, but instead of hiding his gun, he makes a show out of clicking the magazine into place, his attention fixed on Winter. She visibly shivers, her lips parting.

Once we're near the front door, I point at the car, where Boris is behind the wheel. "Go on out ahead of me."

She basically trips over her own feet, still staring at Yan and his gun as she hurries outside. When she passes him, he blows a cloud of smoke in her face that instantly turns red. She doesn't stop, though, until she's next to the car.

The moment she's out of earshot, I grab Yan by the sleeve of his jacket. "What the hell are you doing?"

He grins. "Putting the fear of God in her so she doesn't try anything funny."

"She wouldn't."

"You don't know that."

"You sound just like Adrian right now."

"Hey! I'm younger. I can't possibly sound like him. Besides, he's not entirely wrong. She seems off."

"Because she's scared and homeless. Anyone would be off in that situation. Stop making it worse."

"We'll see."

"I mean it, Yan."

"I mean it, too. If she poses any type of threat, I'm shooting her between the eyes." He motions outside. "Time to go."

I shake my head as we leave the safe house. Winter is fidgeting by the car, probably contemplating whether she wants to be inside the same vehicle with Boris. However, upon seeing Yan, she opens the door with trembling fingers and slips inside.

Yan tilts his head to watch her and I snap my fingers in front of his face. "Stop it."

He lifts his shoulder and gets into the passenger seat. I'm about to join Winter when a little voice calls me, "Mommy!"

I crouch as Jeremy throws himself at me in a hug. Resting my nose against his scalp, I inhale his marshmallow scent. "I'm going to miss you, my angel."

"It's okay, Mommy. I'll play with Papa."

"I'm sure you will." I straighten and glimpse at Adrian who's standing behind him.

A scowl is etched across his beautiful features and his shoulders crowd with tension. If it were up to him, he would've chained me to the bed or at least come with me. But due to everything that's happened within the Bratva, he's under close scrutiny and will get a visit from the brotherhood's kings today.

But he also said he'll play with Jeremy while I'm out with Winter.

After stroking Jeremy's hair, I take a step toward Adrian and place a hand on his chest. "We'll be fine."

He makes a vague sound but says nothing.

"Adrian…I told you I dislike your silent treatment."

"It's not a silent treatment. I just don't want you out there and in danger."

"I won't be. Do you have so little faith in Boris and Yan?"

"After they went against my orders, yes, I do. That's why I'm sending Fedor and two others in a separate car."

"I'm not even surprised."

"As you shouldn't be."

I touch my lips to his, careful to not reopen the cut on the corner of his mouth, but Adrian wraps his arm around my waist and nibbles on my bottom lip until I open them with a moan.

By the time he releases me, I'm dizzy. Adrian's mouth finds my ear and he whispers, "Be good."

I bite my lower lip. "Do I get a reward for that?"

"Depends on how good you are," his voice drops with dark dominance.

Jeremy tugs on my coat and Adrian reluctantly lets me go.

After kissing my son one last time, I get in the back seat beside Winter. She's glued to the farthest corner of the vehicle, her attention on Yan, who has his gun on his lap. I poke him, and he pretends not to notice.

I didn't think I'd ever say this about my friend, but he can be a major jerk.

During the ride, I try to distract Winter from the two men in the front and the car following behind us. At first, she seems too scared to even listen, but with time, she starts talking, too.

As we round a corner, something catches in my peripheral vision. I stare out the window because I swear I just saw a man in black leather clothes, a black baseball cap, and a mask, riding a motorcycle, staring at our car despite the tinted windows.

I strain my neck to search the crowd of people and cars, but there's no trace of him.

That was my imagination, right? Otherwise, I think I just saw Luca.

THIRTY

Lia

WE'RE AT A PARTY.

Well, not exactly, but it's something similar to one. Sergei is throwing a banquet to celebrate the unification of the Bratva and the Luciano families.

As in, *my* family.

I'm still unable to wrap my head around that idea, but I guess it's too soon.

It's been a week since I nearly lost Adrian. A week since I met my father for the first time and asked him to help me.

My husband, who's currently placing a firm hand at the small of my back, is wearing his tux that might be responsible for making me fall further in love with him. He just looks so delectable in formal wear, as if he was born for this type of appearance. Add his sharp features and his untouchable aura, and he's a sight to behold.

I'm wearing on a knee-length satin gown with a somewhat deep neckline that reveals a hint of my cleavage. Its dark blue color compliments my skin tone and makes me look elegant. When I was getting dressed, Adrian kept glaring at the neckline and asked me to change. But we were already late, so I put on a scarf, then removed it as soon as we were in the car.

That's one reason for his sour mood, but the main reason is that I insisted on coming to this celebration.

He was against it, saying that Sergei will only be angrier if he sees me and that Lazlo won't leave me alone. While both of those are true, I'm done hiding away like a porcelain doll.

If there's anything I learned from temporarily losing my identity and everything that followed, it's that I can't keep watching my life like a spectator. I have to take action, even if it ends up being wrong. At least I will have tried, not sat around, waiting for someone else to make the decisions.

Besides, a marriage is for two. I need to stand tall beside Adrian and help him as Rai does with her husband, Kyle.

So what if Adrian always had the last word before? That won't be happening anymore and I proved that by insisting on coming here. I had to pay for it when he turned my ass red with his belt last night—to the point where I can barely sit to-day—but it was worth it.

We stop in front of the lounge area where Sergei is sitting with Igor and Mikhail. He lets Adrian kiss his hand, but when it's my turn, he pulls it away and glares at me. "Why, isn't this the reason Adrian is losing his logic?"

A muscle works in Adrian's jaw. "*Pakhan*. I told you—"

He lifts a hand, shushing my husband without saying it and fixes me with a harsh stare. "Do you have an explanation about your implication in this situation, Lia? An apology?"

I take a deep breath. "I was a victim, and I will not apologize for that. Adrian did what he had to."

"Are you talking back to me?"

"I'm only answering your question." I square my shoulders even though my hand trembles around my clutch bag. "We took vows, *Pakhan*, to care for and protect each other, and those vows are as precious to me as the brotherhood's codes of honor. I'm not asking you to like me, since I know that won't be possible, but please try to understand our situation."

He narrows his eyes on me as if he's contemplating whether or not to punish me for the insolence. Adrian tightens his hold on my waist until it hurts. I'm not sure if it's in anticipation of Sergei's next words or because of how I spoke.

Maybe both.

A few seconds pass before Sergei waves me away. I nod, congratulating him on the deal with the Lucianos and step back.

At first, Adrian doesn't release me, but then he whispers in my ear, "Stay close and don't cause any trouble."

"You, too," I whisper back and get on my tiptoes to kiss him on the cheek.

His expression falters for a bit as he's taken aback. Since he makes it his mission to keep his distance from me in front of his precious Bratva, I've done the same and have never shown any PDA before.

However, now is different. Now, I intend for the world to learn that he belongs to me as much as I belong to him.

I slip from his hold and head back to the party.

The place buzzes with a lot of invitees in formal attire. There's soft piano music playing, but it's somewhat drowned out by the constant chatter.

As per Sergei's other gatherings, this one is heavily guarded and has an open bar and scattered tables where guests can sit and chat.

I used to dislike such events with a passion. Partly because Adrian treated me like a stranger at them and partly because it always felt like I was an outsider, a fraud.

That I'd taken another woman's man.

But I think I'm able to rise above that now. As screwed up as it is, I believe Adrian and I were always meant to be together.

He wouldn't have been as compatible with Kristina. Just like I wouldn't be with any other man.

I'm about to get something to drink when Rai waves at me from across the hall. I wave back, meeting her and her husband halfway.

She's cradling her growing belly while Kyle holds her arm to help her balance as she hurries toward me.

He's tall and muscled in a lean kind of way. He has brown hair and deep cobalt eyes that seem bottomless sometimes, almost like there are no emotions behind them. He used to scare me, because even though he has an outgoing personality, it always felt like he used it as a façade to hide his darker, more twisted side.

A side that Rai embraced without attempting to change him.

"Easy, Princess." Kyle scolds in a loveable kind of way. "You can't keep walking in the fast pace you're used to."

"Whose fault is it that I'm bloated?" She pokes him.

"Mine?"

"Exactly. So stop nagging."

His eyes gleam with mischievousness. "No."

She glares at him playfully, then shakes her head. "You're hopeless."

"For you? Fuck right, I am, Princess." He stares at her with a mysterious look that she obviously understands, because red rises from her neck to her cheeks.

Wow. This is the first time I've seen her blush. I thought she was stronger than the world and incapable of feeling embarrassment or anything similar.

Seems she only feels that way around her husband. She looks impossibly feminine right now, unlike the tough, take-no-nonsense Rai I'm used to.

She clears her throat, elbowing Kyle. "I'm thirsty."

"I'll be right back." He winks at her, then nods at me. "Mrs. Volkov."

As soon as he disappears, Rai takes my hands in hers. "How have you been? Are you okay?"

"I'm supposed to ask you that. How far along are you?"

"Second trimester and it's kicking my ass, I swear." She smiles. "Kyle is making it more tolerable."

"I'm glad you have him by your side."

"Me, too. I wouldn't have been able to do it without him. Did Adrian help you during your pregnancy?"

"Tremendously. He took care of everything."

"He seems disinterested, but I'm starting to think it was all a façade. No one would've thought he would go against Granduncle for you, but he refused to divorce you, even if it meant saving his life."

My lips part. "He did?"

"Yeah. Everyone called him stupid, including Kirill, who's his ally. Me, however? I was impressed. Even Sergei is."

"Sergei?"

"Yes."

"The same Sergei who seems to want my head?"

"It's all an act. If there's anything my granduncle appreciates more than the brotherhood, it's loyalty. Adrian showed loyalty to you and was ready to pay for his actions with his life and Sergei didn't miss that. Give him time and he'll come around."

"You think?"

"I'm sure." She pauses. "Now, tell me, how do I stop myself from wanting to pee all the time?"

I laugh as she intertwines her arm with mine. I always loved Rai's company and I feel she's the ally I need the most in the brotherhood.

After talking about her pregnancy for some time and giving her tips from when I was expecting Jeremy, I clear my throat. "Can I ask you something personal, Rai?"

"I'm interested to see what you think is personal. Shoot."

"I know you and Kyle had an arranged marriage, but it

seems that you've always been equal in your relationship. Is it because of your personality? Or did you do something to get there?"

She runs her gaze over me as if only just now figuring out something. "I know what this is about."

"You...do?"

"You want to be Adrian's equal."

"Am I that obvious?"

"Sort of. But hey, Kyle and I go way back, so the dynamics have been different from the get-go and can't be compared to you and Adrian."

"But he always makes the decisions and he's so closed off about it, it hurts sometimes." My chin trembles. "I know he cares and he proves it with his actions, but whenever I ask something that goes against his agenda, it's like I'm dealing with a completely different man."

"That's because he's used to having his orders followed and reacts badly to the opposite. He's a man of power and has been for as long as I've known him."

"Does that mean I have to keep my mouth shut?"

"Hell no." She frowns as if what I just said is blasphemy. "However, you might have to use unconventional methods."

"Like...tempt him?"

She smirks. "That would work, too. But think about why Adrian is so smitten with you."

"He's smitten with me?"

"He is."

"Which part?"

"Your softness, Lia. Your finesse, your elegance. He sometimes watches you as if he wants to stab the air for making you cold."

Flames explode in my cheeks. "No, he doesn't."

"Yes, he does. At first, I chalked it up to something insignificant, but ever since I started looking closely, it's so obvious."

"Really?"

"Definitely. So you don't have to resort to any methods to win him over. Just be yourself." She rubs my arm. "Did I mention how proud I am of you for speaking up lately?"

"Thanks."

"If Kirill or Damien cause you any trouble, I'll stab them for you."

"I'm sure Adrian would beat you to it."

"He would! Also, I'm sorry about Vlad. He only has the brotherhood's best interests in mind, but he can be such a mule sometimes."

Yes, he can. And the only reason Rai would apologize on his behalf is because he's her lifelong protector and ally. Now that I know he's been hunting Adrian down with the intent to remove him and even kill him, I'll never trust him again.

My husband's enemy is my enemy.

I spend some more time with Rai, but soon after, Kyle comes to fetch her so she can sit down. I wave at them as I head to the buffet for some food, and I nod at some of the members of the Luciano family, like Lazlo's wife, Sofia, and two of his brothers.

Not sure if he told them about me, but they don't show a reaction, considering who I am to them.

I find myself searching for the man himself; I haven't seen him since Adrian and I got here. He wouldn't possibly miss this gathering since it is basically in his honor.

Even though it's been a week, I still don't know how to deal with the knowledge that my father is a Don. That this is some sort of a screwed-up version of *The Godfather*.

Adrian was furious when he learned that I promised to have a father-daughter relationship with Lazlo in exchange for saving him. But it was bound to happen sooner or later. No secret can be buried forever, and that includes my ties with the Luciano family.

Though, I have no clue how to deal with such ties. If Adrian hadn't been disapproving of everything I've done since I left Russia, he would've been the one to help me brainstorm.

"*Carina.*"

I swallow my piece of lobster at Lazlo's distinctive voice as I turn around to face him.

He smiles at me, the wrinkles around his eyes hinting at the many years he's spent on Earth, probably ruining the lives of people like my own husband.

My father takes my hand and kisses the back of it with clear affection that paints a smile on my lips.

"Hi," I greet. "How are you?"

"Not good. I learn that I have a daughter and yet she doesn't seem to want to talk to me."

"That's not true. It's just…" I lower my voice, getting closer to him so no one else hears us. "Sergei doesn't know about you and me, and if he finds out, he won't forgive Adrian."

He releases a disapproving sound. "That makes two of us."

"You promised not to reproach him about that."

"Of course I will. He'll answer for hiding you from me."

"But you promised."

"This has nothing to do with my promise. I need his explanation of why he married my daughter."

"I thought you wanted a relationship with me."

"I do, and that's why I'm being patient and haven't made a move." He takes my hand in his and pats it, the scar on his face not as hideous as I thought, even under so much light. "But I will, *Carina*. You're a Luciano and you need to meet your family."

"What if I'm not ready?"

"Are those your words or Adrian's?"

"Mine."

"Then I will wait for you to be ready. And if Adrian gets in the way, I won't stand still."

"You'll really wait?"

"I waited all this time for a child of my own blood. You think I can't wait some more?"

I smile, genuinely this time. "Thank you."

"No, thank you for existing, *Carina*. You made this old man's life worthwhile. Now, come, let me introduce you to your family."

"But I thought you'd wait."

"I am waiting. What does meeting your family have to do with it?" Lazlo leads me forward and introduces me to his wife, brothers, and even their women, as Adrian's wife. *For now*, as he whispered in my ear. Unlike what I expected, it's not awkward and they don't seem malicious. They're more curious than anything else.

Nicolo, Lazlo's brother and the Lucianos' underboss, observes me intently as I talk about the weather and make small talk. Does he already know?

Lazlo only leaves me when Sergei calls him over. I expect them to go upstairs for their usual meeting, but they don't. Soon after, Adrian appears from among the other leaders of the brotherhood and strides in my direction.

At first, I think he's heading to Kolya and Yan, who've been watching from the shadows the entire night, but he comes straight to me.

I blink up at him when he stops in front of me. This is one of the few times he's ever paid attention to me in the midst of the brotherhood's gatherings. Usually, we walk inside and then he ignores me all night until we have to leave.

Are we going home?

Though I miss Jer and Winter since we spend most of our time together now, we can't leave. Sergei would consider it an insolence.

Adrian stares at me and remains silent as his darkening gaze wreaks havoc inside me. Everything he does to me is sexual in its delivery. Whether it's the way he looks at me or how he follows my every more. Even his voice has a special range that he only uses when talking to me. He doesn't have to touch me to please me. Just being there is enough.

I expect him to usher me out, but he offers me his hand. "Dance with me."

I'm speechless for a second, my gaze flitting from his hand to his face. "W-what?"

"May I have this dance, Mrs. Volkov?"

I stare at the floor and realize Tchaikovsky's violin concerto is playing. A few couples are dancing, including Rai and Kyle.

"You really want to dance?" I whisper so no one hears.

"Why else would I ask you?"

"But everyone is here."

"Exactly." He smiles, motioning at his hand.

I take it with a huge grin on my face. I've always watched everyone who dances with envy, wishing Adrian and I were among them, but I've never had the guts to ask, not even when we were on good terms.

My husband wraps a possessive arm around my waist and I place a palm on his strong shoulder as we slowly sway to the music.

"I didn't know you danced, Adrian."

"I don't."

"You are right now."

"Because you look beautiful."

"You're dancing because I look beautiful?"

"It's a perfectly good reason."

"Is that really all?"

"No. I need to stake my claim so that no fucker looks at you."

"You haven't done that before."

"I thought I was protecting you before, but fuck that. If

you're going to be in the limelight anyway, I'll be by your side every step of the way."

"And...you won't try to hide me away again?"

"Believe me, I would if I could. If it were up to me, I would've worshipped you away from onlookers, where you're safe, but you're not happy with only that anymore, and I would never drive you to the edge of a cliff again, Lenochka."

Moisture gathers in my eyes and I hug him, resting my head against his chest. Because I know, I just know that something different just blossomed between us.

Trust.

THIRTY-ONE

Adrian

WHILE I PLANNED THIS ALL NIGHT LONG, executing it is complicated.

I might have escaped Sergei's wrath the other time, *barely*, but this one is entirely different.

He's not the only one involved.

There's also Lazlo, and judging by the way he made Lia do the rounds of meeting his family members, I have no doubt that he'll soon announce to the world that she's his daughter. The only reason he's pulling back is because she probably asked him to. However, Lazlo Luciano was never a patient man, especially when it comes to things he considers his right.

He's known to be brutal and unforgiving when it comes to family matters. And for that alone, I don't have time to waste.

So as soon as we finish dinner, I stand. Lia stares up at me with those huge imploring eyes. She's so beautiful, it physically aches sometimes.

Like right now.

I spent the entire dinner observing her every movement; the flutter of her long lashes, the twitch of her lips when she talked or ate. I even let Damien address her just so I could hear the tenor of her voice and the newly-found spark in her words.

My Lenochka has been slowly but surely evolving, and I don't want to miss any second of it.

Is this a new form of an obsession? Possibly. I have no doubt that just like her character, my obsession with her will keep growing to match it.

Lia gracefully gets to her feet and slips her hand through my arm. Usually, she wouldn't touch me in public—or in private, until recently—but my Lenochka is changing.

It's not only about how she went to her father and faced that part of her life or how she put her foot down to protect my men and Winter. She's been slowly integrating herself into the criminal aspects of my life, which she used to abhor. It's like she's finally accepting her role as my wife without my having to force her.

If anything, she's the one who's been demanding things.

"What are you doing?" she murmurs, flattening her small frame to my side.

The scent of roses fills my nostrils and I breathe her in, engraving her to memory. She'll always be my lone rose—the resilient rose that I'd pluck from the side of the road over and over again, even if her thorns caused me to bleed.

She's *my* rose.

Her thorns as well as her exotic scent are mine and mine alone.

After taking my fill of her scent, I say, "I need to talk to Sergei, Lenochka."

She shakes her head, her delicate throat bobbing with a swallow. "Not yet. He'll kill you."

"Do you have such little faith in me? Hmm. It seems that I haven't punished you thoroughly enough lately."

Her cheeks turn a deep shade of crimson. "Stop it. And you did last night."

"Not enough apparently." I stroke her hand that's looped in my arm. "I'll be fine."

"I want to go with you."

"No. Sergei doesn't react well to you."

"Rai told me it's an act and that he appreciates how you showed loyalty to me."

I raise a brow. Seems that Rai genuinely likes Lia if she went out of her way to placate her. But then again, she wouldn't have gone against me and risked my wrath to help Lia escape if that wasn't the case.

"He appreciates my loyalty, not yours, Lenochka. I don't want you there when he learns who you are."

She pouts. "Because I'm a woman and my existence doesn't matter?"

"Because you're my wife and I'd rather die a thousand times over than put you in danger."

I can tell she's not convinced, but she doesn't press the matter. However, she hesitates before she releases my arm.

Grabbing her cheeks with both hands, I turn her slightly and brush my lips against her temple. I'm well aware of the on-lookers, just like earlier when we danced. They're all shocked by how close I am to Lia tonight compared to all of the other gatherings. Damien and Kirill even asked me about the sudden change.

It's simple.

I'm done treating my wife like a stranger when she's always been the only person who mattered in a room full of people.

The only person I see.

I reluctantly release her and go to Sergei's side. He's been watching me, too, though he's remained quiet about it.

After making sure Lia is in Yan's direct view, I stop beside our Vor. "A word, *Pakhan*."

"Why?"

"It's of interest to you." I stare at Vladimir who's been

observing me all night, no doubt waiting for me to slip up. "You, too."

Kirill slides to our side with quiet steps and readjusts his glasses. "What about me?"

"Me, too." Damien jumps in with less finesse. "Why does everyone leave me out?"

"Not today." I motion at Kirill with a tilt of my head, and he thankfully takes the hint and drags a protesting Damien away.

Vladimir and I follow Sergei into his office while Igor, Mikhail, and even Lazlo and his men stare at us.

Actually, Lazlo's attention is on me. I ignored him as much as possible the past week, and if I don't do something about it, he'll do things his way.

But I need to take care of my own before extending it to outsiders.

At soon as we're in the office, Sergei sits in the lounge area and Vladimir and I join him.

"What is it?" The *Pakhan* leans on his fist. "I assume it has to do with the wife, whom you once mentioned means nothing?"

"Yes. There's something about her you should know."

"What, pray tell, might that be?"

"She's Lazlo Luciano's daughter."

"*What?*"

"What the fuck?" Vladimir says at the same time as Sergei.

The Vor straightens but doesn't release his fist. "Is this a distasteful joke, Volkov?"

"No, *Pakhan*. In fact, she's the reason Lazlo Luciano demanded to only work with me. I'm his son-in-law."

"What is this insolence?" Sergei's voice hardens. "You've been playing me for fool all along?"

"No."

"Then do you deny knowing who she was before you married her?" Vladimir asks.

"No. I knew since the beginning. Lazlo and Lia, however, found out only recently."

"You expect me to believe that?" Sergei hisses.

"I have no interest in lying to you. If I did, I would've kept this a secret."

"Why didn't you?"

"Unlike what you think, I dislike keeping secrets from you, *Pakhan*."

"You don't seem to when it comes to your precious wife."

"I did that to protect her from this life. Until recently, she didn't even know how tightly she's related to our world."

Silence fills the office, but it's neither uncomfortable nor stifling. Vladimir is deep in thought, probably considering ways to finish me off, while Sergei continues sizing me up before he speaks. "When did you figure out her connection to Lazlo?"

"Before I married her. I intended to use her against him."

"Let me guess, you changed your mind?"

"No. I still intend to use Lazlo for the brotherhood's benefit. He has a knack with the South American cartels and that will help us in the long run. My loyalty lies with the Bratva, not him."

"But he's your father-in-law."

"That makes him an ally, not the boss of me."

"Killing Richard doesn't support your theory," Vladimir grunts.

"I already told you why I did that. Stop nagging like an old woman, Vladimir."

He glares. "And now what? You expect us to let this go, too?"

"That's what I hoped for." I meet Sergei's gaze.

"*Pakhan*," Vladimir tightens his hand into a fist. "You can't possibly forgive the bastard for his disrespect two times in a row."

Sergei remains silent but doesn't break eye contact with

me. I'm fully aware that he doesn't want to lose me, and while I haven't revealed my in-law relations with the Lucianos to not involve Lia, Sergei—and even the fucker, Vladimir—know that it would benefit the brotherhood. Especially with how closed off Lazlo and his people can be.

However, Sergei is old-fashioned, and Vladimir is closed off. They wouldn't let me off the hook, no matter how valuable I am, for the sole reason that they don't want to set a precedent.

Countless men were killed for lesser than this and if I'm forgiven easily, it'd reflect badly on Sergei's power and the brotherhood's codes of honor.

It seems that the *Pakhan* needs an incentive, so I say, "All you have to do is turn a blind eye to it like I'm turning a blind eye to the fact that your daughter embezzled money from V Corp and fled."

Both Sergei and Vladimir stare at me with wide eyes. The way they underestimate me is somewhat insulting. Did they really think I wouldn't figure out that Sergei's soft daughter, Anastasia, isn't, in fact, continuing her studies in Russia like they lied about to everyone?

I was the one who investigated the case of embezzlement from V Corp. However, when I was getting closer to revealing the culprit, Rai figured out a way to return the funds with the help of her granduncle and Vladimir. The three of them thought they could fool me, but they must not know how my system works.

Anastasia Sokolov was too sheltered, too submissive, that she never looked the men in their eyes, but she was smart. For a whole year, during her internship with V Corp, she managed to send small amounts of money to a foreign bank account.

She didn't only manage to fool her father, but also Rai and Vladimir, who made it their mission to shelter her even more than she already was.

However, she was never able to fool me.

Vladimir masks his shock. "What the fuck are you talking about, Volkov?"

"I have proof. Documented."

Sergei's face turns red. "Are you threatening me?"

"If I were to threaten you, I would turn the word upside down, find Anastasia, then bring her to her knees in front of the brotherhood so that she pays for her sin. Betrayal's punishment is death—per your words, *Pakhan*."

Vladimir springs up, pulling out his gun and pointing it at me.

I don't even flinch. "Killing me will only bring Anastasia's funeral forward. My men will make it their mission to find and make sure she disappears once and for all."

"Not if I kill them all."

"What makes you think all of my men are here, Vladimir? Maybe a few of them are on Anastasia's tail as we speak."

"Why now?" Sergei asks. "Why didn't you play this card before?"

"Because I get to use it for two purposes now." And it's my last card against him, Vladimir, and Rai. If the three of them are by my side, the others will fall in line, too.

Igor would follow Sergei's lead. Mikhail usually goes with the flow. Kirill and I already exchange information and he's my ally, especially with the secret I'm holding over his head.

That only leaves Damien, but I'll find a way to rein that wild horse in sooner or later.

"He deserves death for threatening you." Vladimir presses his gun against my temple. "Let me kill him, *Pakhan*."

"I'm not threatening my *Pakhan*. I'm suggesting a deal. If you want me to find Anastasia while keeping it under the radar, I will."

"You can?" he asks slowly.

"Yes. All you have to do is give the order."

I see the exact moment Sergei decides that I'm worth more

than the stupid rules, that my system and my existence is one of the brotherhood's greatest assets.

I see the exact moment he trusts me again, even though he would never admit it aloud.

He just motions at Vladimir with a hand. "Sit down. Adrian is talking."

By the time I leave Sergei's office and Vladimir's vexing presence, a weight has been lifted off my chest.

It'll take time, but the rest of the brotherhood will go back to being the chess pieces on my board. They'll continue to be part of my system as they have been from the beginning.

As I'm walking down the hall, my feet come to a halt when I perceive movement in my peripheral vision. In a heartbeat, I'm surrounded by Lazlo, his underboss, Nicolo, and a few of their guards.

Nicolo points his weapon at my stomach. Isn't it the day of being held at gunpoint?

Lazlo glares at me. "A word, Volkov."

THIRTY-TWO

Lia

I'VE HAD A HORRIBLE FEELING EVER SINCE ADRIAN disappeared with Sergei and Vladimir.

They wouldn't hurt him, right?

From what Kolya told me, it was Vladimir who punched Adrian and sent him home looking like that.

Should I go talk to Rai about it since she's close with Vladimir?

No. Adrian wants me to have faith in him. Besides, they wouldn't do something to him with all these guests present.

At least, that's what I tell myself.

I sit down at a table, cradling a glass of champagne that Yan fetched for me. I feel so much better knowing he and Kolya are around.

"My, my, if it isn't the woman of the hour."

I stare up to find Kirill looking down at me before he and Damien casually occupy the chairs across from me.

In the past, I would've been wary of them—scared, even. They're both tall and broad men and their reputation is only of violence, torture, and bloodlust. But after living with Adrian for all these years, I realize that they could never be as terrifying as he can get sometimes.

"The woman of the hour?" I ask Kirill.

"The ever-so-reserved Adrian was ready to give up his life for you. What do you call that?"

"What is Adrian doing with Sergei?" Damien takes a sip from a glass of what I'm sure is vodka that he brought with him. "Is there some action I need to know about?"

"I...don't think so." I bring the glass of champagne to my mouth.

Kirill adjusts his glasses, staring at me intently. "You're surprisingly...*more*."

"More what?" I ask.

"More everything, though I suspected that Adrian was putting on an act when it came to you."

"You did?" Damien wipes the droplets of vodka off his upper lip.

"Of course. Not all of us are idiots."

"Who are you calling a fucking idiot?" Damien clenches his hand in a fist. "Want to go outside and test that?"

"You probably shouldn't," I say absentmindedly, watching the stairs, hoping Adrian will appear, already. "Kirill might not resort to violence, but he was some sort of a captain in the Special Forces and I heard that's a big deal in Russia."

Silence greets me and I glance back to find both men staring at me with peculiar expressions.

"What? Just because I wasn't talkative, doesn't mean I don't know these things."

"Add this fact to your list of things to know, Lia." Damien grins. "I can still kick Kirill's ass and beat him the fuck up."

"Or that's what you wish." Kirill smirks. "You heard Lia. Just because I don't use violence, doesn't mean I can't. I merely leave brute force to fools like you."

"Who are you calling a fucking fool?"

Damien and Kirill continue their bickering, but my attention breaks from them when I notice something happening around me.

First, Lazlo left his circle and headed in the direction of the bathroom. His brother, Nicolo, followed soon after, though in a different direction. Then several Italian guards left their positions and scattered. It could be my paranoia, but I've learned from Adrian how to recognize a pattern. They might not have gone together or to the same place, but there's something going on.

He'll answer to me.

My father's words from earlier cause me to spring to my feet. Damien calls after me, but I'm not hearing him as I quicken my pace up the stairs, ignoring the pain from the heels.

By the time I reach the top, I see Lazlo, Nicolo, and the others forcing Adrian into one of the rooms.

I break out into a sprint and barge inside before they can close the door.

"Stop it," I speak to Lazlo with a firm voice. "You promised."

"Lia, leave," Adrian tells me with a closed off tone.

"No."

"We're only having a chat," Lazlo says.

"Then you won't mind if I join you." I kick the door shut. "After all, I'm the main reason behind this."

"You're not." Lazlo glares at Adrian. "His lies are."

"He didn't lie to you."

"Only hid the truth to serve his agenda," Nicolo steps in. "And I will see the end to that."

My father's second-in-command, Nicolo Luciano, is around my husband's age but has the stare of a wise man who's seen the future and didn't like it. And because of that, he went back in time to slaughter anyone who would contribute to making that future a reality.

In the past, I was always wary of him, even more than I've

been of Lazlo. Because while my father is the Don, everyone in the criminal circuit knows that his underboss, my uncle, is the true mastermind behind the Lucianos' bloody savageness.

Rai once told me about his secret torture chambers that cause Nicolo's enemies to cower in fear. He's known to be sadistic and downright terrifying to those he deems to be a threat to his family.

And I'll do everything in my power to make sure my husband isn't in that category.

Nicolo didn't seem to dislike me when my father introduced me to him earlier, but that could be only a façade.

"We'll speak another time, Lazlo." Adrian comes to my side. "I have to get Lia home."

"No." I step forward. "I'm done playing a secondary role in my own life, so if you have something to discuss, do it now."

Lazlo shakes his head with a smile. "You take your stubbornness after me, it seems."

"Great, then you know I won't give up." I grab Adrian's hand in mine, squeezing to stop the nerves from emerging. "I don't care about what you think he did wrong. This man is my husband and the father of my son, *your grandchild*, and if you hurt him, I will never speak to you again, let alone have any sort of relationship with you."

"Lia." Lazlo steps closer. "He lied to me and kept us apart."

"Because he wanted to protect me from this life. He barely brought me to these gatherings before for the same reason. I'm the one who insisted on being part of his life. If it were up to him, he would've kept me in a gilded cage where no one would reach me, let alone hurt me."

The Don stares at Adrian with what seems like newfound respect, and I smile internally. I knew that no matter how mad he is at Adrian, he would relate to that protective side of him. I guessed it to be a trait they had in common and I guessed correctly.

"That still doesn't give him the right to take you from me."

"I understand, but give it time and you'll get over it."

"No."

"Please, for me?"

He grunts.

I can tell his resolve is faltering, so I resort to one last attempt. My hold tightens on Adrian's hand, and then I whisper, "Please…Papa."

My father's eyes widen and he remains silent for a second before he speaks, "What…did you just call me?"

"If you want me to say it again, give me your word that you will let Adrian go."

"You're surprisingly manipulative, *Carina*."

I learned from the best. I stare up at Adrian with a smile and he's watching me with a blank expression. What does that mean? Is he mad at me?

"Fine." Lazlo steps even closer.

My gaze slides back to him, my hopes soaring. "Give me your word."

"I give you my word that I won't harm Adrian."

"Thank you."

"Now, repeat what you said earlier, *Carina*."

I release Adrian's hand and hug Lazlo for a brief second, then pull back. "Thank you, Papa."

He studies me again, seeming taken aback before he clears his throat. "We'll meet again, Volkov."

And with that, he exits the room, followed by my uncle, who cuts a sharp glare at Adrian, and the rest of their guards.

As soon as the door closes behind them, I sag against the wall, catching my breath. "God. That was close. I should've figured out that Nicolo knew everything."

My heart beats so loud, it's as if I've just finished a workout. While I knew these types of ordeals were scary, I didn't think it'd be downright terrifying.

"Why did you do that?"

I raise my head at Adrian's quiet question. He's staring down at me with a hand in his pocket and the same expression from earlier.

Straightening, I frown. "What do you mean, why? For you."

"Who told you to call him *Papa* for me? Now, he won't let you out of his sight."

"What makes you think I want to be out of his sight? I happen to like him and want a relationship with him. What's wrong with that?"

"I don't know. Let's see. The fact that he's the fucking Don and his life is constantly threatened by the Rozettis, and fuck knows who he makes enemies with?"

"You're being a hypocrite right now, because we both know your life is threatened all the time, too, and yet, I'm still with you, aren't I?"

"I don't put you in harm's way."

"Oh, then how about the attack after I barely gave birth to Jeremy or the other time at Rai's gathering?"

"I protected you."

"After you forced me into this life."

"So that's your problem? The fact that I *forced* you?"

"No. Well, yes. But it's the fact that you're still doing it now. You don't respect me enough or trust me enough to let me make my own decisions."

"It's not about respect or trust. It's about your fucking safety, Lia. I can debate on anything but that."

"But you don't! You just map the road out and expect me to follow it."

"You didn't have a problem with that before."

"Of course I did. Why the hell do you think I jumped off that fucking cliff?" I breathe deeply so I don't have a meltdown. "Just because I didn't speak up, didn't mean I was fine. I was hurt countless times and deeply so. I won't continue to bottle everything inside and let it fester, then eat me alive. I'm not that Lia anymore, Adrian."

He's quiet for a second before his calm voice fills the air. "I can see that."

"Give me something then."

"I won't let you put yourself in harm's way and remain quiet about it, Lia."

"That's not what I meant." I push off the wall and place a hand on his chest. "I'm done settling for scraps. I need more of you."

"You have me, Lenochka. All of me."

"Not where it matters."

"What is that supposed to mean?"

"I might have your care and your protection, but I don't have your heart."

"You do."

"If I did, you would've given me more liberties. But you still have these walls where I don't have the keys to its doors. I know it's because of your childhood, I know you don't trust that I won't leave if you open those doors, but you need to give me those keys. I already opened myself up to you fully, so it's time you do the same. It's time you...let go."

Adrian's chest tightens against my palm, and I can feel his heartbeat skyrocketing even as he tries to hold on to his eternal calm. "You can ask for anything and I'll slaughter everything in my path so it's yours, but I can't give you what I'm incapable of."

Tears barge to my eyes. "Is that really what you think?"

"It's not what I think. It's the truth."

My heart breaks, its pieces splintering into the cavity of my chest and prickling the skin. It doesn't matter if I don't believe what he's saying to be true, that I'm certain he can let go if he tried. If he doesn't believe it himself and keeps his emotions under lock and key, there's no way I'll be able to get inside.

And that hurts more than I ever imagined.

"Lia…" He wipes beneath my eyes, taking away the rolling tears. "Don't cry."

I push his hand away. "Don't touch me."

His jaw clenches. "I know you're upset, but I told you, not touching you is out of the fucking question."

"Even if you repulse me?" I'm trying to be hurtful at this point, but I don't care. He's the one who hurt me first.

I ripped my heart out and placed it on a platter in front of him and he just ignored it.

He grabs me by the chin, tilting my head back so he can peer down at me with his punishing eyes. "Even if I repulse you."

"I hate you."

"Lia," he warns.

"What, Adrian?"

"Take that back."

"No."

"If you don't, I'll fuck it right out of you."

"I'll still hate you."

He backs me against the wall, using his hold on my jaw and I gasp as my behind hits the solid surface.

The sound is swallowed by his lips on mine. His kiss is imploring, dominating, and harsh, meant to punish me and make me fall to my knees in front of him.

I don't, though.

Instead of submitting to him as usual, I bite down hard on his lower lip until a metallic taste explodes on my tongue.

If I thought that would stop him, I'm far from right. He grabs both of my wrists and slams them above my head on the wall, but he doesn't release my mouth.

His tongue darts out, licking the blood before he bites my lip. He doesn't break the skin, but I whimper at the savage force of it.

As if that isn't enough, he slips his other hand between my

legs. I shiver at his wild touch, at how his palm forces its way against the sensitive flesh of my inner thigh.

He bunches my panties, then rips them off. The motion always, without a doubt, gets my pussy wet and aching.

Adrian thrusts two ruthless fingers inside me, ripping a moan from my throat.

Holy shit.

It doesn't matter how many times he touches me, every time he does, my body craves his roughness and mercilessness, his punishments and his sadism.

Maybe I have no hope after all, because the moment he starts pounding inside me, I can't resist the clenching at the base of my stomach or the throbbing of my nipples.

My body readies for the impact and my limbs shake uncontrollably as erotic sounds leave my lips.

Just when the orgasm is about to hit me, Adrian removes his fingers and his mouth, leaving me panting.

My lips tingle, feeling bruised, and my chest rises and falls hard as I stare at him.

He quickly unbuckles his pants and frees his rock-hard cock. I release a needy moan when he effortlessly lifts me up with one hand, urging me to wrap my legs around him.

I do, because I need the orgasm he didn't give me just now. Adrian is usually about giving before he takes, but this is supposed to be a punishment, so he won't give me that pleasure easily.

He thrusts inside me, reawakening the buildup from earlier. His pace is harsh and long, meant to hit as deep as he can go.

With my wrists above my head, I'm completely at his mercy, and right now, he doesn't seem like he has any to spare.

Tingles still erupt at my walls with each delicious plunge, his groin hitting my swollen clit.

Pleasure deepens and mounts until all I can hear is the

sound of the slaps of flesh against flesh and my desperate sobs for more.

I'm close, so...close.

"Tell me you love me," he rasps.

"No..." My voice trembles.

"Say it, Lia."

"N-no."

His pace slows down and I nearly cry from frustration. He can't possibly do this to me now.

"Adrian...don't..."

His gray eyes are the harshest I've seen in a while, like a storm at the point of erupting. "Say the fucking words, Lia."

"I hate you," I sob, moving my hips to keep the friction.

"If you don't say them, I will leave you hot and bothered right here and now."

His pace slows further until he's barely moving inside me.

"Adrian..."

"Say. It."

My walls crumble and I hate myself at this moment and I hate him. Because he made me feel this way and he's using it against me.

But most of all, I hate that I fell so deep that I couldn't find a way out even if I wanted to, even if having these feelings hurt.

"I love you," I whisper between sniffles.

Adrian's pace picks up almost instantly, driving into me with a deeper rhythm that steals my breath. He pulls all the way out, then thrusts back in as he teases my clit. "Again."

"I love you..." Stars form behind my lids as violent as the words out of my mouth. "I love you, Adrian..."

The orgasm isn't only strong, it's unending, going on for so long that I'm crying, tears rolling down my cheeks and chin.

Adrian slams his lips to mine while he powers harder and faster until he finds his own release. My eyelids droop as his hot cum soaks my inner walls.

He doesn't stop devouring my mouth and mixing his blood with my tears and our saliva. His tongue implores mine, his fingers digging harder into the soft flesh of my wrists as he consumes me, kissing me as hard as he fucks me.

By the time he wrenches his mouth from mine, releasing my wrists and pulling out of me, I'm so dazed that I momentarily forget where the hell I am or what just happened.

It isn't until my quivering legs touch the ground that everything comes back to me.

I asked him to open up and he didn't only refuse, but he brutally showed me that he never will.

Adrian grabs some tissues and starts to wipe my thighs. I slap his hand away, fresh tears springing to my eyes.

"Lia…"

"You're so cruel, Adrian."

"I'm cruel for making you admit what you feel?"

"No, you're cruel for using it against me." I lift my chin. "You're not allowed to touch me unless you're ready to let go."

His jaw clenches. "You're my wife and I will touch you whenever I fucking please."

"Not unless you're ready to force me."

And with that, I turn around and head to the door, thankful that my legs don't give out on me.

I head straight outside, wanting to go home. A few guards are scattered around the property and I do my best to avoid them so they don't see my tears. Once I'm in the parking lot, I pull out my phone to call Yan.

As I do, I wipe my tears with the back of my hand, but they keep multiplying.

"Come on, Yan. Pick up." I really don't want to go home with Adrian right now.

I'm heading in the direction of our car when something cold presses to my side.

"Long time no see, Duchess."

THIRTY-THREE

Adrian

I REMAIN STANDING IN THE ROOM FOR A MOMENT AFTER Lia leaves.

Harsh breaths burn my lungs on their way out, even when I try to slow them down.

My movements are jerky as I tuck myself in and buckle my pants.

Did I go too far?

I probably did. I tend to lose my sense of time and space when it comes to Lia. Not to mention everything that happened tonight from Sergei and Vladimir to Lazlo leaving me on edge.

The thought of her being in her father's company all that time didn't sit right with me. It still doesn't.

Not only will that put her in danger, but she'll also be in his entourage all of the time, considering she's his only daughter. Those who have or discover their children when they're old tend to protect them with their lives. That's the case with Sergei and Anastasia. He had her in his forties, and while he brought her up the brotherhood way, he would never inflict its punishments on her.

She's his only offspring and he's ready to defy the very codes of his existence to protect her. That's why I knew he would agree to my plan.

Lazlo won't be any different. If anything, he'll make it his mission to bring Lia closer to him—and away from me.

I was already forming a strategy to separate them, but I didn't count on the fact that she would actually like him and want to be his daughter.

That she would call him Papa.

I was already displeased with that fact and then she started mentioning feelings and that fucking cliff that twists my chest whenever I recall how she jumped off it.

By the time she said she hated me, I lost my cool head and had to touch her, feel her, have her all for myself.

The moment she whispered that she loved me, then shouted it, I was a goner.

It's not lust. Far from it.

She's touched parts of me I thought were long dead. However, that didn't start just now or even recently.

That's the explanation behind the weird sensations I experienced whenever I went to her apartment six years ago, whenever I stared at my watch until I could leave and have dinner with her.

Back then, I thought it was only because of physical needs, because of how much I desired her and how her body came undone around mine.

But no matter how much I fucked her, no matter how much I punished her, there was no satiating the thirst I had for her. On the contrary, it kept growing and sharpening, and that caused me to smother her deep into my darkness, to close all other roads so that she had no choice but to be led to me.

At some point, it was blind obsession, black and endless. It kept getting worse the more I had of her, and my methods to force her to be close intensified until all the lines blurred.

I could tell something was wrong, that I should stop or at least slow down, but the thought of parting from her put me in a worse state of mind and I just…couldn't put an end to it.

She did.

When she stood at the top of that cliff, pain like I never felt before exploded in my chest—fear, too.

Then she jumped.

Everything that happened was because of my inability to slow down. I finally have her back and even her therapist said that her state of mind is improving, despite the stress I put her through last week.

But I know, I just know that if I don't hit the brakes, this time I will lose her for good.

The thought squeezes my chest worse than when I watched her tumbling down that damn cliff like a leaf in the wind.

I open the door and stride outside, my movements precise but hurried.

When I lost Aunt Annika and was stuck with my parents, I realized that I wasn't worthy of love, affection, and general positive emotions. My father taught me that in order to survive in this world, I needed to discard those feelings. It came naturally, probably because of who my parents were.

It wasn't until Lia that I wanted to identify those feelings, to dig under my own skin and understand them better.

Facing them would be difficult, but it's not impossible, especially if it's for her and the family we're building together.

There were times when I thought there was only pain and cold shoulders in our relationship. However, ever since Lia lost her identity, then returned to her old self, I thought maybe we got a second chance.

A chance where we won't give up on each other.

A chance I won't miss.

Kolya and Yan join me at the top of the stairs.

"What the fuck are you doing here?" I ask Yan. "Why aren't you with Lia?"

"Didn't you tell me not to be with her alone?" He retrieves his phone. "Wait. She called me."

Of course she did.

I still hate their friendship. I don't care how many times it's saved her or how much she needs it.

Sucking in a breath, I head outside, checking her tracker on my phone, then freeze.

It's fucking moving away.

THIRTY-FOUR

Lia

"LUCA...STOP."

My feet hurt and it's not only because of the heels.

When my ex-friend showed up and held a gun to my side and told me to follow him, I did. Not because I was scared of his weapon, but because he threatened to kill Adrian.

Besides, I want this whole thing resolved so we can all move on with our lives. Ever since that day at the park, I knew he'd come back and make a move. I just didn't know when.

After what I learned from Papa, I now understand why Luca wishes me harm. He's obviously an enemy of my father's and has been using me all along.

Just like Adrian.

No. My husband might have wanted to use me and even planned to, but he didn't go through with it. In fact, he hates that I got myself involved in the whole scene.

"Luca." I try to pull my hand from his as he drags me forward.

He drove here—after he shoved me in the trunk—so I have no idea where we are.

It mustn't be too far away, though, because it didn't feel like he drove for a long time.

We're in what seems to be a forest, or the outskirts of one. Tall trees are the only things in sight and they appear like monsters' arms in the darkness. The only light illuminating the way is the one coming from the cottage Luca is pulling me into.

It's small with a wooden patio and flooring. He shoves me inside and I stumble, catching myself at the last second before I hit the entrance hall.

I expect someone else to come, but no one does. I remain at the entrance while Luca pulls all the curtains closed with his gun still in hand as he peeks outside through the window.

Goosebumps cover my skin from the cold. I left Sergei's house in a hurry and didn't bring my coat out, so I'm only in my dress.

My gaze flits from Luca, to his gun, and then to the door. If I attempt to escape, he'll catch me in no time, considering he obviously knows the area better than me.

Or maybe he'll hurt me.

Besides, I can't escape before I sort all of this out.

Hugging my arm, I stare at Luca. He's wearing black army fatigues and a baseball cap that casts a shadow on his face. He's removed the mask, so at least he's not a dark shadow anymore.

"Now what?" I ask.

He keeps staring at the window. "Now, you shut the fuck up until your daddy pays a price for you."

"A price?"

Luca spins around and crosses his arms over his chest so that the gun is facing forward. "If he wants to get you back alive, he'll have to give us a share of his South American drug shipments."

"I don't know who you think I am, but I'm not important enough that Lazlo Luciano would sacrifice anything for me."

"Nice try. But you forget that we've been hiding you all along, Duchess. Lazlo won't turn a blind eye on his only blood offspring."

"So it's true? You've been keeping an eye on me?"

"What do you think?"

"How about Adrian? Why did you have me spy on him and then plot to kill him?"

"Because he's a threat to us, too. Not as much as Lazlo, but he's close behind. He's been killing every one of our guards who knows about your identity."

He's been doing that? I scoff internally. Of course he has. He said it himself, that he'll kill people if he thinks they're a danger to me and that I'm not to question him about it.

I focus back on Luca. "And let me guess, you didn't want him to uncover your identity and your plan about using me?"

"Something like that." He throws his weight onto the sofa, swinging his arm to hug the back. "Now be a good little Duchess and sit with me for old time's sake."

"What old times? The ones when you lied to me? Why didn't you tell me you were a Rozetti?"

"You wouldn't have understood."

"I could've tried."

"*Tried?* You should've tried to spy on Adrian or at least not gotten in the way when I went to kill him, but you were more trouble than you were worth."

"You're such an asshole, do you know that?"

"Thanks."

"It wasn't supposed to be a compliment. And if you had told me what type of role I played in your life and was genuine about it, I would've willingly helped you with Papa. But you had to go and stab me in the back."

He retrieves his phone and taps on it as he speaks, "Aren't you the dramatic one, Duchess?"

"Dramatic? Yeah, I guess I can be dramatic if I find out

that the person I thought was my friend was only using me because of family feuds or whatever."

"Family feuds?" He glares at me over his phone. "My fucking parents were murdered by your damn father, and my few remaining family members put me with a make-believe adoptive family of their workers to save me from my parents' fate. Lazlo didn't and will never stop until he erases us off the face of the earth, and while I would rather put a damn bullet in his fucking head, I can't do that, because that monster Nicolo would erase the few family members I have left."

My heart aches for him despite his monstrous deeds. Luca has been angry and bitter since we were kids, and now, I understand why there's always that constant grudge in his gaze.

I inch closer so that I'm not far from him. "So what do you plan to do?"

"Force him to give us a share."

"He won't agree to that."

"He will if he wants you alive."

"Are you serious? This is his business, and he wouldn't choose me over it."

"In that case, he'll have your corpse. Maybe then he'll understand what it means to lose family." He pauses. "My uncle said that hiding you from Lazlo was our secret weapon. He was right."

"Was…my mother forced into it?"

"At first, I think. Then the man who married her betrayed the family and refused to hand you over."

"My stepfather was one of you?"

"Of course. So was your fake grandmother and the man who took you from Italy to the States. Your parents tried to smuggle you out, but my uncle found the man who was supposed to fetch you from the cottage that day, tortured him for the code word, then killed him and took you. We did a good job of hiding you from Lazlo until one of the fucker guards spilled the truth about you to Adrian under torture."

My head swims from the load of information and my legs barely carry me. "My...grandma was fake?"

"Yes. If she had been real, Lazlo would've found you. He searched the whole damn world for your mother."

Oh. So he did search for Mom.

"Let me talk to him, Luca."

He narrows his eyes. "About what?"

"About letting you have the shares."

"It wouldn't make a difference."

"You just said it would."

"Only if your life is threatened, Duchess."

"He will erase your family from the face of the earth if you hurt me."

"If this plan doesn't succeed, he might as well do it, anyway. I'm at a point where I have nothing to lose and everything to gain."

"But—" My protest is interrupted when a sound comes from outside.

Luca leaps up from his position on the couch and yanks me in front of him, using me as a shield while he jams the gun into my temple. The door barges open and my breath catches when I make eye contact with Adrian's intense gray ones.

Kolya, Yan, Boris, and a few of his other guards are with him. All of them have their guns out.

My heart beats fast as Adrian's entire demeanor sharpens and his body turns in my direction.

"You're not supposed to be here." Luca's tone is light, but I can feel his body tightening behind me. "Now drop your weapons before I kill her."

"You need me, Luca," I say in a low voice.

"Not if my life depends on it, Duchess," he tells me, then addresses Adrian. "Your weapons, Volkov."

My husband's gaze meets mine again for a brief second before he motions at his guards to drop their guns. As they do,

Luca drags me to a back door while still using me as a human shield.

I stumble a few times, but Luca's firm hold on me keeps me upright while we cross the distance.

It's so dark outside that I can barely see my hands, but I keep staring at the door until I can make out the shadow of Adrian and the others.

It'd be a lie to say I'm not scared, especially knowing Luca's impulsiveness, but the fact that Adrian is here gives me a small relief.

Pebbles crunch beneath my feet and when the sound of waves hits my ears, I notice that Luca has taken us to the edge of a cliff.

I suck in a deep breath as I stare at the water below violently hitting the rocks.

Just like that night.

My body trembles and tears spring to my eyes. The thought of repeating that experience paralyzes me, causing the world to close in on me until all I can hear is the pounding pulse in my ears.

"Lia."

My head snaps up to find Adrian a small distance away from me and some of my fear lessens.

"Breathe, Lenochka. I'm here."

"Adrian…" I shake my head. "I didn't mean to that time… I don't want to now…"

"Nothing will happen to you."

"Yes, it will if you don't stay away." Luca presses the weapon harder against my temple.

Something glints in the darkness in Adrian's hand and my eyes widen as I recognize the gun.

Luca seems to have noticed it, too, because he pulls me back in one swift movement.

I shriek as a bullet is fired.

Bang!

THIRTY-FIVE

Lia

PATTERNS WORK IN A STRANGE WAY.
I didn't think I believed in them, but my view completely changed after I met someone who considered them a religion.

If it weren't for those patterns, Adrian wouldn't have found me. He wouldn't have inserted himself in my life and refused to leave.

Thanks to the patterns, my life completely changed. Not all of it was good or bearable. At some point, I hated the change, but one thing's for certain. If it weren't for that change, I wouldn't have found the man who not only saved me, but also gave my life meaning. He gave me Jeremy and didn't allow me to run away from him or myself.

And now, we're at that point where we've reached a crossroads, one that only leads in one direction.

It's been two days since Luca went all kamikaze. Adrian shot him and grabbed me, yanking me away from the edge at the last second as Luca fell off the cliff.

They found his body down the river the next day. I cried

when I heard the news because even though he was pathologically manipulative, his childhood wasn't the best, and he only did what he did so that he and his family could survive.

My father was livid when he came to visit me the night of the incident. After he made sure I was all right, he promised to find the rest of the Rozettis and wipe them off the face of the earth. My attempts to sway him didn't matter, because he'd already made up his mind.

Adrian agreed with him, too, for my safety.

He's been so busy the past two days that I've barely caught a glimpse of him. The night of the incident, he drove me home before going back to the cliff. He spent yesterday in long meetings with my father and then with the brotherhood.

I waited for him to return, but he never did. Looks like tonight will be the same.

Sighing, I cover Jeremy, then put on my coat and opt to go for a walk in the garden. I stare at the guest house, contemplating whether or not I should go to Winter, but eventually decide against it.

She goes to sleep early and I'd rather not bother her with my gloomy thoughts.

When I told Adrian not to touch me unless he's ready to open up, I didn't think he'd take it literally.

But whatever, I'm not the one in the wrong. I thought I could have him without feelings before, that I could love him enough for the both of us, but it was so exhausting and painful. So painful that I thought death was better.

So even if I could put up with it for a while, I need to have some sort of hope that he will one day have feelings for me, no matter how far in the future that might be. I'm ready to wait if I know it will happen.

Our marriage has never been a fairytale, but I thought we cared for each other. Even when we hurt one another.

When I asked my therapist if it's normal to cause each

other pain when I obviously love him and he cares about me, she confirmed it.

Apparently, when stressed, we get to take it out on the person closest to us. In my case, that's Adrian.

But I don't want to hurt him anymore. In return, I don't want to be in pain, thinking that he'll never reciprocate my feelings.

The deeper they get, the more terrified I am that we'll go back to that stage of our marriage where the physical connection was all we had.

I loathe that period.

No matter how sexually compatible we are, it'll wane with time and then we'll have nothing.

The cold night air seeps underneath my coat as I walk to the gazebo. I'm at the entrance when a slight rustle comes from behind me.

Adrian.

I don't have to turn around to know it's him. Six years of marriage has attuned me to his presence, even without seeing him.

Swallowing, I stop and face him. He's wearing his cashmere coat over a white shirt and black pants, looking as handsome as ever. The man ages like fine wine, I swear.

"What are you doing outside in the cold?"

I lift a shoulder. "I felt like taking a walk. What? I'm not allowed to come out here without your permission?"

"Lia…" He gets closer until he's standing toe-to-toe with me and I have to tilt my head back to look at him. "Are you still mad at me?"

"I'm not."

"Yes, you are. Did you know that you pout when you're mad?" He strokes my cheek, then the curve of my lips. "It's weirdly adorable."

"Well, I don't feel adorable."

"I'm sorry."

Did he...just apologize to me? I never thought that would happen in a million years. "You're...what?"

"I'm sorry for making you feel bad when I should've done the opposite. I lost the ability to feel love when I was a boy, but you've slowly but surely yanked those feelings out of me. You didn't only yank them out, you also held tight to a part of me I thought was long gone. For you, I want to go back in time and keep that part alive for the moment I met you. In the past, I thought people were destined to leave, so being attached to anyone was useless. And I thought that at some point, you would leave, too. I fought the pull to you. I fought the lure of your rose scent and your breakable softness. But I couldn't fucking last. Not when I craved your presence the moment you were out of sight. Not when my thoughts of breaking your purity turned to a need to protect it. I told you how different my love is, how dark it can get, but I do love you, more than I've ever loved anyone in my life. I don't only need you; I also genuinely cannot live without you and the light you bring to my darkness. I know you deserve better, but I'm unable to let you go, so I'll try my best to be worthy of you, Lenochka."

A muscle tightens in his jaw and a glassy sheen has covered his eyes by the time he finishes. He finally did it.

He...let go.

Tears roll down my cheeks and I don't bother wiping them. "Oh, Adrian. You already are worthy of me. There's no one else out there who understands me better than you do, who'd bring me back, even when I go through a dark tunnel like I did. I just want to be your wife for real and your partner for better or worse, not merely a delicate flower you hide away from the world."

"I'll try to be better. Though I'll probably never be a hero."

"Who says I want a hero? I'm perfectly happy with you, my villain."

"You are?"

"Absolutely." I wrap my arms around his waist. "I love you, Adrian, and though it hurts sometimes, I've never regretted it."

His lips meet mine and I squeal as he picks me up and carries me in his arms.

EPILOGUE 1

Lia

Five months later

I T'S CRAZY HOW LIFE CAN CHANGE IN THE SPAN OF SUCH a short time.

How much...happier it can become.

It's been almost seven years since I first met Adrian. We started with blood and death, but something much more beautiful blossomed from the darkness.

It'd be a lie to say we live a fairytale. If there's anything that won't change about Adrian, it's the fact that he's a villain.

The type who still works in the background to have everyone under his thumb, regardless of whether they're his foe or his ally.

Everyone except me.

He kept his word when he said he'd try harder. He gave me more freedom and supported me when I decided to take a permanent administrative position in the shelter. One where I have to be present every day.

I thought his loathsome controlling side would come out

and he'd refuse, but he only insisted on security. Winter now helps me while she rebuilds her life from scratch. It's harder for her, but I'm holding her hand every step of the way, trying to help her find the will to rise above what she thinks is her fate.

There's no such thing as too late or the end.

When I heard the pop that finished my career, I thought my existence wasn't needed anymore. That the only reason I was on this earth was for ballet and when that reason vanished, I had no purpose in staying.

Adrian proved me wrong, even if his method wasn't the best. Then Jeremy came along, and while that wasn't the magical solution, it played a part of it.

It's how we got this far.

Now, we go out as a family and spend more time together, because no matter how busy we get, we realize our number one priority.

Family.

Not only the three of us, but also Yan, Kolya, Boris, Winter, and even Ogla. I made it a rule that all of us eat together at least once a week and then play Scrabble. Something that Adrian grumbles about, but he still helps me cheat.

My husband and I didn't come from conventional families and I guess that's why we pay more attention to that part of our lives.

Though I do have an extended family now.

Papa hasn't left me alone since he found out about me. He even threw a massive party in my honor to introduce me to the world as his daughter.

At first, I didn't really like the attention, but I'm enjoying getting to know him and his side of the family more than I thought I would.

Adrian says it's because he's spoiling me, but Adrian is just jealous because someone else is doting on me.

He wraps an arm around my waist as he leads me into one

of the brotherhood's gatherings. He looks so dashing in his tuxedo that I wish I could have him all to myself.

It doesn't help things when he stares down at me, offering me one of his rare smiles. "Ready, wife?"

"Of course I am." I grin, then lower my head.

"What?"

I smooth an invisible wrinkle on his jacket. "I just…love being on your arm."

"So do I."

"Says the man who always gave me the cold shoulder in front of the others."

"A mistake that will never happen again."

"Not that I'll let it. I'm not scared of you anymore, you know."

"Is that so?" He raises an amused brow. "I have my monster reputation to maintain."

I bite my lower lip. "Does that mean you'll punish me?"

A deep grunt leaves his lips. "Don't tempt me or I'll do it now."

"Do it then," I whisper provocatively.

"Lia…" he groans in a husky tone.

I grab his hand and pull him to the patio, away from watchful eyes.

Adrian pushes me against the wall and kisses me, his lips brushing against my trembling ones before his tongue finds mine. A whimper escapes my throat like every time he has me in his embrace. It feels like a first, like we're rediscovering each other with every touch.

I pull away, panting, before he deepens it even more and I lose track of my surroundings.

"Adrian…I have something to tell you."

"Later." His lips search for mine again, but I tilt my head and he nibbles on the sensitive skin of my throat.

"Oh…God…"

"Hmm. I love your voice, Lenochka."

"You do?"

"Why is that even a question?"

"Adrian..."

He kisses his way down my neck. "What?"

"I'm pregnant."

He pauses with his lips on my throat before he slowly pulls back, his gray eyes shining in the darkness. "What did you just say?"

I take his hand and place it on my flat stomach. "I took a few tests and they were positive. We have to go to the doctor, but I'm almost sure we're expecting."

We agreed to have a second child not too long ago and Adrian has had a blast trying to impregnate me. He fucks me any chance he gets and whenever I become a brat and whine about it, he says it's to give Jeremy a sibling and that we should both sacrifice for the greater good.

His large hand strokes my stomach. "Our baby is here?"

"Yes. Our baby."

Jeremy might have brought us together, but it was a forced start. This one will be different, this one will be our permanent step into happiness.

Adrian hugs me, then sighs in the crook of my neck before he pulls back to stare at me. "And here I was enjoying the process of impregnating you. But oh well, all good things come to an end."

"Why do they have to end?"

"My, Mrs. Volkov. Are you implying that I should continue?"

"I mean, you have to. If my pregnancy with Jeremy was any indication, you know how responsive I get."

He smiles, eyes shining. "Oh, I remember."

I grab him by the jacket. "Should we start now?"

"Again, why is that a question, wife?"

Then his lips are on mine again.

EPILOGUE 2

Adrian

One year later

I SLOWLY CLOSE THE NURSERY DOOR, MAKING THE CLICK as quiet as possible.

Putting our daughter, Annika, to sleep is a mission all on its own. She's such a handful compared to when Jeremy was an infant. And not only after she was born, but also during the pregnancy.

She often woke Lia in the middle of the night with her furious kicking and refused to go to sleep. Those nights were the longest, but my Lenochka and I got through them by being equally awake.

Ogla says Annika will be a hellion and I believe her.

Jeremy has been over the moon since he found out that he'd have a baby sister, and he's the first one she smiled at. He said he will protect her as her older brother. Our boy is so responsible, even at a young age, and has already learned how to hold his sister properly.

Lia's putting him to bed while I take care of Annika.

Sometimes we switch and other times, I come to find both of them asleep or Annika throwing a tantrum while a half-awake Lia coos her to sleep.

The first months are usually the hardest, but we're getting there. Even if we've forgotten what it means to get a good night's sleep.

All my life, I've known I was expected to have children and heirs, but I never thought it would be such an experience. The fact that I get to live it with my Lenochka is the reason why I not only endure it, but I also enjoy it.

Because this is our family.

My family, the one I would protect with my life.

As soon as I close the door, Lia grabs me by the hand and leads me to our room.

She's naked.

Fully.

Fuck. It doesn't matter how many times I see her unclothed, it still has the same effect as that first time in her apartment.

She's still the most beautiful rose I've ever seen.

Lia pushes me until I'm lying on the bed, unbuckles my pants, and straddles me. Her hands stroke my already hard cock as she bites her lower lip.

"Are you going to use me, Lenochka?" I tease.

"I miss you…" she groans, slowly guiding me inside her wet heat. "I barely get to have you lately…"

Her head tips back with a moan as she lowers herself until I'm fully sheathed inside her.

Her trembling palm rests on my chest while she gives herself a moment to adjust. No matter how much my beast urges me to do something, to fuck her thoroughly, I rein it in, letting Lia have her fill.

She starts moving slowly, her hips rotating with an increasing rhythm while she rides me. My dick thickens inside her and she traps the corner of her bottom lip between her teeth. But it's not only because of the ecstasy etched on her features. It's also everything else. From the way our groins meet with each up and down movement or how her arousal drips down my length.

A sheen of perspiration coats her glowing skin and dampens her dark locks as they swish against her shoulders. Her breasts bounce, her engorged nipples lactating when she picks up her pace. I reach a hand out and pinch them, making her moan, then whimper.

The view from the bottom is the only reason I let her do this sometimes. But even my patience has limits.

Grabbing her by the hips, I roll her over and she squeals as her back meets the mattress. But then she moans when I drive into her fast and hard before going slow and unhurried, the pace that we both enjoy.

Her erotic sounds reverberate through the air, urging me on, begging me, imploring me for more.

The sound of her voice makes me even harder and I give her what she needs. After she deprived me of them in the past, I don't take her noises of pleasure for granted. Whenever she offers them, like now, I engrave each and every one of them in my memory.

"Oh, Adrian…yes…yes…" she cries out as she falls apart around me. Her pleasure hooks on to mine and I join her at almost the same time.

We lie there sprawled over each other, kissing slowly while I touch her anywhere I can reach. Then we just stare at one another as I stroke her hair behind her ear.

"You're so cheap," she pouts, running her fingers over my chest.

"Cheap?"

"You didn't let me finish riding you."

"You don't like finishing riding me. You only like to start it."

"Maybe I do like finishing."

"Is that why you never orgasm in that position?"

"Whatever." She sighs. "I'm just happy we weren't interrupted."

"Don't jinx it. The hellion is one door away."

She laughs softly, then pauses. "Hey, Adrian."

"What?"

"Remember when I lied to you about cheating?"

My mood instantly blackens. I hate that part of our lives, even if it shaped who we are today. But what I hate the most is the feelings from back then. It's true that she didn't cheat, that she was as faithful to me as I was to her, but at one point, I believed it. And that pain split me in two, and because I was miserable, I hurt her.

"Why are you bringing that up?" I ask.

"I'm curious. If you believed I cheated, how come you never let me go? Wouldn't that have been the most logical thing to do?"

"Not to me. I would rather have you, even knowing you cheated, than not having you at all."

Moisture gathers along her lids as she grins. "Oh, Adrian."

I narrow my eyes. "Are you thinking about cheating, Mrs. Volkov?"

"Not even in the next life." She wraps her arms around my neck. "You're not only my lover and my husband, you're also my best friend and my partner in everything."

"And you are mine, Lenochka."

"I love you, Mr. Volkov."

"I love you, Mrs. Volkov."

And I'll spend the rest of my life showing her exactly how deep and raw that love is.

THE END

Next up is a dark taboo New adult, *Red Thorns*.

Curious about Rai and Kyle who appeared in this book? You can read their completed story in *Throne of Power*.

For a sneak peek into Adrian's past, you can download the free prequel, *Dark Deception*.

WHAT'S NEXT?

Thank you so much for reading Consumed by Deception! If
you liked it, please leave a review.
Your support means the world to me.

If you're thirsty for more discussions with other readers of the
series, you can join the Facebook group, Rina's Spoilers Room.

Next up is my most controversial, taboo book to date, a dark
new adult titled *Red Thorns*!

ALSO BY RINA KENT

For more books by the author and a reading order, please visit:

www.rinakent.com/books

ABOUT THE AUTHOR

Rina Kent is a *USA Today*, international, and #1 Amazon bestselling author of everything enemies to lovers romance.

She's known to write unapologetic anti-heroes and villains because she often fell in love with men no one roots for. Her books are sprinkled with a touch of darkness, a pinch of angst, and an unhealthy dose of intensity.

She spends her private days in London laughing like an evil mastermind about adding mayhem to her expanding universe. When she's not writing, Rina travels, hikes, and spoils cats in a pure Cat Lady fashion.

Find Rina Below:

Website: www.rinakent.com

Newsletter: www.subscribepage.com/rinakent

BookBub: www.bookbub.com/profile/rina-kent

Amazon: www.amazon.com/Rina-Kent/e/B07MM54G22

Goodreads: www.goodreads.com/author/show/18697906.
Rina_Kent

Instagram: www.instagram.com/author_rina

Facebook: www.facebook.com/rinaakent

Reader Group: www.facebook.com/groups/rinakent.club

Pinterest: www.pinterest.co.uk/AuthorRina/boards

Tiktok: www.tiktok.com/@rina.kent

Twitter: twitter.com/AuthorRina